ALSO BY ROBBIE COUCH

The Sky Blues

BLAINE
★ FOR ★
THE WIN

ROBBIE COUCH

SIMON & SCHUSTER BFYR

NEW YORK LONDON TORONTO SYDNEY NEW DELHI

SIMON & SCHUSTER BFYR

An imprint of Simon & Schuster Children's Publishing Division
1230 Avenue of the Americas, New York, New York 10020
This book is a work of fiction. Any references to historical events, real people,
or real places are used fictitiously. Other names, characters, places, and events
are products of the author's imagination, and any resemblance to actual events
or places or persons, living or dead, is entirely coincidental.
Text © 2022 by Robbie Couch
Jacket illustration © 2022 by Ana Hard
Jacket design by Krista Vossen © 2022 by Simon & Schuster, Inc.
All rights reserved, including the right of reproduction in whole
or in part in any form.
SIMON & SCHUSTER BOOKS FOR YOUNG READERS
and related marks are trademarks of Simon & Schuster, Inc.
For information about special discounts for bulk purchases, please contact
Simon & Schuster Special Sales at 1-866-506-1949 or
business@simonandschuster.com.
The Simon & Schuster Speakers Bureau can bring authors to your live event.
For more information or to book an event, contact
the Simon & Schuster Speakers Bureau at 1-866-248-3049 or
visit our website at www.simonspeakers.com.
Interior design by Hilary Zarycky
The text for this book was set in ITC New Baskerville.
Manufactured in the United States of America
First Edition
2 4 6 8 10 9 7 5 3 1
CIP data for this book is available from the Library of Congress.
ISBN 9781534497467
ISBN 9781534497481 (ebook)

For the unserious ones

CHAPTER 1

I t's official: a more perfect Friday will never exist.

My spring break has begun. The mural in front of me is turning out to be one of my all-time favorite creations. And, in just a few hours, I'll be on the most magical date of my entire life. Does it get any better?

Days like today are an anomaly, I've learned in my sixteen years. Days like today will stay with me forever. There's no other way to explain a day like today other than to say the universe must be delivering a hefty batch of good karma that I stored up in a previous life.

I am paying back said universe by featuring it on the storefront of Susan's Stationery—and doing a pretty bang-up job, if I do say so myself. The mural is only about halfway done, give or take, but coming along much better than I anticipated, honestly. A bubble-gum-pink Saturn with rings of teal floating in cobalt-colored space; the perfect pick-me-up on a boring block like the one that Susan's Stationery calls home.

Ms. Ritewood, the owner, handed over full creative control to brighten up the greige facade, which has been in desperate, decades-long need of an "aggressive facelift"—her words, not mine (although I wholeheartedly agree). City code would probably call for the crumbly storefront to be bulldozed and built from scratch, but with Ms. Ritewood's limited budget, a high schooler with a big imagination and even bigger paint selection is the next best thing.

"Blaine!"

I jolt at Ms. Ritewood's voice, nearly dropping my brush.

She floats from her store entrance to the middle of the sidewalk to get a better view of my progress. After a good five seconds of contemplation, she breathes, "It's coming along *wonderfully.*"

Relieved, I take a few steps back and attempt to see it through her eyes. "You think so?"

The cheery store owner, barely five feet tall, stands beside me, eyes wide and arms folded across her belly. "The colors are spectacular, Blaine."

"Yeah?"

She shakes her head in amazement, her sculpted, copper bob of hair unshakeable beneath a layer of hair spray. "The rings are mesmerizing."

"They're my favorite part."

"And . . . wait a minute. Is Saturn . . ." She leans forward, peering at the personified planet, with its emerald eyes, button nose, and oversized dimples. "Is Saturn supposed to be . . . me?" She rotates her head to get my answer.

I bite my lower lip, nervous now that the big reveal has finally made itself known. "Yes."

"Ah!" Ms. Ritewood lights up, arms shooting into the air. "I love it!" She goes in for a hug—

"Wait!" I jump back, showing the palms of my hands,

which are covered with smudges of cobalt acrylic. "I don't want to ruin your clothes!"

"Oh, that's right," she says, glancing at my raggedy white shirt, splattered with teal. "Smart move." She turns her attention back to the wall with a grin and a sigh.

This moment—the thrill in her eyes, the hanging jaw, the pregnant pause filled with all the possibilities an aggressive facelift like this one could mean for Susan's Stationery—is a big reason why I paint murals for local businesses around town. I also enjoy the aesthetic rewards of sprucing up my weathered corner of northwest Chicago, of course, and getting lost in my own fictional worlds of color is a form of therapy for me. But watching a business owner in real time taking in their new storefront? I'm not sure if there's a more rewarding feeling in the world.

Ms. Ritewood looks up at me, cheeks flushed with excitement. "Was your—" But an L train zooms along on the rusted tracks above, rattling the liquid surfaces of my paint cans and blanketing our conversation in a deafening roar. Ms. Ritewood finishes her thought, but I don't hear a word.

"Sorry," I say with a grin. "You'll have to repeat that."

"I said"—she raises her voice—"was your anniversary dinner canceled?"

"No . . . ?" I reply slowly, confused. "Why would it be?"

She glances at her phone. "Well, it's already six o'clock, Blaine, and I thought—"

I gasp. "What?"

"Yes, dear." She checks her phone again. "It's 6:09, to be exact—"

"I've got to go!" I begin hammering on the lids of my paint and throwing items into my reliable utility cart—the four-wheeled metal wagon that I've been dragging around Chicago since my first mural.

The biggest dinner *of my life* is tonight, and I'm running behind.

"Can I help you pack up?" she asks, glancing around anxiously.

I consider requesting that she gather up my drop cloth, before reminding myself that Ms. Ritewood is a sixty-something-year-old with lower back pain, persistent carpal tunnel, and the agility of a tortoise. "I've got it!"

"You're sure?"

"Definitely."

Once my cart is full and the cleanup is complete, I snag the cart handle and dash down the sidewalk for home. "I'm making good progress!" I shout over my shoulder. "I should be able to finish up in the next week or two!"

"Sounds good, Blaine," Ms. Ritewood calls after me, eyeing my cart with concern. "But take it easy with that thing! I want you to make it to your dinner alive—and in one piece!"

I jog as fast as my tattered cart will allow, without its wheels spinning off into oncoming traffic. Although they're the least efficient way back home, cozy side streets lined with brownstones are my preferred medium of travel, as the shade from the overhead trees breaks up the late-afternoon sunshine, and you'll likely see more dogs being walked by their humans that way. But there's no time for befriending strangers' pets when you're racing against the clock, so I veer right onto congested Milwaukee Avenue and pick up the pace, daring my aging cart to rebel.

I can't be late tonight. Not for the date night of all date nights.

This dinner could very well be one of the highlights of my high school experience, after all, the one-year anniversary of—

"Agh!" I hear the terror in my victim's voice before I see their face.

My guess is, someone turned the sidewalk corner a half second after I zoomed by going the perpendicular direction. And that suspicion is confirmed another half second later, when I feel something slam into the side of my cart behind me.

I turn around just in time to witness several paint cans fall over, and a human body, roughly my size, stumble toward the ground, dropping their plant. The plant pot slams into the sidewalk and shatters into a million pieces. Fresh, dark soil and shards of ceramic scatter everywhere.

"Oh no!" I yell, reaching down to help the victim up. To my horror, I realize that I know this very unlucky person. "Danny?"

Danny Nguyen ignores my outstretched hand. "Oof," he huffs, popping up from the concrete on his own and glancing around to see if passersby witnessed our crash. "Maybe you should slow down with that thing, Blaine."

"You're right," I say, lifting my paint cans back into their upright positions. Fortunately, none of the lids popped off in the crash. Acrylic crisis averted.

He sighs, eyes narrowed on me as he folds his arms against the front of his indigo puffer vest. I smile guiltily, unsure how to steer this painfully awkward interaction to a better place.

Danny falls (literally) into the category of acquaintance that makes a shameful disaster like this as bad as can be. He's not a friend of mine—someone who could immediately laugh this off and agree to hang out soon—nor is he one of the three million strangers in this city who'd go on their way as I go mine, both of us eager to put the embarrassment behind us. Nope, Danny is smack-dab in the middle—a fellow junior at Wicker West High School who's just vaguely aware enough of my existence to make this peak cringeworthy.

"Damn," he says, suddenly aware of what happened to his little cactus plant thing (which I assume is now on its deathbed). "My aloe vera."

"Your al-uh-what?"

"My aloe vera plant," he says, bending at the knees to assess the damage. "I just bought it."

"When?"

"Five minutes ago."

I gulp. "Oh. Dang. Well, Danny . . . I'm—"

"Sorry," he sighs, irritated. "Yeah, I bet you are."

"Really, though! I am."

With no remaining pot for the plant to call home, Danny carefully holds it in the palms of his hands like he's cradling a newborn chick. He looks up at me, expressionless, hoping I'll say or do something that will help make this unbearable moment a little less nails-on-a-chalkboard terrible.

I check my phone, grimacing. It's 6:20. I'm going to be so late. *So, so late.* "I've got to go!" I say, snagging the handle of my cart and darting off.

"Really?" he calls after me. "That's it?"

"I'll get you a new aloha plant, I promise!"

"Aloe vera!"

"What?"

"Never mind."

Welp, add "buy new al-uh-whatever plant for Danny Nguyen" to my running list of things to do, right after "finish Ms. Ritewood's mural." Alternatively, I could avoid him like the plague through graduation day, a year and some odd months from now, which—at a school as large as Wicker West—isn't entirely out of the question.

I finally make it home—a boring brick town house not unlike the sea of forgettable apartments near Susan's Stationery. (Maybe my next mural should be on my *own* block—a magenta Jupiter, floating in a turquoise solar system, surrounded by golden stars.) I drop the handle of my cart in front of the stone steps, race up, and blast through the front door.

My aunt Starr, standing a few feet away in her plush,

lavender bathrobe, looks just as frazzled as I am. I open my
mouth to explain how I lost track of time and then crashed
my cart into a classmate, but—

"It doesn't matter," she cuts in, holding up a finger.
"We've got fifteen minutes to make you sparkle. Let's go."

CHAPTER 2

My feet, achy from the sprint home, race up the stairs as fast as they can carry me. I slip my shirt and sneakers off as I speed down the hall, half-naked before I reach the bathroom.

"I hung your shirt up in there!" Aunt Starr calls after me from the foyer.

"And I put the rest of your outfit in there too!" my best friend, Trish, adds from my bedroom as I race by without glancing inside.

"Thank you!" I yell back to both of them, then slam the bathroom door, strip off the rest of my clothes, and jump into the shower.

First things first: washing the hues of Ms. Ritewood's psychedelic universe from my skin. I can't show up looking like a used paint palette tonight—not when everything needs to be perfect. So I lather up and start scrubbing with the gritty bar soap that Aunt Starr got me for my birthday. Once I've successfully transitioned back from a rainbow-spotted Martian to a peach-colored Earthling, I hop out and towel off.

Someone knocks. "Are you almost ready?" It's Trish.

"Yes!" I exclaim, rubbing lotion into my forearms. "Give me two minutes."

"Hurry up. You're cutting it close."

I rub in the lotion faster. "I know, I know."

I sigh and face my outfit, hung neatly on the back of the bathroom door. Much like Ms. Ritewood's mural on that snooze-fest of a block, this look likely won't harmonize all that well among the bland fabrics worn by Chicago's one percent tonight. But also like with Ms. Ritewood's mural, where's the fun in fitting in?

I push my fists through the sleeves of the white-and-yellow-checkered button-up and pull on the dark corduroy pants. Next come the complementing suspenders, and after a few frustrating failed attempts, I finally get my bow tie just right. I massage grooming clay into my sandy hair before carefully parting it the way I like (Don Draper style), add a subtle swipe of mascara to make my eyes pop, and walk through falling droplets of my favorite cologne—sandalwood with a hint of vanilla.

"Here we go," I mutter to myself, twisting the doorknob, and head down the hallway to my bedroom. I close my eyes as I approach the open doorway, knowing Trish and Aunt Starr are waiting inside to see the finished look.

"Well?" I say, nervous that they'll hate the outfit now that it's on me instead of just colorful pieces dangling from hangers.

I pop one eye open.

Trish, half-buried in a mound of pillows on my bed, pops her head up. Her round face, framed by springy, black curls, melts when she sees me. "It's perfect."

"You swear?" My lips sneak up into a grin. "You like?"

"That's it, Blaine. That's the look. And the mascara is the perfect touch."

I hope she's right.

Because this is *not* just another date night. It's the date night of all the date nights: my one-year anniversary with Joey Oliver. It's been 365 days, and I'm still pinching myself.

I glance at Aunt Starr, sitting in the chair at my desk, for final approval. "What about you?"

Aunt Starr's eyes travel up and down my outfit, studying each inch as she tightens the belt of her bathrobe and flicks a strand of blond hair off her face. She pauses dramatically before lifting a frosted chocolate doughnut to her lips, mulling over her answer. (We all know that Trish has a big say in my fashion choices, but Aunt Starr's two cents reign supreme.)

"Blaine," she finally breathes, carrying the weight of the room. "You look amazing."

I dash over to my bedroom mirror, where—unlike in the foggy bathroom—I can actually get a good look at myself. I let out a little shriek before twisting my socked heels against the slippery hardwood to face Aunt Starr and Trish again. Not to sound conceited, but they aren't wrong; I *do* look pretty great. "All right." I exhale. "This is happening."

Tonight is going to be filled with Fancy. The boy of my dreams is picking me up any second now, wearing his signature charcoal suit (Fancy). We're celebrating our big day in downtown Chicago on the most gloriously sunny spring evening ever (Fancy). We're having dinner at Grey Kettle, on the Windy City Center's seventy-eighth floor, overlooking a glittery Lake Michigan (Fancy AF). People like me, from ordinary families like mine, don't do Fancy like this. But tonight is an exception.

"They don't have a dress code, right?" Aunt Starr asks, popping the final bite of doughnut into her mouth. "Not that you don't look top-notch, but sometimes these hoity-toity places are annoying like that."

I take another hard look at myself.

It might not be the most conventional outfit for a Michelin Star restaurant, but understated ties and grayscale tones desperate to fit in have never been my thing. Joey knows my style anyway—would he take me to a place where I couldn't be myself?

I don't know if the ensemble reaches Grey Kettle's standards, but it exceeds mine. I hope that's enough.

Aunt Starr, probably sensing my nerves, flicks her wrist at me. "Forget I said a thing. They're idiots if they don't let you in looking like that."

I'm not sure how a goofy junior like me ended up with Joey Oliver—the It Boy of Wicker West High School's senior class. One impromptu dance together at the winter formal last year, and everything just fell into place, I guess.

Our first date was at Pequod's. (I laughed until my cheeks were numb, and I nearly choked on my slice of pepperoni deep-dish multiple times.) Date two was gulping down ginger beers in the park near my town house. (We shared our first kiss next to a patch of roses.) A week later, we made it official over hot chocolates and *The Umbrella Academy*.

It's been a fairy tale ever since.

Okay, a fairy tale that makes zero sense, I'll admit it.

Because on paper, we shouldn't be together. Joey's a straight-A student; I'm lucky landing Bs. He wears collared shirts and polished shoes; I'm more of a black-denim-jacket-and-pink-sneakers kind of guy. His family lives in a penthouse unit with views of the downtown skyline; mine lives in a greige town house with views of a fire hydrant. He's got a twenty-year plan to become president; I spend summers painting murals on places like Susan's Stationery as a side hustle.

We're two very different peas in a pod. But somehow it works.

"I can't believe that in, like, forty-eight hours, you'll be flying first-class to Cabo San Lucas," Trish squeals, rolling off the mattress and landing gracefully on her feet next to me. "You need to take photos by those big rocks off the shoreline. . . . What's that area called?"

"Land's End?"

"Yeah! Just imagine the sunsets you'll see there." Trish, eye-to-eye with me in her mint-green platform sneakers, grabs both my shoulders with a grin. "*Cabo*, Blaine. Cabo! With the Olivers."

"I know."

"This is big."

"I know!"

"An entire week with his family."

"Well, five days, but yeah—"

"Hold up." Aunt Starr slides across the room in her bunny slippers and plops onto the corner of my bed. Somehow there's another doughnut in her hand that came out of nowhere (this one, vanilla with sprinkles). "Uh, what? Five days with the Olivers in Cabo? Please explain."

"He didn't tell you?" Trish turns to her. "Tonight Joey's asking him to go on his big, annual family trip to Mexico over spring break."

Aunt Starr stares, jaw fully dropped. "Excuse me?"

I turn pink. "Yeah. Well, maybe! I think it's going to happen tonight. Joey's been dropping hints."

"*Big* hints," Trish says, striking various poses in front of my mirror.

"Do your mom and dad know about this?" Aunt Starr asks. "And isn't spring break like . . . now?"

"Know about what?" Mom says, appearing in the doorframe with a smile. Her light blue scrubs are dotted with stains and smudges from a long shift in the hospital's ICU.

"Your son's apparently going to Mexico with the Oliver family," Aunt Starr explains before I can, her eyes widening. "For a whole week, too—"

"Five days," I say, correcting her, straightening my bow tie in the mirror next to Trish, who's now trying on discarded belts and hats I left on the floor. "Please don't freak, Mom. It's not official. Joey hasn't asked me yet."

"But he is tonight," Aunt Starr whispers at her.

Mom takes a moment to process this admittedly pretty

big spring break update, which I hadn't planned on dropping on my parents like this—in front of Trish and Aunt
Starr, no less.

I pause and watch in the mirror as Mom mulls it over. I
can sense her hesitation.

"Well," she finally breathes. "Assuming Mr. and Mrs. Oli-
ver would be footing the bill, that would be awfully nice of
Joey to offer . . . ," she says, trailing off in thought. "But it's
Friday. Spring break started today. When are they leaving?"

"So this is where the party is." Dad pops up next to her,
a can of Coke in one hand, sandwich in the other. Just like
Mom's, his shirt—soiled with grime from a construction
site—reflects an extra-long day on his feet. "Sorry I missed
dinner."

"I just got home too," Mom sighs his way. They exchange
strained smiles that confirm it's been a long week for both
of them.

I usually hate when my bedroom suddenly becomes the
family hangout spot like this. But I can't complain, given the
exciting circumstances of tonight and the fact that it's rare
to have both Mom and Dad home at the same time. Having
them here adds to the thrill.

"These paninis are great," Dad says, taking an extra-big
bite. "Your handiwork, Starr?"

She winks at him. "Chef Starr at your service. There's one
for you in the fridge for later, Blaine, but I doubt you'll want
ham and cheese after feasting like royalty tonight."

"Feasting like what now?" Dad asks, wiping crumbs from

his mustache and letting out a burp. Trish giggles at him. Mom glances his way, giving him a chance to remember why tonight is so important, before clearly mouthing *the anniversary.*

"Oh!" He lights up. "That's right, the big one-year. Joey must be taking you somewhere nice, dressed like that. Crab Legs on Clark?"

Aunt Starr lets out a howl, raising the tip of her nose into the air and shifting her tone to sound like she's a pompous rich lady in an old black-and-white film. "Crab Legs on Clark?" she jabs with a grin. "Who do you think your son is, Kevin? A peasant?" She rolls over on the bed to get more comfortable, and her robe slips open, revealing the same silky lime-green pajamas she's been wearing for the past week. "Try Grey Kettle."

Mom gasps.

Aunt Starr nods.

"Blaine." Dad looks at me like she can't be serious. "Grey Kettle? Is your aunt lying?"

"I would never lie to my brother-in-law," Aunt Starr snaps back playfully, picking a sprinkle off the doughnut to toss into her mouth. Trish is giggling at her now too.

"She's not lying," I say, turning to Mom and Dad, my pink cheeks undoubtedly shifting to red. "Joey's taking me to Grey Kettle."

They both seem legitimately stunned.

Because in Chicago, landing a table for two on a Friday night at Grey Kettle downtown is basically like dining at the Obamas' private residence in Hyde Park. Unless you're from a power family, it just doesn't happen. I keep having to remind myself that tonight isn't that extraordinary, though—at least for Joey. The Olivers *are* a power family.

Does this mean I'm part of a power family too?

"Well, dang. Grey Kettle. Are we *sure* he's asking about Mexico and not your hand in marriage?" Mom laughs, half-serious. She pauses. "Wait . . . he's not going to propose, right, Blaine?"

The doorbell rings downstairs. Aunt Starr gasps. My heart starts pounding. Hard.

My little brown rescue mutt, Fudge, comes storming into the room to protect us with the ferocity of an angry grizzly bear.

"It's okay, bud, it's okay," I laugh, reassuring him with a quick pat on the head and a belly rub. "It's just Joey."

I glance over my hands to be extra sure I got every last speck of paint, fix one rebellious strand of hair in the mirror, and let out a long, excited sigh.

"How're you feeling?" Mom asks, beaming at me from the doorway.

"Good."

"Keys, wallet, phone?" Trish asks, grinning from ear to ear in my red bucket hat, which, knowing her, she'll likely wear home.

I pat my pockets before grinning back.

She gives me a big hug. "Deep breaths, okay? Just have fun."

"Yes, have *fun*," Aunt Starr says, rubbing the back of

my head. She stops abruptly, realizing it's ruining my Don Draper look. "Focus on the fun, doll. You're sixteen, not getting married—to your mom's relief. Have a good time."

"But not *too* good a time," Dad emphasizes. "Be home by eleven."

"Yes, Dad."

Mom kisses me on the cheek as I slip through them on the way out. "Love you, kiddo."

Why has the buildup leading to tonight felt so special? Sure, Cabo will be wonderful, and celebrating a one-year is inherently momentous—especially at an unforgettable place like Grey Kettle. But even so, these butterflies in my stomach are weirdly intense. They must know something I don't.

I open the front door, and there he is, glowing in the porch light.

The boy of my dreams.

Joey's lips crack into a small grin. The charcoal suit fits him just right—like a fashion designer sketched it directly onto his strapping frame. His eyes, crackling like fires, wander up my outfit before meeting my gaze. His thick, wavy hair is sculpted so perfectly, he might just be a real-life prince standing on the doormat (which, I'm just now realizing, is absolutely covered in Fudge's fur).

"Hi, Blaine," he says.

And that's all it takes for me to immediately melt into a puddle of goo.

CHAPTER 3

We peel onto the expressway in Joey's new black BMW, the sky outside painted in pinks, purples, and the perfect number of wispy white clouds. The galaxy I'm creating on the outside of Susan's Stationery crept off the wall and glued itself onto the real abyss above, it seems.

I want to keep my window down—the first smells of spring always hit right in the muggy Midwest—but I want to be able to hear Joey on the off chance he brings up Cabo during the drive there, and eighty-mile-an-hour air whipping into your face isn't the best facilitator for a meaningful conversation. So I roll the window up nearly all the way. Joey smirks, like he's up to something, before turning on the knob for the air conditioner. I sigh to myself dreamily, taking in the Fancy.

My eyes dance across the oncoming skyscrapers, their towering glass casting orange beams on Joey's chiseled jaw. I wish I were a sponge right now, soaking in every ray of light so that I could reimagine this scene perfectly in a future mural. Downtown views are such a cliché when they're regurgitated as street art, I know, but Chicago mom-and-pop stores love a good hometown skyline painted on their storefront.

"Happy to be on spring break?" Joey asks, glancing between me and the road.

My hand finds his thigh. "Of course. You?"

"Like you wouldn't believe."

For a second I think he *is* going to ask about Cabo, but the silence lasts a bit too long for comfort. So I move on.

"I know you're worried about student council stuff," I say. "But high school is drawing to a close for you—and fast. Try to enjoy it."

He takes a sharp breath in, which confirms that my suggestion that he try to relax had just the opposite effect. "Ashtyn is stressing me out with prom planning, AP Calc might ruin my GPA, and the elections for next year's class executive board are kicking into high gear the week we get back to class. A lot is happening."

"You're allowed to get a little senioritis." I grin at him.

He doesn't notice. "Not when you're an Oliver, you're not."

I look away, resisting the urge to roll my eyes. "No offense, but the school will be fine without you. Soak in these last couple of months while you still can, is all I'm saying." The car zooms over a maroon bridge, trembling on its metal beams, and the Chicago River plows through the concrete below. "At least you'll only be at Northwestern."

"*Only* be?"

"Yeah. Only be." I look at him. Again, he doesn't seem to notice. "As in . . . you know, Evanston's only about a half hour away?"

He's quiet.

"As in, we'll *only* be a half hour away from each other?"

He swallows hard, Adam's apple rising in his throat. I think he wants to say something else, but all he mutters is, "True."

That was . . . weird.

Maybe it's just student council stress. Or maybe he's nervous about asking me to Mexico.

This is a big night for him, too, after all. Joey's only dated one other guy before me—some dude named Aaron he met at a leadership conference—for a brief, chaotic six weeks, and it ended in disaster. I'll be the first guy he's bringing on his family's annual trip. Maybe butterflies have been batting through his stomach just as intensely as the ones fluttering in mine since I nearly killed Danny (and *actually* killed his aloha plant) with my cart earlier.

Three minutes and one wrong turn later, we pull up to the front entrance of the Windy City Center—a narrow, pitch-black needle of a building that shoots straight into the ozone. It's the newest and third-tallest skyscraper in Chicago, but when I'm standing down here, engulfed in its vast shadow, it might as well be a million stories high. I'm in total awe just being here, but remind myself to keep outwardly chill, seeing as literally every person around me is far more Fancy. My suspenders and checkered shirt are enough to make me stand out; I can't also look like a starry-eyed local kid who ventures downtown for special occasions no more than three times a year, tops (even though it's true).

Joey tosses his keys at the valet—which, yes, feels as cool to witness as you'd think it would—and we breeze through

revolving doors into the lobby. Everything, and I mean everything, is glass inside. We cross the room and tell a red-vested
worker—the bellhop? concierge? elevator dude? I have no
idea what sort of Fancy title he has—that we're headed to
Grey Kettle.

He recognizes Joey. "How's it going, Mr. Oliver?" he asks,
pressing the button for floor seventy-eight.

"Doing well, thanks," Joey replies.

"Enjoy, gentlemen."

I smile to say thanks too—and nearly curtsy. What can I
say? My body involuntarily reacts when I'm feeling awkward.
That's how out of my comfort zone I am in places like this!

"How did your parents get us a reservation again?" I
ask as we zoom into the sky and my ears pop. Elevator dude
becomes a tiny red dot on the shiny white tile below, until
our all-glass elevator plunges into the blackness of the higher
floors. "My mom and dad were shocked when I told them we
were going here."

His face crinkles in thought. "The owner was a client of my
mom's, maybe? Or a childhood friend of my dad's? Not sure."

I nod. "Gotcha."

Something feels off.

Joey doesn't seem *upset*. Maybe just . . . distant? Like his
body's here, but his mind is still at school on a Wednesday
afternoon, consumed by student council election prep and
graduating-senior stress.

I decide to just come out and address it. "Hey." My shoulder bumps his. "You okay?"

The elevator arrives at seventy-eight, and the doors crack open.

"Yeah," he says, forcing a smile. "Why?"

I take his hand in mine as we step inside. "Just wondering."

Grey Kettle looks exactly how I imagined. Well, I Googled it just about every day since Joey asked me about coming here, so it's not like my mind was starting from scratch. But still, it's even more stunning in person.

The first thing I notice are the views. Large windows line the exterior walls, with an endless Lake Michigan extending to the east, and a concrete jungle, draped in the colors of a setting sun, surrounding us on the other three sides. Somewhere people are playing a piano and a violin, soothing the bustling restaurant floor into a calming lull. The lighting is soft. Every table has a flickering candle on it, and every guest is dressed like tonight means something important.

The host glances at my shirt, surely about to make a remark—my whole body tenses up, because maybe Aunt Starr was right to raise a flag. But the host stops herself when she realizes who I'm with. "Oh, Mr. Oliver. Nice to see you again."

"Hi, Wendy."

"Happy anniversary, you two."

"Thanks."

"Right this way."

Wendy seats us at our table, which is nestled in the far corner. I might be biased, but I'm sure we have the best view in the house. Looking straight down, which forces my stomach up into my chest, I see where the lake intersects with the river. Following the urban grid north and south is like Christmas morning for my eyes, absorbing new buildings, new colors, and new art. We're high enough that we could be floating on a cloud, yet still low enough to appreciate the street-level details. I've lived in this city my whole life, but I've never seen it like this.

"Wow," I mutter, pulling my phone out for a pic. I look to Joey. "This is crazy, huh?"

His eyes, focused intensely on the drink selection, don't leave his menu. "Yeah," he says, unbothered by the views. "Wild."

Okay. I've experienced Anxious Joey before—usually he surfaces ahead of big speeches in front of the school or the nights before exams—but this attitude is truly next-level. I'd rather he ask me about Cabo now and get it over with so we can enjoy the night, instead of putting up with this human ball of nerves sitting in front of me for hours on end.

A waiter comes and takes our drink order. I stick with water; Joey goes for Sprite.

Then we sit in silence.

"So . . . ," I begin, already feeling like I'm scraping the bottom of the barrel for things to talk about. I decide to lean in to the student council drama, thinking he may need to talk it out before he can enjoy himself. "How are the upcoming elections going?"

He sighs, exasperated, and I immediately regret my strategy.

"It's ridiculous that they make seniors help organize the juniors' races for next year's executive board, you know?" he says, increasingly irritable. "I won't even be at Wicker West. Why should it fall on me? Mr. Wells is being so lazy about it too."

"Mr. Wells? The math teacher?"

"Yes, but . . ." He looks at me like I should know this by now. "He's also our student council adviser?"

"Oh, right, right, sorry."

Keeping up with Joey's student council stuff is the least-interesting boyfriend responsibility that falls onto my plate. I'm constantly forgetting who's who and what's what. It's not my fault my mind wanders the moment Joey starts talking speeches and prom budgets. More times than not, it drifts off to whatever mural I'm working on. And up here, with these spectacular sights fueling my right brain, I have a feeling it'll be extra easy to get distracted.

"Zach Chesterton is going to win in a landslide anyway," Joey continues.

I pull my mind away from Saturn's rings outside Susan's Stationery. "Win what?"

"The class presidency for your grade." The waiter places our drinks on the table, and Joey goes in for a sip. "We might as well not even have an election. I mean, a bunch of juniors are trying to get on the ballot to be next year's senior class president too, but Zach has the experience, the name recognition, the look."

"The look?"

"Yeah. He just *looks* like a class president. You know?"

I stop myself, yet again, from rolling my eyes.

"I know it's a sad reality," Joey adds, probably sensing my

annoyance. "But let's be real: looks matter when it comes to this stuff. If anyone knows that, it's me. If people can't *see* you as class president, you probably can't *become* class president." He sits up and straightens his tie before adjusting his fork and knife on the table. "That—uh," he stammers, and sips his Sprite again. "That kind of brings me to my next point."

I can tell by the way the words move off his lips that, whatever his next point is, he means business.

My stomach drops.

"Blaine." He reaches out and grabs my hand on the table. His palms are a bit sweaty, but I don't mind.

My heartbeat is in my throat.

Wait. Is this the Cabo moment? I'm not sure what Zach Chesterton becoming class president has to do with our spring break, but I roll with it.

I sit up straight too, swallowing hard. We may be floating a million feet high in Illinois, but my mind flashes to scenes at sea level in Mexico, surrounded by white sand and swaying palm trees. I exhale, accidentally too hard, and it nearly blows out the candle on our table.

"I . . ." He glances down at the table, finding the right words.

Just ask, I think, unable to stop grinning. *You know I'll say yes. Just go for it.*

"Blaine, I . . ." He looks back up again, his eyes finding mine. "I think we should break up."

I snort, a little relieved that he decided to ease the tension. "Good one."

He's not smiling anymore. He's not saying anything.

He's just staring at me, each second lingering longer than the one before it.

"Wait," I say, my stomach now dropping much, much faster—through my chair, through the floor, all the way down to the lobby. It's chilling next to red-vested elevator dude right now.

Joey licks his lips before biting the bottom one. "I think it's best."

I yank my hand away from his.

"I'm sorry," he says.

"But . . ."

"I know."

"I . . ."

"Don't be angry."

"I thought you were asking me to go to Cabo!"

His face contorts into a confused ball of mush. "Cabo? Blaine, my family's flying there on Sunday."

"And?"

He grins. He dares to *actually grin* right now. "I would have asked you months ago if I had plans to take you to Cabo."

My head is spinning. I'm starting to hyperventilate. "Oh my God. I can't believe you took me *here*—to *Grey Kettle* on our *anniversary*—to dump me."

"Babe, don't freak out."

"*Babe*, don't call me 'babe' right now."

"It's just . . . ," He starts speaking in a hushed way, sensing eyes from across the restaurant falling on us. "You know

I have a lot going on, and my parents aren't making it any easier."

"Okay? So?"

He leans into our table, speaking in a near whisper. "My family? My mom, the real estate tycoon who's shooting a pilot for HGTV? My dad, the most famous attorney in the Midwest? Their expectations of me are higher than the Windy City Center!"

I realize my mouth is hanging open. I want to close it, but can't.

"My neurosurgeon brother graduated at the top of his class at Columbia," he barrels on, working himself into a frenzy. "My sister launched her own nonprofit that just partnered with the *Gates Foundation*, Blaine. Bill Gates! And my parents are *still* disappointed in them."

"Again . . . *so*?" I feel tears collecting in my eyes. "What do your brother and sister have to do with us? What does *any of that* have to do with us?"

"I'm my parents' last shot at big-time success." He nods at a few onlookers with a grin, uncomfortable with their prying eyes.

I can't believe what I'm hearing. "Neurosurgery and BFFs with Bill Gates don't qualify as success?"

He exhales in frustration—like he's explaining something simple to a stubborn five-year-old. "You don't get it. You don't get how high the bar is for me. If I'm going to become the first openly gay president someday—"

This time, I can't help it—I actually roll my eyes.

"See!" He notices. "You think my dreams are a joke!"

"No, I don't!"

His voice shoots up about a hundred octaves. "You just rolled your eyes!"

"I didn't mean it like that. But you have impossibly high standards for yourself, Joey."

Beads of sweat are forming on his brow, and his cheeks are getting increasingly flushed. "If I'm going to make it through pre-law at Northwestern, then law school on the East Coast, then win a seat in Congress, then take the White House, I *have* to have impossibly high standards for myself, Blaine. That's how the world works."

I close my eyes, holding my head in my hands for a second.

Is this really happening?

"Okay, but . . ." I swallow hard, wishing I had stayed to keep working on Ms. Ritewood's mural instead of hurrying off to get dumped seventy-eight stories high in the air. "I'm still trying to figure out how you hypothetically winning the presidency, like, *decades* from now has anything to do with me—anything to do with *us*."

He shakes his head. "Don't you get it?"

"What am I supposed to get?"

"Blaine. Come on." He glances around again, leaning in even closer. "If I'm going to do big things, with a life in the public eye, I need to start dating . . . you know . . . serious guys."

Huh? "Are you kidding me?"

He gives me a look that confirms he is definitely not kidding me.

"So you're breaking up with me because I'm too . . . *unserious?*"

He considers the allegation. "I wouldn't put it that way, but—"

"I can't believe you're doing this," I mutter to myself. "I can't believe you're letting your tyrannical parents dictate your dating life."

"Don't put words in my mouth."

"Isn't that what's happening, though?" I say. "Mr. and Mrs. Oliver are the puppet masters controlling your life, Joey—puppet masters that apparently hate my guts."

"It's not like that," Joey retorts. "They like you. Don't take it personally."

Don't take it *personally?* I want to scream.

"Did you have to do this tonight?" I ask.

"I—"

"And here, in *literally* the most romantic restaurant in Chicago?"

"Well—"

"And to think that—"

"Look at your shirt, Blaine!" he explodes. Someone at a nearby table drops their fork. The restaurant falls silent. "Why would you wear that shirt, with those cheap-looking suspenders, to a place like this? Huh? It's not Halloween. And look at your hands! I know you were working on a mural after school, but you couldn't even manage to get all the paint off for our one-year anniversary?"

I glance down at my palms and spot a few specks of Ms.

Ritewood's cobalt universe that I somehow missed in the shower.

"See, this is why I have to do this—why this needs to end," he continues. "I need a right-hand man—not some artsy kid who paints pictures on buildings for less than minimum wage and calls it a job."

I would have preferred that he punch me in the gut. That would have felt better than this. He's spent the past year bottling everything up, clearly, and it all just came pouring out of his mouth like gasoline on a fire.

My world is moving in slow motion, a nightmare stuck in molasses. Every patron in our corner of the restaurant is staring at us—staring at *me*. I may have felt Fancy tonight, but obviously I'm not Fancy enough for them. Or Joey Oliver.

"Okay," I say softly, standing. "I'm going to go now."

"Hold on," Joey says guiltily, now keenly aware of all the unwanted attention he's garnered. "I didn't mean to—I want to be friends, Blaine. That came out wrong. I like your shirt. And I don't really care about the paint on your hands! Blaine?"

My legs are completely numb, but they somehow get me to the elevator. The host is staring at me like I'm the most pitiful thing she's ever seen as the glass doors close between us. I descend to the lobby, unable to fully grasp what just happened.

"Sir?" elevator dude asks, confused, as I breeze past him toward the exit. I must not be hiding my grief all that well. I need to get out of here, and I need to get out of here *fast*—

But I don't have a way home.

A Lyft to my neighborhood would cost a day of work on a mural, easy, so that's off the table. I'd call Trish, but she has plans with her girlfriend, Camilla—a date night that's undoubtedly going much better than mine. I don't want to ruin their evening.

I pull out my phone and frantically find Aunt Starr in my contacts.

"Blaine?" she asks, surprised.

"Hi."

"Oh no," she says. I must sound absolutely awful. "What happened?"

"He . . . uh . . ." My voice cracks. My mouth can't even find the right words. "I'm not doing so great."

"You're at Grey Kettle?"

"Yeah."

"Don't move," she says. "I'll be right there."

I hang up.

Eyeballs are piercing me from Fancy passersby in the lobby; old men doused in thick colognes and ladies in trench coats staring like I'm the rainbow-colored Martian who crash-landed in their world of normal. Haven't they seen a distraught sixteen-year-old with paint on his hands before?

"Sir?"

I jump, startled. It's elevator dude. "Yeah?"

He lowers his voice, holding out a tissue. "For your eyes?"

Oh my God. My mascara!

I flip my camera phone lens to see myself. I look like a complete and total hot *freaking* mess. I take the tissue and wipe away the streams of black collecting around my eyes. "Thank you."

"Not a problem, sir." He lingers a moment longer, as if to ask if everything is all right.

"I'm okay," I assure him. He and I both know it's obviously a lie. But it's enough to get him to leave me alone.

I look up at the all-glass elevators zooming up and down the far wall of the lobby. Joey has to be on his way down. Even if it's just to make sure I make it home okay. Surely, Joey Oliver isn't the kind of prick to enjoy our *anniversary dinner* by himself at Grey Kettle after dumping me. Right?

Right?

One minute goes by.

Five minutes go by.

I stop counting the minutes.

The screeching of tires outside breaks the lobby's white noise, confirming Aunt Starr's arrival. I take one last glance at a final descending elevator to make sure Joey's not in it (he's not) before spinning through the revolving doors.

The valet guys look mortified by Aunt Starr's rusting 2003 Volvo. It's loud, its exhaust is particularly smelly, it absolutely does not belong anywhere near the Windy City Center—and I've never been happier to see it. It might not be Joey's BMW, but screw Joey's BMW.

The passenger-side window rolls down, and Fudge's slobbery face appears.

Aunt Starr bends her neck from behind the steering wheel to see me on the sidewalk. "Let's get the hell out of here."

CHAPTER 4

Thank God for dogs. More specifically, rescues. Bushy, brown mutt rescues. Whose names are Fudge.

He's nestled up against my chest in bed, fast asleep, little belly expanding and contracting with each breath. Every few minutes, a muffled bark escapes his mouth as he chases a squirrel or cat in his dream (although, he gets along great with most felines in real life). Maybe he's chasing after Joey for me.

It's been exactly one week since the Worst Day Ever, and I have yet to leave my bedroom. Well, except for meals, bathroom breaks, and taking out the trash in my pajamas (an involuntary chore enforced by Dad). Instead of rolling around in the sand on a tropical beach with Joey, I've been rolling around in an unkempt bed with Fudge. Seven days later, and I still can't believe it happened.

And that it happened *that way.*

What kind of monster takes his boyfriend to one of the most beautiful restaurants in town—on their anniversary—to throw him under the bus? The night keeps recycling through my consciousness like a horror movie stuck on repeat. The rattled stares from other diners; the way he sipped his Sprite before delivering the news he must have known would ruin my year; the look in his eyes as he explained his need to start dating Serious Guys.

Serious Guys.

The worst part? I'm not over him! Not even a little. I'm still madly, sadly in love.

And I want him back.

I pull out my phone for approximately the 347th time today (I have to type in the passcode, as the phone can't identify my smushed, tear-streaked face, half-hidden by pillows), and open my email. Bad, bad mistake.

I'm immediately filled with dread.

Ms. Ritewood messaged, wondering when I'll be able to finish her universe. The most candidly cruel part of me wants to reply with a simple "never," but the guilt of abandoning an unfinished project would haunt me forever—not to mention the fact that the criminality of treating Ms. Ritewood as though she's anything other than the stationery queen that she is would guarantee a lifetime of bad karma.

The truth is, I haven't felt this creatively depleted in a very long time.

Do I even *want* to paint anymore?

As difficult as it was to hear, Joey made a valid point at Grey Kettle: Serious Guys don't wander around town bringing fantastical scenes to life on aging brick buildings. And they especially don't do it way below market rates, as I'm sure Joey's business-savvy mom would tell me.

Maybe I'll take this season off.

Although it's a rule of mine to never leave a client hanging, I scroll past Ms. Ritewood's email, convincing myself I'll deal with it later.

My finger taps Instagram.

And there he is. The very first thing I see on my refreshed feed.

Joey, shirtless and sun-kissed standing near a palm tree, has a drink in his hand, with a slice of pineapple peeking out the top. Just the latest photographic evidence of the Olivers' magical spring break without me. Posted seven minutes ago.

The worst decision I make every spring break is deciding to go back home! #JustKidding #ILoveChicago, he captions, followed by a row of sun and orange-heart emojis.

I suppress the urge to projectile-vomit all over Fudge and my bedspread.

"Oh. My. God." A voice says to my right. I jump.

It's Trish. She's standing in the doorway, completely mortified, next to her girlfriend, Camilla. And okay, whatever, the looks on their faces are definitely warranted, I admit.

Dirty clothes are everywhere. Also, dirty dishes. My "Melancholy Mood" playlist is humming along, Taylor Swift's *Folklore* confirming I'm still spiraling.

"Blaine," Camilla says with a sigh. "Dude."

"This room smells like a barn," Trish says, walking over to my side of the bed, Camilla following behind her. "We've got to get you out of here."

"My parents and Aunt Starr already tried—many, *many* times throughout the week," I answer. "If they couldn't motivate me with promises of Jeni's ice cream or that new Pixar movie, what do you think your chances are?"

Trish and Camilla exchange knowing looks.

Seeing them in real clothes makes me realize how wholly unfit I am for public consumption, sitting here in dingy sweats and a stained hoodie. Trish's pineapple-yellow, faux-leather jacket complements her earrings, while her golden eye shadow, sparkly on her brown skin, is the perfect contrast to my Oscar the Grouch aesthetic. Camilla has on an emerald baseball cap that draws out the green in her eyes, a silver *T. rex* necklace (she's obsessed with dinosaurs), and a spaghetti--strap shirt.

They're carrying large drinks with bright pink straws from our go-to coffee shop nearby, Biggest Bean. Trish hands me the third cup. "Your fave—mocha."

I mumble out a "No."

Trish doesn't care, pushing it into my palm anyway. So I take a sip. I don't admit it out loud, but its chilled creaminess definitely hits just right.

"Blaine, this is unacceptable," Camilla says, poking my butt to get a rise out of me. "It's been an entire week. Your whole spring break is gone."

"And?" I ask.

"*And?* What, are you planning on dying in here?"

"Yes."

Trish turns off Taylor Swift with a sad sigh before sitting next to me and rubbing Fudge's face. "Look. Remember when Camilla dumped me last year and I fell into a depression spiral?"

Camilla swivels her head, forcing her chestnut hair, pulled into a tight ponytail, to flip in front of her shoulder. "Why do you have to drag me into this?"

"I'm getting at something, I swear," Trish responds, turning back to me. "Well, we did get back together, obviously, but you gave me some solid advice that helped me put my head back on straight. Well, put it back on *queer*, I guess is more like it. Do you remember what it was?"

I rack my brain. "That you could do better than Camilla?"

Camilla's eyes pop open.

I smirk. "Just kidding."

They both light up, relieved I'm still capable of making a joke.

"So?" Trish says after I don't respond. "Do you remember?"

I squint in thought, but my mind is incapable of revisiting a single coherent memory prior to the Worst Day Ever (which, tragically, I can recall in very great detail—down to the bubbles fizzing on the surface of Joey's Sprite).

"Never give someone else the authority to dictate your self-worth," Trish says after it's abundantly clear that my mind is malfunctioning. "Now I'm reciprocating that same advice to you. Don't let Joey dictate your self-worth."

I sigh.

It was a nice attempt at a pep talk, but I'm not having it.

"Blaine, c'mon." Trish begins yanking me out of bed by my arm, but I'm resisting. Hard. She gives up after a minute. "There will be other boys!"

"*Lots* of other boys," Camilla says.

"Boys on boys on boys."

I pout for a second, which I know annoys the hell out of Trish. "I don't want other boys, though. I want Joey."

They fall silent, setting down their drinks. Trish looks to Camilla. Camilla catches her eye. Then their gazes find mine and I know that something's up.

"Wait. . . ." A scheme is unraveling before me. "What are you two about to do?"

"Blaine," Trish says, pulling my mocha out of my grasp and placing it on the bedside table. "We're sorry."

Before I can defend myself, Camilla rolls me onto my stomach and pounces onto my back. She's as strong as hell. "What the—?"

Trish quickly wraps a blindfold around my head, and ties it tight. *Real* tight. I can't see a thing. "We have a surprise for you."

"Does it involve taking me into the woods and murdering me?" I gasp, struggling to breathe. "Because it feels like that's what's happening right now!"

"No. It only involves you putting on flip-flops."

"That's it," Camilla notes, all her body weight pressing me into the mattress. "You don't need to bring a thing."

"Can I at least shower first?" I ask into a mouthful of bedding.

"No. You'll slip out of the bathroom and escape."

They know me too well.

Camilla pulls my arms back, and I feel cold metal click around my wrists. "Wait, are those handcuffs?"

"Yes."

"You two cannot be serious."

"The surprise will be worth it," Trish says unconvincingly. "I promise."

Camilla climbs off—I can finally take a full breath again—and guides me to my shoes. I slip them on because there's no sense in fighting a losing battle now. With one of them on either side of me, they direct my steps downstairs and through the foyer.

"What're you three up to?" Aunt Starr asks, presumably from the couch. I hear her crunching on popcorn as *Bridgerton* plays in the background.

"They're taking me hostage! Please help, Aunt Starr!" I plead.

There's a brief pause.

"I'm happy someone's finally able to get you out of the house," she says, cranking up the TV. "Have him back by dinner, ladies."

I'm guessing it's a nice day on the northwest side of Chicago, as the birds are chirping, and the sun feels warm on my forehead. But Trish wrapped the blindfold so tight, I might as well be trekking along the L's underground train tracks.

"When we get back to your room, you're doing your laundry, by the way," Trish orders.

"And taking all the dishes to the kitchen," Camilla adds.

"My room's not *that* bad," I retort.

"Yes," they say forcefully in unison, "it is."

We walk a few more minutes, and—judging by the total

time in transit and the familiar scent of baked sweets in the air—I think I know where they're taking me.

"Biggest Bean?" I ask as we come to a complete stop.

Camilla unlocks the handcuffs.

Trish pulls off the blindfold.

It takes a few seconds for my eyes to adjust to the sun, but I'm finally able to squint and confirm my suspicions. Yep, Biggest Bean Roasters. Except we're standing on the side of the building, in the empty, grassy lot next door. There used to be a laundromat here, Mom told me once, but it burned down when I was a little kid. Now it's just a barren, rectangular eyesore with more fortunate businesses remaining on three of its sides.

"Um . . ." I look between the two of them. "How is this the surprise? Weren't you two *just* here getting our drinks?"

"*This* is your surprise," Camilla says, gesturing to Biggest Bean's exterior brick wall. "Bao hired you to paint it."

Oh. Whoa. "For real?"

"Yes," Trish says, the sparkles in her eye shadow extra glittery in the sunlight. "And you can paint anything you want too. He trusts you."

"I mean, maybe keep it PG-rated," Camilla clarifies out of the corner of her mouth. "But yeah, basically anything. Trish asked him about it earlier, and he seems super chill about the whole thing."

"I'd say even excited," Trish adds.

"My vote is for a scene out of the Jurassic period," Camilla says, nudging me.

Trish rolls her eyes. "Of course you'd go dinosaur-themed."

"Maybe a few brachiosaurs eating lunch near a lake?" Camilla adds, geeking out. "I don't know, something serene."

"Why would a coffee shop want *brachiosaurs* on their wall, babe?" Trish asks.

"I *am* doing a psychedelic Saturn outside Susan's Stationery," I explain. "The solar system doesn't have a direct relation with paper, so it's not like the mural has to be relevant to the store."

"See?" Camilla smirks. "Brachiosaurs it is."

They spin off into a discussion about coffee and dinosaurs, leaving me alone with my thoughts. My mind races through the possibilities of the towering canvas staring back at me.

There's no doubt the store's smiley owner, Bao, enjoys our near-daily visits (which probably has a lot to do with how much money we spend in there, come to think of it). But, unlike Susan's Stationery, his Vietnamese-American fusion café and bakery is on a prominent street corner in a commercial building that attracts a ton of eyeballs. Surely there are much better Chicago artists—professional artists—who are up for this job.

He wants *me?*

I scan the exterior. For someone who's constantly on the prowl for blank walls to make over, I'm almost embarrassed I've never considered Biggest Bean before. The building is aged, to be sure, its chipped bricks ranging from red to burnt orange and charcoal. A few lingering remnants from murals past are left fading too, but overall the building is still in decent shape.

It's a big wall, though. A *very* big wall. Most of my murals are on the smaller side; this would take me all summer to finish.

"I—"

"Don't worry," Trish says, reading my mind. "He's not expecting you to paint the whole thing. Just the bottom corner closest to the sidewalk, where most pedestrians walk by."

"You can go bigger, if you want," Camilla says. "But he said even, like, an eight-by-eight-foot piece would work. Just to give the wall some *oomph*."

I think a moment longer.

There must be a catch.

"I bet he's not offering to pay me, though, is he?" I ask with a grin. I've learned that some business owners in well-trafficked areas are still under the impression that "exposure" is the same as cash to an artist.

"One thousand," Camilla says flatly.

I stare. "One thousand . . . what?"

"Dollars," Trish says. "His offer, not ours."

"You're kidding."

"Nope."

"I mean . . ." I've never been paid $1,000 for a job before. "Are you sure?"

They laugh. "Yes."

I made $400 recreating the Hollywood sign on Filmore Films' entrance last summer, and $500 for a depiction of

RuPaul's Drag Race on Betty's Wigs in Uptown. But $1,000?

My decision from this morning comes crashing down on me. "Wait, I can't."

They look confused.

"Why not?" Trish asks.

"I don't think I'm going to paint this season."

"How come?" she prods.

Camilla gapes. "You didn't mention this before."

"I know, sorry." I start moseying up the edge of the building toward the sidewalk. "I decided this, like, today."

"Does this have to do with Joey?" Trish asks.

"No! I mean, yes. Well, sort of." I'm not sure how to articulate it all. "I've been thinking about what I'm doing with my life—"

"Blaine."

"—and, although I love painting, I barely make any money from it, and—"

"Blaine."

"—it's a lot more work than you two realize, honestly, with getting the right paint and equipment and all the labor that's involved—"

"Bl—"

"Please, stop! Okay? I'm just trying to figure things out!" I burst, plopping down onto the grass next to the sidewalk.

Trish and Camilla go quiet for a moment before joining me cross-legged on the grass.

"I'm sorry," I say to them, a bit embarrassed. "I didn't mean to go off like that."

"It's cool," Trish says. "We got you."

"Thank you for asking Bao about it," I say, glancing between them. "But I want to take a break from painting. If not for the whole season, at least for just a minute. All right?"

They both lean in for a group hug.

"Of course," Camilla whispers.

"Love you," Trish says.

The hug is an especially long one. And after a week of nearly zero human interaction—and almost *too much* Fudge interaction—it's exactly what I need. We stay down there on the edge of the grass a bit longer, watching pedestrian ankles trot by. Trish and Camilla fill me in on the stuff I missed over break because I was too mopey to leave the house. Most of it wasn't too FOMO-worthy, except that they went to a drive-in to see the original *Frankenstein*. I wish I'd gone to that.

My mind starts wandering off, distracted by the breeze, and the swaying trees, and all the hustle and bustle. Business-people dashing from Biggest Bean, lattes in hand; skate-boarders enjoying the final stretch of spring break doing tricks against the curb nearby.

I wish I were with Joey.

I shouldn't even be thinking that, I know; he broke up with me in the most monstrous of ways (speaking of *Franken-stein*). But the heart wants what the heart wants. Mine still wants Joey Oliver.

Last Friday was a fluke. That's not who he really is, I don't think. He's been stressed over student council, and prom planning, and Northwestern. And it's not like he was lying about the pressures from his family; the bar truly *is* sky-high for the Oliver kids.

I want him back.

The bell on Biggest Bean's front door jingles as a group of college guys wearing DePaul University shirts pours out from the coffee shop.

"I can't believe he beat Tucker Randolph, though," I overhear one of them say, sipping his coffee. "Jeff is going places, man."

"Today it's DePaul vice president of student government," another chimes in. "Tomorrow it'll be the freaking mayor of Chicago."

"What a badass."

"Right?"

They carry on out of earshot, but I'm stuck on Jeff—whoever the heck he is.

Jeff. DePaul vice president. The guy who's going places.

The future freaking mayor of Chicago, maybe.

A *badass.*

I can see him now, with his khaki pants, his beaming disingenuous smile, and a knack for arriving fifteen minutes early. Vice President Jeff is the exact kind of running mate Joey would want on his ticket someday. Heck, I bet Jeff is the exact kind of Serious Guy that Joey would want *to come home to* someday. . . .

I gasp.

Trish and Camilla gasp too.

"Don't scare me like that!" Trish yells, flicking me on the shoulder. "What's wrong?"

I stand and begin pacing the patch of sidewalk in front of us, my brain firing on all cylinders.

If the key to being with a Joey is becoming a Jeff, who says I can't become a Jeff?

"Blaine, you okay?" Camilla asks, looking concerned.

"You're freaking us out," Trish says.

I stop, smiling wide. "I know what I have to do."

"You're going to paint Bao's wall?" Camilla asks excitedly.

"No."

Her lips curve into a frown.

"I know what I have to do to win Joey back." I stand taller, inhale deeper. "Trish. Camilla. I'm running for senior class president."

CHAPTER 5

Oh, wow." Trish plucks a purple sucker from her lips, scanning me up and down. It's quite the contrasting reaction to the one she gave my Grey Kettle look, but I expected this one would spark a different response. "You really were serious about this senior class president thing, huh?"

I shrug sheepishly, glancing around to see if this outfit is garnering anyone else's attention. The hallway is especially raucous the first morning back at school, as everyone's reuniting with friends and dishing on their spring breaks. I suspect many students have heard about the breakup by now, although no one's asked me about it yet. Not too many people care about me getting dumped, to be clear, but Joey Oliver being single again? Wicker West High School absolutely *does* care about that.

"You hate it, don't you?" I ask Trish, squishing my face into a cringe.

She closes her orange locker door with a bang, turning to face me head-on. "It's, uh . . . it's different."

"So you *do* hate it."

"No. It's rare that I see you in a suit, is all. And it's . . . Isn't it a little . . . ?"

"Big?"

She grimaces. "Yeah."

"Dang it."

"It's okay, though!" She attempts to backtrack, shifting her textbooks from one hip to the other and giving her sucker another lick. "It's on the roomier side. But you can pull it off."

"Roomier side" is one way to put it. Who am I kidding? Another whole Blaine could fit inside this suit jacket with me—and we'd probably have space for a third.

The white button-up tucked into my baggy slacks nearly reaches my knees, and these black dress shoes belong on a circus performer. I'm the funeral version of Bozo the Clown, more or less. But hey, this is what you get when you're limited to your dad's closet to find professional-looking attire. If this is the Serious Guy aesthetic Joey wants, this is the Serious Guy aesthetic Joey will get.

"Okay." I straighten my tie, which is basically the width of my neck. "I'm ready."

"You're *sure* you want to do this?"

"Yes."

"Because I think running for class president is like, a *thing*."

"I know."

"As in, it's a commitment," she says. "A big one."

"I understand that."

"Here's the thing." She adjusts my tie a little more, careful to keep the sucker between her fingers from touching it. "Remember when Camilla dumped me last year and, for like forty-eight hours, I was hell-bent on spending my entire summer in Seoul for some reason?"

My eyes dart upward in thought. "Yes," I reply slowly. "What's that got to do with anything?"

"Humans tend to do impulsive things when they're in a slump," she says, brushing lint off my shoulders. "And right now, you're in a slump. Just like I was post-breakup."

"Are you implying that my running for senior class president may be a stupid rash decision based solely on Joey dumping me, and one that I'll potentially grow to regret forever?"

She opens her mouth ever so slightly, rocking her head from side to side. "Well, I'm not *not* saying that."

"Trish." I put her hands in mine. "Trust me. Does Joey have something to do with all this? Sure," I admit, knowing that was the understatement of the year. "But I want to run. Okay?"

She stares so deeply into my eyes, I'm pretty sure she's seeing through the back of my head. "All right, then," she says, nudging me with her elbow—her way of giving me a high five.

I march down the hallway alongside Trish, to where Joey is manning the student council elections table prior to first period. No, I haven't seen him since the Worst Day Ever. And no, I can't be entirely sure how I'm going to react when talking to him again. Will I get the urge to slap him? Kiss him? Both, consecutively? We're about to find out.

A crowd of freshmen departs from the front of the table, and there he is.

Still the boy of my dreams.

His Cabo sunburn has faded into a golden glow. A

maroon sweater vest pairs perfectly with the cute, brown glasses he sports on Mondays, when he's too tired to put in his contacts but still wants to look polished. Even standing a few feet away, I catch a subtle whiff of his cologne, and it makes me nostalgic for what we were a mere two weeks ago.

His face drops when he sees mine. "Blaine?"

I try to put an extra pep in my step as I approach—and nearly trip into the elections table from walking in my clown shoes. "Hi, Joey."

He nods behind me. "Hey, Trish."

Trish is not excited to see him, which her tone makes abundantly clear. "Joey."

"That's an interesting jacket you have on," he says, trying to interpret my outfit. "Why . . . ?" His voice trails off, jaw hanging slightly ajar.

I give him a second to finish. "Why . . . what?"

"Why are you wearing it?"

I take a deep breath. Trish gives me a supportive shove from behind, probably sensing my nerves.

"Joey," I say, exhaling. "I've decided to run for class president."

He stares. "I'm sorry, what?"

"I'm entering the race."

The staring continues, my words apparently not registering.

Trish steps up, and stands shoulder to shoulder with me. "What's so difficult to get? Blaine would like to learn more about entering the race for senior class president." She gestures around at the table, which is covered in sign-up sheets and candy dishes to lure prospective council members. "Isn't that what y'all are doing here?"

Joey, jaw still ajar, looks from her to me. "*You* want to be senior class president?"

I grin. "What, like it's hard?"

The conversation falls flat. Our eyes are locked. I wish our spark was still there—like when he was looking at me on my front porch two Fridays ago—but it's more like he truly can't compute the words leaving my mouth. Like I'm speaking Elvish to a hobbit.

"Hi, Blaine." Mr. Wells, scratching at his white beard, pops up next to Joey. He raises his chin to see me through the bottoms of his bifocals. "Have a nice spring break?"

"A terrific one," I lie.

"Really? *Terrific?*" Joey's friend Ashtyn Nevercrop appears on the other side of Joey. "That wasn't the answer I was expecting. Did I just hear you're running for class president?"

Ashtyn is the absolute worst.

She and Joey go way back. Like, their parents were best friends in middle school, back. She's unforgiving, deeply cynical, and incredibly protective of her friends. If you cross her, she'll throw you under the bus. And not like a camper van. One of those massive SEE CHICAGO! buses, where the tourists sit outside, on top, as it rolls through the Magnificent Mile. Ashtyn only tolerated my existence while me and Joey were together; now I'm undoubtedly on her enemies list.

"Hi, Ashtyn," I say with a smile, refusing to play her

ROBBIE COUCH

games. "You are correct. I'd like to learn more about running for senior class president."

She tosses her dirty-blond hair behind one shoulder. "You do realize you'll be entering the race incredibly late, right?"

"And?" Trish interjects without missing a beat.

Ashtyn's ice-blue eyes pierce Trish with a menacing glare. "*And*, a million other juniors are running already."

"Well, let's not be hyperbolic, Ashtyn," Mr. Wells says, attempting to lower the temperature. "Many have expressed interest, but so far only six have met the signatures requirement."

"Signatures requirement?" I ask, glancing between the three of them.

Joey, finally finding his voice again, adjusts his glasses. "You'll have to get fifty signatures from fellow juniors who approve of your candidacy," he says.

"What exactly does 'approve of your candidacy' mean, though?" Trish asks.

"It doesn't mean they're committing to voting for you," Mr. Wells says, handing me a sheet with slots for fifty names. "It just means they're open to considering it. See?"

He points at the language typed across the top of the page.

I, _____, believe the candidacy of _____ for senior class president deserves to be considered by the Wicker West High School Student Council.

54

"Please don't make up or forge names—yes, we do check to make sure they're valid," Mr. Wells continues, clearly having had to explain this a hundred times before. "As Ashtyn noted, you'll be a little under the gun, Blaine. We'll need your fifty signatures by Wednesday."

My eyes pop. "As in, like, two-days-from-now Wednesday?"

Ashtyn, sensing my panic, grins. "Yes."

I lean toward Trish. "Do we even know fifty people?" I whisper.

"Of course," she says, knowing Joey and Ashtyn are listening.

"Okay," I say, turning back. "So if I get the fifty signatures, I'm on the ballot?"

"No," Ashtyn cuts in.

"Maybe if you'd listened when I talked about student council stuff, you'd know that already," Joey says with a passive-aggressive laugh.

He and I both know there's nothing funny about this.

"Sorry," I say, easing the tension with a laugh myself. "Then what happens after the fifty signatures?"

"If you get fifty valid signatures, you'll then give a three-minute speech in front of the student council," Mr. Wells says.

"Holy"—I catch myself—"crap. Sorry. I just, I didn't know a speech was involved. In front of the whole council?"

"Well, we don't want just *anyone* running for class president, do we?" Ashtyn retorts.

"The speech should note why you're running and what you'll bring to the office," Mr. Wells explains.

"The type of president you'd be, the theme of your campaign, the expertise you'd bring to the table," Joey lists, knowing full well that I've never given a thought to any one of those things.

"Okay," I say, racking my brain. "And then I'm on the ballot?"

"And *then*," Ashtyn says, unable to contain her glee as she watches me flounder under the weight of all these revelations, "the council will vote. At least half of the student council has to vote yes to putting you on the ballot."

"This year there are ninety-four student council members in total," Mr. Wells says, "which means at least forty-seven of them must like your speech enough to think your name deserves to be on the ballot."

"Forty-seven seems like it'd be difficult to pull off, no?" I ask.

Mr. Wells nods. "Should you get your fifty signatures and make it to that point, I'd highly recommend you put a lot of thought into your speech and platform, Blaine. Plus, the more work you put into your speech, the better prepared you'll be for the debate."

"The what now?" I ask.

A *debate*? As in, I stand under a bunch of bright lights and argue with other people for an extended amount of time?

Joey sighs. "C'mon, Blaine. You know this. The final candidates debate in front of the school. Don't you remember mine last year?"

Yes, I do. But I totally forgot about it until this very second. "Of course I do."

"Blaine," Joey says, lowering his voice. "Why are you doing this? Is this about us?"

"Joey," I whisper back confidently, although I am feeling anything but confident right now. "No. This is about me wanting to be senior class president."

Mr. Wells hands me a packet. "Here are all the details about how our elections work—dates to keep in mind, requirements for each candidate, those sorts of things."

"It's especially useful for rookies who've decided to run with zero experience," Ashtyn adds with a bite. "I'd keep it handy."

"Awesome, thanks for all your help," I say, taking it from Mr. Wells. I give them all one last smile and begin to shuffle away, and trip in my clown shoes as I leave.

Once we're out of earshot, Trish leans in to me. "What did you just sign up for?"

Fifty signatures by Wednesday.

A speech in front of the student council.

A debate in front of the entire *school.*

"I don't know," I say, on the verge of either laughing or crying, I'm not sure which. "But I need to get serious if I'm going to pull this off."

★ ⭐ ★

CHAPTER 6

To say I'll be out of my comfort zone for the next month isn't quite accurate. It's more like I've been shoved—catapulted, really—into my discomfort dystopia, and I've only got myself to blame. Petitioning classmates for signatures? Giving a speech to the student council? Debating a bunch of brainy kids onstage? I'm the oddball with earbuds in, painting murals by himself—*not* a handshaking politician in the making.

I've got to get serious, though. Starting now.

Like, literally. *Right now.* I don't have an hour to waste.

I begin with the most immediate hurdle I need to overcome: the fifty signatures.

At lunch I snag a table in the cafeteria all to myself and pull out the sign I made at the end of first-period art. It reads BLAINE FOR SENIOR CLASS PRESIDENT! in big, blue letters. Juniors will spot it, come over to chat, and sign on the dotted line.

Or so my theory goes.

"What's this?" Carly Eggman asks, strolling by while sipping a Diet Coke.

"Hi, Carly! Thanks for asking. I've decided to run for senior class president, and I . . . Oh, okay, see ya." She's already drifting away with Caleb Kresky, who's distracting her with a cheeseburger and fries. "Let's chat later!"

I tape up my sign so it's hanging at the most optimal angle to take advantage of cafeteria foot traffic, and display a pen and the sheet of paper that Mr. Wells gave me to collect signatures. I roll up the sleeves of my dad's oversized suit jacket, strap on a smile, and start glancing around awkwardly, hoping at least a few fellow juniors care enough to acknowledge my existence.

Then I wait. And I wait. And I wait some more.

Five excruciating minutes go by before Matt Hattle stops in front of my table and confusedly furrows his brow, popping a pretzel into his mouth.

"Hey, Matt," I say after he remains silent. "I'm running for senior class president."

"I see that. But aren't you a junior, like me?"

"Yes. These are the elections to determine *next* year's class leaders, and—"

"I heard Joey dumped you, by the way. Sorry. That must be rough."

I feel my cheeks getting hot. I laugh to ease the weirdness. "Thanks. It's, uh, it's not a big deal, though—"

"I heard he did it on your anniversary, too. Is that true or just a rumor?"

I clear my throat. "Yeah, it's not a rumor."

He leans in, lowering his voice. "Dude, that *blows*."

"It's okay. Things are looking up! I'm running for senior class president, and I'll need signatures to—"

"Fill me in on this later. I've got to run! But keep up the good work, Blaine."

And he's off.

Welp, oh-for-two.

I didn't expect that convincing people would be easy, of course, seeing as BLAINE FOR SENIOR CLASS PRESIDENT! probably reads as akin to TORTOISE RUNNING IN 50-YARD DASH! to most. But at this rate, I'll be in college before I can get fifty people to get on board.

Ashtyn is awful, but maybe she's right for scoffing at my attempt to take the reins from Joey. She's been in student council since middle school, after all, and understands the politics of Wicker West High School, arguably better than anyone else—Joey included. I assume the only reason she's not running herself is because she's secretary of the National Honor Society, French club chair, and captain of the varsity softball team. (If she could clone herself to lead every extracurricular group at WWHS, though, you'd better believe that becoming Joey's successor would be her top priority.)

She may be a lot of things, but stupid isn't one of them. And if Ashtyn thinks my presence in this race would be a joke, maybe I should quit while I'm ahead.

Wait, no. *Stop it, Blaine.*

To avoid falling down a regret rabbit hole, I dig into my bag and pull out the packet Mr. Wells gave me with important election info. It lays out the big dates to keep in mind— notably the student council speech, and the debate the day before the election. On the packet's third page, there's a list of requirements each candidate needs to meet in order to run. *Candidates must have a GPA of at least 2.0.* Check. *Candidates must refrain from using profanity in campaign rhetoric, including speeches, debates, and hallway posters.* Tempting, but okay. *Candidates must choose a campaign captain before submitting their signatures.*

Oh, that's right. I need one of those. Joey chose his freakishly organized, anal-retentive friend Ralph to be his last year. He would have chosen Ashtyn, I'm sure, but she was a sophomore, like me, and campaign captains need to be in the candidate's same grade.

I flip the page to read up on the role's specific duties. The conventional campaign captain will help the candidate *craft a message and campaign theme for their time in office,* the packet reads, as well as assist with a handful of logistical responsibilities on the day of the election.

Trish appears by my table next to Camilla. "I know you told me earlier that you wanted to do this alone today, but . . ." She pauses, trying to read my face. "How's it going?"

I push the paper that theoretically should have signatures on it their way. "Not great," I say. They glance down to see that exactly zero people have signed. "Only two people have stopped to talk."

"Who were they?" Trish asks.

"Matt Hattle and Carly Eggman."

Camilla shrugs them off in support of me. "Would you even *want* Matt Hattle and Carly Eggman to be your first signatures anyway?"

"I mean . . ." I think for a second. "Yeah?"

"We'll be your first," Trish says, picking up the pen and signing on the first line.

Camilla jots down her name too before peeling off half her string cheese and handing it to me.

I inhale it all in one gulp. "Hey, by the way," I say, looking at Trish, "how do you feel about being my campaign captain?"

She looks back suspiciously.

I hand her the packet, which is open to the page outlining the role's responsibilities. She takes it to read. "'A campaign captain will help the candidate craft a message and campaign theme for their time in office'? 'A campaign captain may take a candidate's spot, should the candidate forfeit their right to lead after they've qualified for the ballot'?" She drops the packet and gives me a look. "What, does Mr. Wells expect you to get assassinated?"

I roll my eyes with a grin, taking the packet back. "So that's a no from you?"

"It seems pretty involved," Trish says, turning to Camilla. "I feel like you'd be a better fit for this than I would."

"No, no, *no*," Camilla says, immediately pushing back. "No offense, Blaine, but all *this*"—she gestures at the sign on my table—"is not my thing."

I sigh. "I mean, same. And I'm learning that the hard way."

"Plus, I have a lot of internship hours at the Field Museum for the rest of the semester," Camilla says, dropping the remaining string of cheese onto her tongue.

My eyes wander back to Trish. I let a frown of desperation push the corners of my lips into my chin. "Pretty please?" I ask softly.

Trish contemplates for another moment, staring off into the cafeteria in thought. Camilla nudges her arm, encouraging her to say yes.

"Okay, fine," Trish surrenders. "As long as you know *why* I'm saying yes to you."

I try to read her face, puzzled. "Why are you saying yes to me?"

"Because you are my best friend, I love you, and I will have your back until the day I die. If I do this, I will go hard for you, and leave it all on the table."

"Aw," I say, feeling a bit tingly. "That's so cute, Tri—"

"*However.*" She lifts a finger to add an important caveat (which I should have seen coming). "I am not saying yes because I support your reasons for running. I don't think winning class president should be a prerequisite for winning back an ex-boyfriend, and I think it's important you understand that. Okay?"

Camilla turns to me, hesitant, to gauge my response.

I contemplate, unsure what option I really even have. "Well . . . okay. Deal."

Trish nods. "Deal."

Camilla exhales with relief.

"Now." Trish folds her arms across her chest, looking down at my BLAINE FOR SENIOR CLASS PRESIDENT! sign. "As your campaign captain now, can I make my first official suggestion?"

"Oh no." I stand and hop around to the front of the table in my clown shoes to give the sign another look, terrified I misspelled my name. "Where's the typo?"

ROBBIE COUCH

"No, nothing like that. I think it should be . . . different."

"What do you mean?"

"'Blaine for Senior Class President.' That's fine, I guess. But what's motivating people to stop and talk to you? What's motivating them to support you?"

I think. "I don't know. Joey put candy out on his elections table before first period. Do you think M&M's could do the trick?"

"Yes," Camilla says quickly before taking a swig of her almond milk. "Candy sells."

Trish gives her a look. "No. Okay. Blaine. My boo." She suddenly gets serious. "Can I be real with you?"

I nod before sitting down again.

"These are the types of campaign signs that make most people roll their eyes at student council elections," Trish says. "This sign is all about you. It's peak narcissism."

"Agreed," Camilla adds.

I guess I never thought about it that way. These are the types of signs that blanket the hallways every election season; I just made the poster I thought I was supposed to make.

"Well, let's think of something better, then," Camilla says, eyes narrowed in thought. "Vote Blaine. He'll . . . bring back Snow Cone Fridays?"

"Vote Blaine Bowers, the boy who will . . ." I pick up the pen and start doodling mindlessly on the corner of my signatures sheet. "Paint his way to victory? No, that's terrible, don't listen to me."

Without my conscious effort, the ink from my pen recreates Ms. Ritewood's Saturn before shading in its rings and dotting some subtle stars in the background. Clearly my brain defaults to my murals whenever I give it the space to wander. And despite my best attempt to put painting on the forgotten back burner, my unfinished work outside Susan's Stationery is still simmering just a daydream away.

Focus, Blaine. You've got a presidential campaign to run.

"How about . . . ," Trish says, bringing me back to our conversation. "'Let's talk'?"

The three of us pause.

"You're just getting started," Trish follows up. "Your campaign needs a pulse. Maybe the best way to do that is to talk to people. Get a sense of what's on their minds, what issues they'd like a class president to lead on." She shrugs. "Like, yes, the real reason you're running has to do with Joey, but you shouldn't let them see that."

"'Let's talk,'" Camilla mutters, mulling it over. "I don't hate it."

Neither do I. "'Let's talk.' Simple. To the point. I like it."

Trish is right. If I need fifty signatures—not to mention a campaign speech that resonates with actual students—I might as well focus my campaign on them.

I grab my bag and snag the same blue marker I used to make the sign in art, then pull down my sign. I flip it over and start fresh on the blank side. This time the words are all caps and extra big: LET'S TALK.

"Are you sure you don't want us to stick around?" Trish asks as I finish off the last letter. "We don't mind."

"I can bring you more string cheese?" Camilla adds.

"Nah," I say, using the same tape to reattach the sign in front of the table. "I think it's good for me to do this on my own. But thank you."

They wander off toward our usual table in the cafeteria. I barely sit back down again before someone approaches.

"'Let's talk,'" Bobby Wilson reads. "Talk about what?"

I'm caught a little off guard. What *do* I want to talk to students about? "I guess we can talk about anything you want. I'm running for senior class president and want to know what issues are important to stu—"

"Mr. Anderson's coffee breath," he says way too quickly, as if he's been bottling it up for years. Bobby moves his blond bangs away from his eyes. "He's got bad, *bad* coffee breath. I sit in the first row, right next to his desk, and the smell ruins my morning every day."

I pause, unsure if he's joking. But his lingering silence and dead-serious direct eye contact confirms that he is not, in fact, going for a laugh.

"Well . . ." I pause to swallow, finding the right tone to sound empathetic. "As class president, I'm not sure how much sway I'd have over Mr. Anderson's hygiene choices— although, I don't mean to trivialize its negative effect on your mornings."

"It's brutal."

"Are there any other issues that I might be able to control through student government?"

He folds his arms in thought. "No one's ever asked me."

He presses his lips together and pushes them from side to side, pondering. "Exams, maybe?"

"Exams," I repeat. "What about them?"

"They're awful," he says. "This school puts way too much emphasis on them. The stress level is unbearable. I hardly sleep during exam week because I'm so anxious. And when I don't sleep, it throws everything else off too—my appetite, my mood, my focus at practice. And then I end up doing *worse* on my exams because of it!"

"Wow, yeah. I mean, I hear you. I'm a terrible test-taker in general. Exam week exacerbates it all."

"Right?" Bobby picks up the pen and starts signing to the right of Ms. Ritewood's Saturn sketch, just below Camilla's name.

"Oh, signing that means you're in support of my—"

"I know," he says, giving me a smile. He starts walking off. "If you can ban exams, you'll get my vote, Bowers!"

Huh. My first campaign supporter who's *not* a friend.

Maybe Trish was onto something here.

Not even ten seconds go by before Maggie Dorris wanders up with her friends Tracy Sheets and Elle Palms.

"Hey, Blaine," Maggie says. "What's this all about?"

"I'm running for class president and want to know what's on your mind," I say.

Maggie and her friends stare back—maybe a bit surprised.

"You want to know what's on *our* minds?" she says with a smirk. "What gives?"

I laugh. "I'm trying to gauge what issues people care about, what changes they'd like to see, those sorts of things."

They look among each other.

"I mean, everyone's being awful online lately, but what's new?" Tracy says.

"I feel like it's been really bad lately, though," Maggie adds.

"How so?" I ask.

Elle leans in and lowers her voice. "You know, the shady comments and the subtweets and the leaked screenshots of other people's convos and pics. . . ."

"Seriously," Tracy confirms. "It's gotten so cliquey this year."

Then they look at me—like *I'm* the one who should have a solution.

Oh, wait. When you're running for class president, you *are* the one who should have the solutions.

"Um," I say, swallowing hard.

Does Blaine Bowers, candidate for senior class president, have an official stance on social media drama? "How does all of that make you feel?"

Oof. *Stupid question, Blaine.* Ridiculously stupid question. But the three of them don't seem to take it that way.

"I dread even opening Insta now," Maggie admits, glancing between Tracy and Elle. "Like, it's not fun anymore because of all the meanness, but then there's also this pressure to always be on and always be posting, you know?"

"And if you're not posting, it's like you're irrelevant, or

you basically don't even exist," Elle says. She laughs. "That sounds like an exaggeration . . ."

"No, I get it," I say, recalling how I felt over spring break watching Joey frolicking on the beach as I rolled around in my filthy bed. "Instagram can make you feel terrible sometimes."

Maggie picks up the pen and jots down her name. Elle and Tracy follow suit.

"Appreciate you asking us," Elle says with a grin. She bends in close so she can whisper, "And screw Joey. You can do better than him anyway, Blaine."

They skip off.

Holy crap. The sign is actually working!

A few moments later, Joshua Golden confides that he feels as though hazing on the varsity baseball team has gotten out of hand—but he's too embarrassed to bring it up to any teacher or his parents. Rachel Rugg says fatphobic comments run rampant around school, worsening body-image issues, but nobody's addressing it. Jesse Rodriguez notes that, although Wicker West is a big and diverse school, being second-generation is always stressing him out in ways that his white friends don't get. At one point, there's a line of students forming in front of the table who want to talk to me.

An actual, literal *line*.

With just a few minutes left before the lunch bell rings, I'm at twenty-seven signatures. Twenty-seven! Maybe fifty by Wednesday *is* doable.

With a slight lull in the pace of students approaching the table, I open the notes app on my phone and start jotting down the feedback I've gotten, before it all goes in one ear and out the other.

"Hey—" I say, feeling a presence near me and looking up to my next visitor. Oh.

It's Danny.

"'Let's talk,'" he reads aloud, eyes shifting from the sign to my face. "How about we talk about the aloe vera plant that you owe me?"

It's like someone dumped a bucket of ice-cold awkward onto my head. My cheeks get flushed and my mind spirals into overdrive, concocting a plan I can tell Danny about buying him an aloha (or whatever) plant. I completely blanked on the cactus-looking thing that I killed on the Worst Day Ever. "Danny, I promise that I'll get one to you ASAP. I've just been busy."

He smirks, and I can't tell if it's playful or serious. "I'll believe it when I see it." Danny is lean and handsome, with full lips, kind eyes, and black hair buzzed in an enviable fade. His gray, striped shirt is crinkled beneath the straps of a bulky book bag hanging off his shoulder.

"So," he says. "You're running to be our class president?"

"I am."

"What for?"

"Well." I point toward my sign. "That's why I want to talk to students. I want to know how I can be a good president for them."

His eyebrows perk up, and his mouth dips into an impressed frown. His fingers trace the signatures on my paper, his head nodding ever so slightly as he murmurs the names of my potential supporters.

"Why do I feel like I'm being judged?" I ask.

"Because you are," he says. "Isn't that the whole point of an election? We're supposed to assess the candidates and choose which one we think would be best?"

I consider his take. "Touché." I push the sheet of paper a few inches toward him. "I need a few more signatures to officially enter the race. What can I do to win your support?"

He licks his lips, adjusting the straps of his backpack. "You've never been in student council before, right?" he asks.

I pause. "No, but—"

"And you want to go from student government novice to senior class president"—he snaps his fingers—"just like that?"

"Well, I—"

"Get me a new aloe vera plant. Then we can talk about me *maybe* signing." He nudges the paper back. "See you later."

Danny spins around on his sneakers and disappears into the crowd of drifting bodies and food trays.

Okay, so one clever sign can't make up for killing a person's plant, it seems. But if I have forty-nine signatures by Tuesday night, you'd better believe I'm showing up on Danny's doorstep with an entire forest to win his support.

I pull out my phone to Google "plant shops near me" but feel another hovering presence arrive in front of the table.

"Hi, Blaine."

It's Zach Chesterton. Current junior class president—and clear front-runner for next year's senior class president, according to Joey.

My mouth dries up.

This should be interesting.

"Nice jacket," he says sweetly—but there's some spice behind it.

Zach is dressed how I probably *should* be, with a faded salmon blazer fitted nicely over a textured white turtleneck. A silver watch is strapped around his thin wrist, and curls of his wavy, dark brown hair frame his narrow face. As much as I hate to admit it, Joey wasn't totally off base at Grey Kettle; Zach *does* carry himself in a way that demands the respect of a leader.

"'Let's talk,'" he says, glancing down at my sign. "That's cute. What would you like to talk about?"

I clear my throat and smile. "Anything you'd like to talk about, Zach."

"Okay," he says, smirking. "What brings you into the race for class president? It feels a bit . . ." He pauses. "Random."

"That's an excellent question. I've never been involved in student council, but I've always been curious," I say, although it's not really the truth. "Why not go big senior year?"

He laughs, amused. "Well, I hope you plan on going *really* big." He rests his palms on the table and leans toward me. "You know I got ninety-seven signatures in support of my candidacy, right?"

"I did not. Why, though, if we only need fifty?"

He ignores my question. "Maybe you heard that I've already gotten verbal commitments of support from many of the most influential juniors, including several varsity football team members and a plurality of the cheerleading squad?"

"I didn't get that memo, sorry."

He bends in even closer. "Did you know I've been our class president since we were freshmen?"

"That I *did* know."

"And I've led our grade to first-place victories in the homecoming float competition every year since?"

"The *Flintstones*-themed one last year truly was remarkable. Good work."

"My point is"—he's now so close that I can smell his strawberry gum—"if this election is some game to you that involves Joey, you might as well quit right now." Zach picks up the pen and signs his name. "Because I'm always in it to win it."

And there he goes. My twenty-eighth supporter.

I didn't expect Zach to welcome me into the race with open arms, but even so, that was one of the weirdest interactions of my life.

I watch him find a spot to stand in near the cafeteria doors as I begin to pack up my stuff, a bit frazzled from whatever the heck just happened. Because, like, why am *I* such a serious threat deserving of an attack? If Mr. Wells is correct and I become one of seven candidates in the running, why would Zach's ire be directed at an underdog like me?

Joey appears in the cafeteria doorway as I'm about to pull down my sign. I pause to see if he'll walk over to say hi. I mean, sure, he seemed appalled by my decision to run this morning, but maybe he's coming around to it now.

Joey doesn't seem to notice me or my sign. He does, however, notice Zach.

They smile at each other, take a step closer together—and share a kiss.

As in, their mouths touch.

As in, I think maybe their tongues do too.

As in, *what the hell is going on?*

I get light-headed and crash down into my seat, grateful I didn't land on the floor instead. I blink away the shock in time to see the two of them walking away, hand in hand.

CHAPTER 7

You and zach??? Are you for real??

I don't even think about it. I just hit send.

it's been 10 DAYS, Joey. you found another boy-friend IN 10 DAYS???

I fire that one off too.

Did you think the movie HOW TO LOSE A GUY IN 10 DAYS was written for you??

I don't know if that last text even makes sense, but it's in Joey's inbox before I can stop myself. I'm rage-typing a fourth when Trish returns to the sofa in the corner of Biggest Bean with my mocha and her latte.

"Blaine," she says threateningly. "Are you texting him?"

"No."

"Blaine!"

"Maybe."

She puts her drink down on the coffee table and swipes my phone in a flash. "Get yourself together!"

How could Joey do this to me? How could he be this cruel?

He dumped me in the trash like moldy bread at Grey Kettle, sped off to Cabo San Lucas to show off his upper torso on Instagram, and then returned home with a tan and another boyfriend—all in just over a week? I've had feuds with Fudge that have lasted longer than one week. And of course Joey'd pair up with Zach, too—the most serious of all the Serious Guys at Wicker West.

Wait.

"Do you think he was cheating on me with him?" I blurt—way too loudly.

"I don't know," Trish says, exhausted with me. She hands over my mocha before slipping off her red raincoat. "But even if he did cheat on you—right here, right now, you've got to chill out, because you're scaring the other customers."

I glance around Biggest Bean and spot more than a few curious onlookers. My petulant mood doesn't match the vibes inside. It's cozy and warm, per usual, with the soothing smell of fresh coffee and baked sweets wafting over from the counter up front. Trish and I snagged our favorite corner in the far back, away from the hustle and bustle, where we've claimed a spongy couch and oversized beanbags as our own next to the wall that Bao turned into a stuffed bookcase. Alicia Keys is humming along from the speakers above, and raindrops are splattering the window nearby. Typically this would be my pure bliss. But not today.

"Sorry I'm late," Camilla says, tossing her coat and bag aside and falling onto the beanbag next to Trish. She's wearing her internship uniform—a white polo and navy pants—and looks like she normally does after a long day at the Field Museum: tired but content. "What did I miss?"

Trish is looking at my phone, her almond-shaped eyes practically bulging out of their sockets. Clearly, she's horrified by my texts. "You didn't miss much, just Blaine firing off a bunch of unhinged messages to Joey that he'll regret in a half hour."

"Uh-oh." Camilla bends her neck to read too, her bushy eyebrows furrowed with dread. "Hoo boy."

"Can I have my phone back if I promise not to text him anything else?" I ask.

"No," they say in unison.

"He's a total douchewad, Blaine," Camilla says. "He's not worth your time, your energy, or your angry texts. Screw Joey *Golden Child* Oliver."

She's right. Joey *Golden Child* Oliver deserves to get screwed.

Still, I'm gutted. Totally, completely, full-stop gutted.

Somehow today is even worse than the night at Grey Kettle. Because now I'm even further up Breakup Creek without a stupid paddle, having put my whole life on the line for this dude. I've stopped painting murals and left Ms. Ritewood hanging, just for Joey. I'm running for class president, just for Joey. I'm wearing clown shoes and a tie that could fit an elephant, just for Joey.

And he's got Zach Chesterton's tongue down his throat?

"I'm not running for president," I decide aloud. "I can't do it now."

"No!" Camilla gasps. "You can't drop out because of Joey."

"Why not?" I say, taking a swig of my mocha. "I decided to run because of him."

"You got nearly thirty signatures at lunch, Blaine," Trish says. "You can get fifty by Wednesday, easy. What you did today struck a chord. Why give up now?"

"Hold on." I blink, long and slow, to underscore my surprise. "Weren't you just telling me that I shouldn't be running for president to win back an ex-boyfriend?"

"Yes." Trish blinks back at me—equally long and slow. "And?"

I grin, because her rationale isn't adding up. "So if I wanted to enter the race for the wrong reasons, wouldn't you be happy if I decided to drop out?"

She ponders, eyes following a few pedestrians rushing through the rain outside. "I guess I don't want you dropping out for the wrong reasons either." She sips her drink, turning her gaze to meet mine again. "Honestly? The cafeteria was buzzing over at your table today, Blaine."

"It really was," Camilla adds.

"Okay, okay." I roll my eyes. "But it was buzzing over *your* 'Let's Talk' sign. You deserve most of the credit for my signatures today."

Trish rocks her head back and forth, considering the idea. "Regardless, juniors apparently like someone in student government asking about what's on their minds, right?" She shrugs. "I don't know, maybe you should listen to them—and then be in this race for the right reasons?"

The soft buzzing of Biggest Bean fills the silence in our corner.

She may be onto something, but I'm mentally and emotionally drained from the day, and the more we talk about student council stuff, the more I'm imagining Joey and Zach swapping spit.

"Let me think on it," I say, sitting up. "Let's talk about something other than the election. *Anything else.* How'd the internship go?"

Camilla sighs. "Good. Busy. They're redesigning the dinosaur exhibits to include more interactive features, and I'm helping out with that."

"That's awesome, babe, look at you," Trish says, rubbing her back.

"It is pretty cool," Camilla says with a grin. "I'm the youngest person in the internship program—everyone else from other high schools is a graduating senior."

"That's badass," I say.

"Maybe. But it also means I constantly feel completely in over my head. Impostor Syndrome is *real.*"

"Camilla," I say, gently kicking the bottom of her shoe beneath the coffee table. "You are one of the smartest people slash brainiest future scientists at Wicker West. If anyone deserves this internship, it's you."

"No lies detected." Trish pecks her girlfriend on the cheek.

"Aw, thanks, guys." Camilla's face lights up. "Oh! I almost forgot." She reaches into her pocket and pulls out a business card. "This is my boss's info. There's a new job opening in our department, and I think it'd be perfect for Aunt Starr."

"Oh yeah?" I say, taking the card from her. Camilla's

written *Cool gig for your aunt!* above the dude's name.

Aunt Starr has been living at our house since Thanks-giving, after getting laid off meant she could no longer afford rent for her apartment in Logan Square. Now she spends her days cleaning with a podcast on, cooking with an audiobook blaring, or watching every show on every stream-ing service repeatedly, usually with chilled wine and a treat in hand. I'm not sure how much Aunt Starr has loved her "sea-son of change," as she's optimistically calling it, but I know I've loved every second. Normally, with Mom and Dad both working a ton, I'm home alone with Fudge most evenings. That changed when Aunt Starr came into the picture.

If she gets a new job, it'll be back to heating up leftovers solo for me.

"What's the position?" I ask Camilla.

"Aunt Starr does event planning, right?"

"Yeah, I think so."

"This new role is director of events for children's pro-grams," Camilla explains. "So she'd be organizing all the ador-able events and activities at the museum for twelve-and-unders. I told my boss how amazing Aunt Starr is, and he said she should email him to set up an interview. Pretty perfect, huh?"

Unfortunately, yes. This *does* sound perfect for Aunt Starr. Part of me wants to trash the business card and never relay the job opening info, just to ensure I get a few more months with her at home. But that would be cruel. I'll pass it along (but then secretly wish Camilla's boss retracts his inter-view offer).

We finish our drinks and call it quits for the evening. I decide to stay back and thank Bao for offering me the job to paint the exterior building wall, because—even though I'm still not going to do it—the opportunity deserves a thank-you. I don't see anyone working up front, so I tap the bell next to the register with a loud *ding.*

Someone pops up from the other side of the counter, startled. "Ah!"

"Oh!" I jump too.

What the heck? It's *Danny.*

Danny freaking Nguyen.

"Are you kidding me?" I blurt.

He holds a hand over his chest and exhales, setting down a stack of napkins he was retrieving beneath the counter. "You really love terrifying me, huh, Blaine?"

I look around, as if there's a prank unfolding and I'm the victim. "Are you just . . . everywhere? All the time?"

His forehead crinkles. "If by 'everywhere' you mean 'where I work,' then yes," he answers. "Although 'all the time' is a bit extreme. I usually get about twenty hours a week."

My brain is still trying to compute the fact that Danny is standing behind the counter of my go-to coffee shop like he owns the place, an apron dusted with flour tied around his middle. "You must have just started working here, then," I assess.

His forehead crinkles even more, as he is clearly enjoying the toll this confusion is taking on me. "No . . . ? I've worked at Biggest Bean since my dad opened it."

My chin drops. "You're Bao's son?"

He grins devilishly, pulling on plastic gloves. "As much as it pains me to report this, you're not losing your mind," he says, pushing a plate of fried golden balls of bread to the front of the display case so customers can get a good look. "I only worked in the kitchen up until a few days ago, so it makes sense that you wouldn't have seen me around here." He nudges each bread ball so that its best side is facing outward.

"What are those?" I ask, nodding at the display case. "They look amazing."

"Bánh Tiêu," Danny answers. "Vietnamese doughnuts."

I watch him move on to a tray of carrot cake. He glides around behind the counter so effortlessly, as if he's been doing it for decades. "Is Bao—er, your dad—around?"

"Errands," Danny says, now on to a row of freshly baked blondies that smell like heaven. "He'll be back in an hour or so. Shall I give you a heads-up so you can jump out and startle him?"

I drop my chin, giving him a look.

"Or, better yet, you can ram him with your paint cart when he's least expecting it."

"Ha-*ha*."

"If you're lucky, he'll be carrying a tray of cookies and he'll drop the whole thing," Danny says, pouring it on. "Blaine strikes again."

"Okay, you made your point. I just wanted to thank him. He offered to let me paint the side of your building, and—"

"Ohhhh." Danny pauses and straightens his back, an

epiphany washing over his face. "*You're* the guy."

"Uh." I push my lips out and squint, unsure who "the guy" is. "Maybe?"

"That makes sense." He moves on from the blondies and begins sorting a group of chilled containers that have colorful ingredients and slush inside. "Chè ba màu," he notes after spotting my curiosity. "Red and mung beans, green jelly, coconut milk, and straight-up deliciousness."

I'm practically salivating.

"Anyway," he continues. "My dad said one of our regulars wanted to paint a mural on the side of the building. I should have assumed it was the mural kid."

The mural kid?

"Is that really my nickname at school?" I ask, watching him wipe down the countertop. "*Mural* kid?"

"In my head it is," he says nonchalantly, gathering a pile of crumbs. "Actually." He pauses again to think. "Now it's 'the Boy Who Still Owes Me an Aloe Vera.'"

I roll my eyes. "For the millionth time, I will get you your plant. I will get you an entire *field* of those things if it means you'll stop bringing it up every chance you get."

He pushes the crumbs into a trash can. "So, when are you starting on the mural?" he asks.

"Well, that's the thing," I say, a bit embarrassed to be turning down the offer. "Can you tell Bao—er, *your dad*—that I won't be able to do it after all?"

"How come?"

"I have a lot going on."

"The election?" He leans forward against the counter.

That's a much more straightforward answer than the whole truth, so I roll with it. "Yeah. It turns out there's a lot more to campaigning than you might think."

"Oh, I know there is," he says. "That's why I've never run for a class executive board position, even though I've been a member for a while."

"You're in student council?"

"Yep."

Danny shifts gears to rearrange a group of mason jars filled with baking ingredients.

"I won't keep you," I say, backing away from the counter and turning to leave. "But please let your dad know I appreciate his offer—"

"I liked your sign in the cafeteria, by the way," he says, looking up from a container of dark brown sugar.

I can't tell if it's a sincere comment or yet another setup for him to dunk on me again.

I stare.

He stares back.

"Thanks?" I finally say.

He lowers his voice, as if paying me a genuine compliment is a source of embarrassment. "I was giving you a hard time by not signing your sheet. But I will tomorrow. 'Let's talk.' . . . That's a cool way to launch a campaign."

"You think so?"

"Yeah. It's refreshing to see someone running for class president with that kind of mindset. More focus on what students care about, less letting their ego run the show. You know?"

A *refreshing* candidate? That has a nice ring to it. A bubble of pride begins rising in my chest. I open my mouth to thank him, but—

"I mean, let's not get it twisted," Danny says, cutting me off with a smirk. "It's very clear what you're doing, Blaine."

I pause. "Huh?"

His eyes drop back down to the brown sugar, but his smirk sticks to his face. "You're running because Joey Oliver broke up with you."

The bubble of pride bursts into a waterfall of shame. "What?" I laugh, as if the idea is ridiculous. "What makes you think that?"

"It's pretty obvious, dude," he says, scooping the sugar into a different container. "Why else would *you*—a person who's never been within a mile of a student council meeting before—suddenly want to run as Senior Class President Joey Oliver's successor mere days after he dumped you?"

I'm speechless. Exposed. A little bit mortified.

Is it really that obvious?

Of course Trish and Camilla know that's at the core of why I'm running. But am I being naive in thinking that they're the only ones? Can all of Wicker West High see straight through the facade?

"Hey." He looks back up with a sigh, probably sensing how hard he just read me for filth, and feeling bad about it. "Like I said, I'll gladly sign in support of your candidacy." One corner of his lips creeps up into his cheek. "Just because you're running to get revenge on Joey Oliver doesn't mean you can't also be running a worthwhile campaign."

"I'm not running to get *revenge* on Joey," I clarify. "I'm running to win him back and—" I catch myself.

But it's too late.

Danny's eyes widen with glee as his jaw drops. "I knew it!"

I shake my head with a sheepish chuckle, feeling the heat surface on my face. "Okay, yes, whatever. I want to win Joey back. Feel better?"

Danny considers the question before nodding. "Actually, yeah."

"Like you said," I emphasize. "Just because that's what motivated me to enter the race doesn't mean I can't run a worthwhile campaign."

"Agreed."

The store phone starts ringing. Danny lifts his pointer finger at me to hit pause on our conversation and picks up. "Biggest Bean Roasters."

I don't want to wait there awkwardly until he's finished listing off the bakery's gluten-free options. So I quietly nod goodbye and slip out the front, popping in my earbuds with the smallest of grins.

Trish and Danny have both made excellent points about my being a candidate who truly resonates with people. I should have put two and two together sooner.

The best way I can win Joey back is by running an inspiring campaign. A campaign that can get both student council veterans like Danny and uninterested students like Trish fired up for the future. A campaign run by a *Serious* Guy.

A campaign that has a real shot at beating Zach Chesterton.

CHAPTER 8

I plop my bag and coat down on the countertop with a wet *thud*. Aunt Starr can immediately tell that my first Monday back after spring break was as messy as my sopping-wet hair is.

"Uh-oh," she says from her chair at the kitchen island. She puts her Kindle down and pulls off her reading glasses. "What happened?"

"Welllll," I sigh. "Are you ready for this?"

"I was born ready."

"Joey has a new boyfriend."

"Stop!"

"Yep."

"Who?"

"Zach Chesterton."

She pauses to think. "Okay, I don't know who that is, but it doesn't matter. Here." She hops off the chair and pulls me over so I can sit down instead. "I'm making us brinner."

"Really?"

"Yes."

Aunt Starr's famous brinners (breakfast foods for dinner) were once an exclusively Christmas Day affair. But she's become more lenient in seasonality over the years—especially since she's moved in with us. Now Aunt Starr cooks up brinner at least once a month, always as a way to celebrate an occasion worth remembering or, like today, to bury our pain in buttery, salty-sweet comfort foods. When Mom single-handedly saved a teenager who literally had a one-in-a-million shot at survival? Chocolate chip pancakes. When Dad needed five stitches after crashing his bike attempting to go no-hands on the 606 trail? Nutella-stuffed French toast.

"Bacon-and-egg sandwiches," Aunt Starr announces, diving into the cupboard and pulling out a loaf of sourdough. "That sound good to you?"

"Perfect. Are you making some for Mom and Dad?"

She gives me a pity smile. "They're both working late tonight. It's just us."

I pull out my phone and mull over the unanswered texts I sent Joey earlier. And yes, they read even more desperate now than they did an hour ago at Biggest Bean, as Trish predicted. Damn it, I wish she'd taken my phone away one minute sooner.

"So, what's this Zach Chesterton kid got that you don't?" Aunt Starr's lopsided ponytail falls apart more as she pulls open the refrigerator door. "Besides the most pretentious last name in Chicago."

"A significantly higher GPA and a large trust fund, probably." I lay my head down on the counter. "He's our current class president and, from what people are saying, the clear shoo-in for the job next year. Plus, Zach is a *Serious Guy*."

"A Serious Guy?"

"You know, the kind of guy Joey says he needs to start dating if he's going to be president someday."

"President? Of *America*?" Aunt Starr's eyes roll so hard, for a second I think they might be stuck like that forever. It's moments like these when I see how we're family.

She lines up a row of extra-thick bacon on a skillet, and the wonderfully intense smell of sizzling meat fills the room in seconds. "How do you know Joey and *Mr. Chesterton*"—she mocks Zach's last name in a terrible English accent—"are officially boyfriends?"

"They were all cozied up at lunch."

"Cozied up?" She flicks a limp wrist at me while her other hand butters the bread. "That can mean a lot of things."

"They also kissed."

She sucks her teeth, cringing. "Okay, well . . . kissing sounds a bit more substantial."

Aunt Starr's phone *dings*—the specific sound that I've learned signifies a new email. She yelps excitedly, wiping her hands off on a paper towel before picking her phone up and scrolling. "It's probably Lincoln Park Zoo!"

"Why would the zoo be emailing you?"

"I had a second interview for an events director job there yesterday, and they said I should know by—" The color drains from her face. She takes a deep breath in before exhaling long and slow, tossing her phone back onto her bright purple purse. "Never mind. I was a *great candidate*, apparently, but not quite great enough." She looks up at me. "Oh well. Zoos are bad for animals anyways, right?"

I give her a sad smile.

"Can this sad brinner be in honor of the both of us?" she asks.

"Definitely."

Aunt Starr slides in her slippers back to the stovetop. She attempts to snap back into her usual bubbly self by humming a song and dancing in place, cracking a couple of eggs into a pan that's adjacent to the bacon. But I know it's a performance. As much as Aunt Starr tries to exude joy around me 24/7, I know she gets down on herself sometimes too. I know she wants a new job, ending her "season of change." I reach into my pocket for the business card that Camilla gave me—but stop and reconsider. I don't pull it out.

Tonight is for commiserating in our sad brinners together, I decide. Aunt Starr can worry about job stuff tomorrow. Plus, is it so bad that another day when she doesn't know about Camilla's Field Museum opportunity means another day guaranteed that she'll be living under the same roof with me?

Aunt Starr finishes up the breakfast sandwiches and plates them for us at the island. My first bite is glorious—buttery toasted bread, caramelized bacon, and an egg the perfect amount of runny, resting on a thin bed of arugula and sliced ripe tomatoes. Delicious, multiplied ten times.

"You've outdone yourself," I say with my mouth full. "Not that I'm surprised."

She gives me a wink and takes a sip of her orange juice (the only acceptable brinner drink). "So, what's your game plan?" she asks.

"Game plan for . . . ?"

"Breaking up Joey and *Mr. Chesterton*"—she does the English accent again—"and winning back the boy you deserve."

I snort.

"What?" she asks.

"You want me to try to break them up?" I say. "Have you been drinking?"

"Well, maybe, but that's beside the point." She drops her chin at me. "You can't *not* do anything. *Mr. Chesterton* stole your man. You've got to fight for what's yours."

I swallow a big bite and think through my intentions. "Yes, I want to *win* Joey back," I say. "But I don't want to, like . . . aggressively *steal* him back. You know?"

"And what exactly is the difference between those two things?" She waits for a response.

"I don't know, Aunt Starr," I say, sipping juice. "Earlier, I was thinking about dropping out of the race anyway, so—"

She drops her glass with a *thud.* "Excuse me?"

"Yes?"

"*Please* tell me you're kidding."

I take another bite, shaking my head.

"Blaine!" She kicks me under the counter.

"Ouch!"

"You cannot even *consider* doing that!"

"Why not?"

"You can't drop out of the race just because this *Mr. Chesterton* thing is throwing you a curveball." She reaches across the counter and grabs my hands—both hers and mine are slippery from the buttery bread—and looks me square in the eye. "Listen to me. You are brave, and smart, and funny, and compassionate, and *all the things* the kids at Wicker West High School deserve in a class president."

I look away because it's getting intense. "*Eh* . . . I mean, I—"

"No," she says flatly, pulling her hands away. "You're not allowed to do this, Blaine."

"Do what?"

She pauses for a beat, eyes beaming into mine like lasers. "You're not allowed to quit just because you're scared, doll."

My stomach crinkles.

Because we've had this discussion before.

"Remember when you quit the after-school art club when you were a freshman because you were intimidated by those senior girls who were better at ceramics than you?"

"'Better at ceramics' is an understatement," I say, defending myself. "I was way out of my league—"

"And then you quit the photography club because you had *one* bad day?"

"A *bad day*? I ruined everyone's photos in the darkroom!" I squeal, turning pink. "I didn't realize the room was in use, and when I went to open the door, I—"

"My point is," she says, cutting me off. "I love you more than I love frozen Snickers bars, which says a lot, but you have a tendency to quit when fear takes hold—whether that fear is of being shown up by a bunch of seniors in art, or facing the photographers whose pics you destroyed." She exhales. "You're an amazing muralist, Blaine, and you can be a great class president if you want to too. I say, go win Joey Oliver back."

I finish my sandwich, give Aunt Starr the biggest hug on the planet, and head upstairs to take a long, hot shower and wash off the day. Once in bed, I toss and turn for hours, though, thinking through my options.

I mean, c'mon. Do I have a real shot at convincing Joey I can be serious?

Do I have a real shot at beating Zach Chesterton?

Aunt Starr obviously thinks so. But apparently Trish does too. Heck, even Danny—who may or may not hate my guts— saw a spark in the potential of my campaign. Maybe Wicker West is ready for a *refreshing* candidate to step up. Maybe I do have what it takes to win back the boy who broke my heart— and the senior class presidency with him.

I wake up the next morning knowing exactly what I need to do.

I get to school, snag my sign out of my locker, and take it with me to first-hour art class for a slight retouch. Three anxious hours later, I arrive at the cafeteria extra early and hang my sign up before any other students come in for lunch.

LET'S TALK, it reads above the letters I added this morning: ABOUT CHANGING THE STATUS QUO!

There's even more interest in me today. More heart-to-hearts. More confessions from shy students I've never spoken to before. More curious student council veterans who sign my sheet in support, like Danny ends up doing—pencil in one hand, turkey sub in the other. More juniors eager to find someone—*anyone*—who is willing to simply listen to them.

As lunch comes to an end, I count the total number of signatures on my sheet—all sixty-eight—and breeze by Zach on my way out of the cafeteria.

"Looks like you passed fifty, huh?" he calls after me.

I turn, smile, and nod.

"Nice," he says—a bit *too* friendly for my comfort. "Welcome to the race, Blaine."

CHAPTER 9

★ ☆ ★

With my shoes hovering above the hardwood floor, I lean even farther over the front counter at Biggest Bean and look down, just to be extra certain there's not a person stocking items out of sight. Because how terrible would it be if I gave Danny a heart attack for a second day in a row—mere days after killing his aloha (or whatever) plant?

Once I see that the coast is clear, I hit the bell with a *ding*.

Bao comes bouncing out of the kitchen with his typical contagious smile and a tray of fresh chocolate chip cookies. His apron is sparkling white—an FBI detective with a black light couldn't spot a smudge, spot, or stain on that thing— and his dark hair, sprinkled with a few grays near his ears, has been parted and slicked back carefully.

"How's it going, Blaine?" he asks cheerily, placing the tray on the counter in front of me. The aroma hits my nostrils like a freight train of sugary bliss.

"It's going okay," I say. "How about you?"

"Can't complain." One by one, Bao begins dropping the cookies—flat and crispy on the outer rim and soft and gooey in the middle—into the display case. "I noticed that Trish and Camilla came in a few times last week without their third. Out of town with your parents over break?"

"Nah, just busy," I lie, because that sounds better than, *I spent it wallowing in my bedroom like a baby.* "Hey, how come you never told me that you're Danny's dad?"

He laughs. "I didn't realize you went to Wicker West, or I would have mentioned it sooner. He told me you stopped by."

"Is he around today?"

"He's in back. I'll get him."

"Thanks. Oh, also—I, um," I stammer, suddenly a bit embarrassed. "In case he didn't mention it, thanks about the mural opportunity. That was nice of you to offer."

He tosses a hand towel over his shoulder. "Danny told me you decided not to do it. How come?"

"Just busy," I say. "Honestly."

But he doesn't believe for a second that I'm being honest. "Trish told you I'd pay, right?"

"It's not a money thing."

"And there's no time frame. You can take as long as you want to finish."

"Yeah, it's just . . ."

"You wouldn't have to do the whole wall. Even something small in the bottom corner near the entrance, just to spruce it up a bit."

I'm running out of excuses! And he's making this more difficult than it needs to be. "I have a lot on my plate right now, Bao."

He plops the last chocolate chip cookie into the display case and lifts the empty tray off the counter. "Well, the offer remains, Blaine. Just let me know. I'll grab Danny."

Oof, that was not comfortable. But what am I going to tell him? The *truth*? The ex-boyfriend I'm trying to win back hates that I have a crappy, unserious side hustle I practically lose money doing, so I'm taking some time to rethink my life choices?

Danny emerges from the kitchen, his apron in a laughably different state than his dad's. It looks like a hundred Hershey's Kisses melted in a pool of caramel before someone took a s'more and spread the concoction around his entire torso.

"Wow." I giggle, nodding at his chest. "Your apron's seen better days."

He glances down before rolling his eyes. "We catered a kindergartner's birthday party."

"Was the theme Milk Chocolate Massacre?"

"Very funny."

"How many marshmallows lost their lives in your kitchen today?"

He sighs. I sense that he's holding back a laugh. "Can I help you with something?"

I notice a row of small plants lining the window facing the sidewalk. "Oh, hello, little ones."

He glances over. "I'm building up my succulent stockpile."

"They're coming along nicely."

"Thanks. All I'm missing is . . ." He tilts his head, waiting for me to finish his sentence.

I bite my lower lip awkwardly. "Why can't I ever remember the name? I want to say 'olive oil plant,' but clearly that's not right."

"Aloe vera."

"Aloe vera!" I smack my forehead. "Aloe vera, aloe vera," I repeat to myself. "Like the stuff you put on sunburns."

He nods, unsure what to make of my eagerness to chat.

"I really like that one," I say, pointing to one whose rigid leaves look like rose petals with hints of pink. "It's lovely."

"Yeah," he says. "Echeverias are a fave."

"Uh-huh," I say, like that name makes any sense to me.

"I'm stoked about my zebra plant." He points to a bigger one with deep-green leaves with white veins. "They're native to Brazil and like warm, muggy, bright climates."

"So Chicago's probably not ideal?" I ask with a grin.

"Not at all. But I'm up for the challenge." He doesn't grin back. I think he knows I'm up to something. "Can I help you, Blaine?"

"Yes." I shove my hands into my pockets nervously, not knowing where else to put them. "I turned in my fifty signatures today for the election." I wait for him to respond.

He doesn't.

"So this means my campaign is, you know, *official* now," I continue. "I'm hoping to build out a legitimate campaign team."

He keeps staring at me blankly.

"And, uh." I keep going. "You're a junior who's in student council, and you also mentioned you liked my 'Let's Talk' sign from yesterday."

He nods.

"So it seems like, *hypothetically*, you might be open to

supporting someone like me for senior class president?"

He thinks for a second, looking at his succulents. "Maybe. Hypothetically, of course."

"Hypothetically, yes." I clear my throat. "So, let's say you don't hate the idea of supporting me for class president. Would you be open to, like . . . helping out with my campaign? Hypothetically?"

"Are you asking me to be your campaign captain?"

"No, no, no," I say, waving my hands with a chuckle. "I've already asked Trish to be my campaign captain. It's just, neither of us have the kind of student council experience you'd bring to the table. I think you'd be a great asset."

He thinks a bit more. "What's in it for me?"

"Oh. Well . . ." *That,* I'm not really sure. "You'd get to help shape the presidential platform of Wicker West's incoming senior class president?"

One of his eyebrows darts upward. He's unconvinced.

I shrug.

"How about this," he proposes. "You follow through on a new aloe vera plant for me, I'll help with your campaign, and we'll call it even?"

I light up. "Yes!" I exclaim. "I mean, I *of course* was going to get you one anyway. But I'll get an extra-perfect one as a thank-you. I'll get you *two,* even."

"It's okay." He shakes his head. "One aloe vera plant is plenty."

"Really?" I say. "You're sure?"

"Yeah."

"Fantastic!"

"I just have one request, though," he says.

"Anything!" I bellow. "Well, maybe not *anything*, but—"

"You've got to move."

"Huh?"

He nods behind me. I turn to find a line of irritated customers waiting to order, each one giving me a slightly different dirty look.

"Oh my gosh, I'm sorry!" I squeal, turning red and jumping out of the way.

I look at Danny as I glide backward toward the exit. "I'll let you know when our first campaign meeting is!"

"I'll be there," he says. I think he's hiding a smile. "Hypothetically."

CHAPTER 10

★ ☆ ★

I decide that I simply cannot do another day of clown shoes and suit jackets made to fit a linebacker on the Chicago Bears. As inconvenient as it may be for me and my fashion preferences, Joey has a point: if I want to be senior class president, students have got to *see* me as senior class president. That means no more Dad clothes.

The problem is, my options are limited.

I decide to gut my entire closet and sprawl everything out on my bed, just to see what I'm working with. Spoiler: it's not a lot. There are turquoise angel wings, yellow knee-high socks, and a whole pile of fanny packs in pastels, but not a single normal necktie. How can I have eight fanny packs—*eight fanny packs*—and not a single freaking necktie?

Fudge is curled up next to a pillow and one of my crop tops, judging the fashion disaster surrounding him.

"What?" I ask defensively.

He barks.

I sigh, pulling out my phone to text Trish. 8 fanny packs, I write. Is that too many for a class president to have in their closet?

Writing bubbles pop up immediately. Not enough, boo, she responds. Need at least 10 to get my vote tbh.

I reply with a skull emoji.

Btw, am I officially your campaign captain? she asks.

Yup, I text back. Returned my signatures to Mr. Wells and submitted your name. <3

She reacts with a row of hearts and rainbows.

Heads up that I asked Danny to help out with the campaign too, I write.

Danny . . . ? she responds.

Nguyen. Did you know he's Bao's son? He works at Biggest Bean. . . .

There's a pause. oh that's right, I've seen him carry trays out of the kitchen before. Another pause. He's kinda cute, B . . . , She adds a smiley face.

I write back: lol it's not like that. trust me. I think he still sort of hates me for killing one of his plants before spring break.

Clearly she doesn't believe me—as evidenced by the smirking face she sends. You know he came out as bi last year . . . , she follows up.

Yeah. So? I reply.

She responds with a whole row of smirking faces.

I roll my eyes—Trish is extra motivated to force me to forget about Joey, it seems—and toss my phone onto my comforter.

After a few minutes of organizing outfits for my speech, a potential debate, and all the days in between, I'm pleasantly surprised to learn I *do* have the basic items to flesh out a handful of conventional campaign looks. Sure, they may not be quite as refined as Zach, in his salmon blazers and turtlenecks, but I have what it takes to pull off presidential.

I hope. We'll see.

"What do you think?" I ask Fudge, holding up a light blue button-up and navy pants. He barks his approval.

So really, the only essential item I'm missing is a necktie. And I refuse to wear Dad's from Monday again. (That one can go to hell.)

I head down to the kitchen, where Aunt Starr is chopping cucumbers for our salad in a leopard-print shirt and leggings with ice-cream cones on them. Dad, a bit sunburnt and still wearing an orange construction vest after a long day at one of his sites, is layering lasagna noodles into a baking pan. It's nice to have him home at a reasonable hour.

"Hey, kiddo," he says, pulling me in to kiss the top of my head like I'm ten. I try to resist, but his strength advantage prevails. "How was school?"

"Good," I say, leaning over the big pot of starchy pasta water to get a mini facial. "It'd be better if I had more ties, though."

I glance up at him.

He glances back. "Just come out with it, Blaine."

"Can we go to William's Outfitters this weekend?"

"William's Outfitters?" Dad laughs sharply. "Why in the world would you need an eighty-dollar tie?"

"You can find some on sale there in the sixty-dollar range," Aunt Starr chimes in, popping a cucumber into her mouth.

Dad doesn't say anything, scooping a ladle of meat sauce.

"Blaine is in the *presidential* race!" she follows up cheerily.

"Kevin, that means your son's got to look—as the kids are calling it these days—*fierce*."

I smile at her.

I know Dad wants to smile too, but remains silent to prove a point.

"Well, all righty, then," Aunt Starr says softly. She abandons the cucumbers and backs away into the adjacent dining room with a bowl of shredded cheese and her iPad. "I will see myself out."

Once she's gone, Dad gives me a look. "Sixty bucks is still a lot for a tie, Blaine."

"I know," I say, finding a seat at the kitchen island, feeling a bit guilty. "Maybe they have some closer to fifty bucks?"

They avoid addressing it head-on with me, but I know that Mom and Dad have been feeling a financial crunch the past few years, which explains the overworking. They're trying to save up for my college tuition while paying off some debt and dealing with our area of Chicago getting pricier with each passing year. Sure, it's nice when charming storefronts pop up, but it also means that making ends meet gets harder to do for families like ours. The Olivers and Chestertons may appreciate juice bars with ten-dollar drinks, but my dad certainly doesn't. To his credit, it's easy to see why a bougie tie from William's is *very* far down on our family's financial priority list these days.

"Didn't you wear one of my ties earlier this week?" Dad asks. "Why do you need another one?"

"That one's way too wide for my neck. I looked like a toddler playing dress-up."

"I have others."

"They're all shaped the same way, Dad."

He opens the oven door and pushes the pan onto the middle rack. "I'm getting the sense that this isn't so much about ties as it is about something else." He straightens back up, wipes the sweat off his face with his forearm, and stares me down. "This doesn't have anything to do with Joey, does it?"

We hear the front door swing open. "Hello?" Mom asks loudly from the foyer. She appears a few seconds later in her scrubs, blond hair bunched into a ball atop her head, carrying a baguette that's nearly as long as she is tall. "Good news: I didn't forget the bread for once."

"Hey, Mom," I say as she pecks me on the forehead. I can't remember the last time both she and Dad were home for dinner. I've missed the feeling of a full kitchen.

"Hey, Sis!" Aunt Starr bellows from the dining room over an episode of *Big Brother* on her iPad. "How was your day dealing with mean sick people?" She leans back in her chair to see me in the kitchen. "Is that awful to say?" she whispers.

I chuckle.

"Yes, it is awful to say," Mom answers with a grin, pulling dishes out of a cupboard. "I dealt with mostly *nice* sick people today. Did you email Don about the job?"

Aunt Starr groans loudly.

"Starr!" Mom shouts back. "Why not?"

"Because I'd rather have every one of my eyebrow hairs plucked out individually than work the front desk in that dentist's office."

Dad stifles a laugh.

"Starr," Mom scolds, holding back a laugh too. "I told him you'd be in touch."

"*Eyebrow* hairs, Sis."

"A job's a job," Dad says, finding the Parmesan cheese on the refrigerator door.

"Kevin, would *you* want to work as a secretary for Don Drake, with those creepy flamingo paintings all over the walls and his gross halitosis breath? What *dentist* has halitosis?"

Dad looks at Mom with a shrug. "She's got a point."

"Will you at least email him to say thanks for the offer, Starr?" Mom asks, a bit of desperation in her voice. "Even if you don't end up taking the position, it was a nice gesture."

"Sure thing," Aunt Starr answers, before shaking her head and mouthing *nope* at me.

I smile—and then I'm suddenly and uncomfortably aware that the business card Camilla gave me is still upstairs, on my dresser. I keep forgetting to tell Aunt Starr about the director of events gig at the Field. Well, it's either that I'm forgetting or that I'm conveniently not remembering and am putting it off. Maybe it's a bit of both?

Later tonight, I promise myself. *I will tell Aunt Starr about the job tonight.*

"What else did I miss around here?" Mom asks.

"Not too much," Dad replies, giving her shoulders a quick massage as he passes by to the silverware drawer. "Except your son wants an eighty-dollar tie from William's Outfitters."

"Eighty dollars?" Mom drops her jaw at me. "Is it made out of gold?"

"You can find some in the sixty-dollar range," I say, stealing Aunt Starr's defense. "I'm running for senior class president, Mom. I want to dress like it."

"Honey." She starts slicing up the baguette. "You know we're thrilled about you running for president, but you don't need an eighty-dollar tie to do it."

"Wicker West is brutal when it comes to this stuff, Mom. You know how nice Joey dresses as senior class president, and I'm running against Zach Chesterton, who—"

"Wait." Mom stops cutting and looks up at me. "This has to do with Joey?"

She exchanges a look with Dad.

"No!" I say. "Of course not."

I mean, the more accurate answer is *Yes, of course it does*—but only in that I need to be taken seriously enough to become senior class president and win him back. That's all.

"You don't need a tie to impress that little turd nugget," Dad says, taking plates and silverware out for us to use.

"Turd nugget? Really?" Mom looks at me, clearly feeling like the only grown-up in the house. "I agree with your father, though. Any boy that makes you feel like you have to own a pricey piece of clothing just to impress him is not worth your time."

"I told you, it's not about Joey," I say, getting frustrated that they can see right through me. "It's about the election. I want to be taken seriously."

"How about we go to the mall on Saturday and pick something out there?" Dad suggests. "I could probably use a new dress shirt anyway."

"I thought you're working on Saturday?" Mom asks him.

He scrunches his face, remembering. "That's right. It's next Saturday I have off."

"I could take you?" Mom suggests, smiling at me hesitantly. "I don't know if you want it to be a father-son thing, but—"

"I thought you're working too?" Dad says, folding his arms against his chest.

She pauses to think. "Am I?"

"That's what you said yesterday."

"I think I work on Sunday."

"Are you sure?"

They both step toward the calendar hanging on the fridge, which is absolutely destroyed in black and red pen markings that reflect the lives of Chicago's two biggest workaholics.

I close my eyes and exhale, long and slow, knowing all too well that whenever work schedules bleed into the conversation, there's no turning back. I might as well send a letter to Santa asking for a new tie, because I've surely missed my opportunity with Mom and Dad.

I miss painting my murals.

The thought comes out of nowhere but feels so urgent and true that I spend a moment questioning whether I just said it aloud. Even though I know that Joey would rather have a boyfriend who wears ties from William's Outfitters than an unserious boyfriend who paints murals, the fact is, I'd rather be sliding a cobalt-colored paintbrush against the storefront of Susan's Stationery than doing just about anything else in the world right now. I *really* miss painting my murals.

Look at your hands! I remember, in horror, Joey's scathing words at Grey Kettle. *You couldn't even manage to get all the paint off for our one-year anniversary?*

I jolt back to reality.

There's no time for distractions—or cobalt-speckled hands. I've got to stay focused.

I've got to stay Serious.

I rise to my feet.

"I'm going to take Fudge for a quick walk before we eat," I announce. Between *Big Brother* blaring in the dining room and Mom and Dad still bickering in front of the fridge, I don't think anyone hears me. Oh well. Wicker West may just have a senior class president next year who doesn't own a tie, and everyone will have to deal.

CHAPTER 11

O rder, order," I joke, tapping my mug of mocha on the coffee table. Camilla giggles, Trish shakes her head at my corniness, and Danny looks like he doesn't know what to make of me. I clear my throat. "That was funnier in my head."

We're huddled together in our corner of the coffee shop, Danny sitting on the other end of the sofa, Trish and Camilla curled up on the beanbags across from us. It's especially hectic in here today, with big families buying baked goods in bulk and an unruly kids' soccer team playing tag throughout the store, spilling crumbs and bubble teas as they dash between chairs and tables.

The chaos isn't helping my anxiety about our first campaign meeting.

Spending entire summer afternoons painting brick walls with no one else except whichever music artist is serenading me through my headphones? That's more my speed. Leading an official campaign launch, where people are looking to *me* as the Person in Charge? I could not be further outside my wheelhouse. I know it's just three people—two of whom are my best friends—but the expectation is different now. I need to become my inner Joey Oliver, and that's no easy feat.

"We may technically all know each other, but let's do

quick intros, now that we're on a team," I say, feeling like that's a thing the Person in Charge would do. I point to Trish. "Want to start?"

She adjusts the straps of her black overalls and gives me a salute. "Trish Macintosh, campaign captain, reporting for duty," she says with a serious face. She already has her laptop out, ready to take notes.

"Dang, sergeant," Camilla says, twirling her *T. rex* necklace with her fingertips. She looks at Danny. "We had geometry together, but I don't think we ever formally met. I'm Camilla."

"Hi, Camilla. I'm Danny," Danny replies with a nod and a smile, munching on a ham-and-cheese croissant. He's immediately much warmer to her than he's been to me (maybe because Camilla hasn't killed one of his plants). Although I'd never say this aloud because it'd get Trish all fired up, I think Danny is distractingly cute today, snug in a yellow polo beneath his apron.

"I think Danny will be a huge help for us, seeing as none of us have student council experience," I yell over a screaming nine-year-old soccer player. "And on that note, let's get started at square one: What do you think my first priority should be if I'm going to have a shot at winning this thing?" I ask him.

"Zach Chesterton," he says at once and without question.

I wait for him to elaborate, but he doesn't. "Can you explain?"

"I know there are other people running for president,

but forget about all of them," he says. "Right now Zach is on a completely unobstructed path to win. He's your sole competition."

"How can you know that for sure, though?" Trish asks. "It's not like the student council does polling to tell us who's up and who's down."

I laugh for a second. "Wait, does the council do that?" I ask.

Danny hides a grin. "No. I don't mean to come off as arrogant, but I've been in student council long enough to know how elections work at Wicker West. It's a numbers game, and we have to play catch-up, big-time, because Zach's been working the numbers in his favor for years now."

"How so?" Camilla says.

Danny finishes the last bite of his croissant. "Wicker West is massive. There are about five hundred fifty students in our class. To get at least a plurality of votes and win, you need a clear, coherent strategy. And from all the elections I've witnessed at a school this big, every winner does one of two things really well." He holds up a single finger. "One, either you inspire people to support you through your vision." He holds up another finger. "Or, two, you just *hammer away relentlessly* with name recognition to stand out."

I hear the rapid clicking of Trish's laptop and glance over to see her taking notes like a boss. I've never seen Trish do her *homework* with such focus. Where is this newfound determination coming from? "Which one of those is Zach?" she asks.

Danny looks at her like the answer's obvious. "Can you name a single thing he's fought for as our class president the past three years? A single policy or idea he ran on, a single thing he stands for? Zach is a name-recognition candidate, and name recognition *only*."

"That makes sense," Camilla says, sipping her drink. "Hell, I'm pretty sure *I* voted for him last year, just because I wasn't exactly sure who the other candidates were."

"See?" Danny says. "I mean, I give him credit. He knows how to work the system. Why do you think he's an office aide?"

Trish, Camilla, and I glance at each other, none of us having a clue.

"When you're an office aide, you're in the know about everything that's going on," Danny explains. "All the gossip, teacher drama, updates on student organizations—the main office hears most of it first. Student aides can even see the *security footage* throughout the whole school. Zach uses all of that access to his advantage." Danny wipes croissant crumbs off his pants. "Plus, he's ridiculously good at schmoozing—cozying up to athletes, staying on good terms with the various social circles. No one *loves* the guy, but no one really *dislikes* him either, you know? Last year he visited every extracurricular club in the entire school for at least one of their meetings to kiss ass. I'm telling you, he's a very good politician."

"And an absolutely terrible change-maker," Trish adds.

"Exactly," Danny says, nodding at her. "What has he done? Nothing, really. He doesn't stay in office to make things better for students—he stays in office to pad his résumé for Ivy League admissions."

"Sounds like someone else I know," I mutter, thinking of Joey. They all look at me. "Anyway. So how do we compete with that? How do we compete with the kid who's basically been preparing for this moment since birth?"

Danny takes another sip of water and sighs. "I don't know, dude. I'm here to help, but at the same time, I want to be real with you all. Beating Zach?" He cringes a bit. "It's going to be tough."

We pause to think, the screeches of stressed parents and their rambunctious children filling my ears.

"How about . . . ," Camilla begins, brainstorming, "we make, like, a *million* posters for you, Blaine. Just plaster them throughout the school. That'd boost name recognition, huh?"

I nod in consideration before turning to Danny.

"Potentially," he says. "Posters could be part of a bigger strategy, but I don't think they can win an election on their own."

"Maybe you're right," Camilla says, twirling her necklace in thought. "It seems like people get used to seeing them after a couple of days. At least I do, anyway. They lose their luster."

"I think we need to take the other track you mentioned, Danny," Trish says, concentrating on her computer screen before her eyes find mine. "Zach has name recognition locked down, and honestly? I don't think we can beat him at his own game at this point. But we could fill the *vision* lane. What's your vision? Why should students feel inspired to support *you* as president?"

Danny and Camilla turn toward me as well. The heat immediately begins rising in my cheeks. This is a question I should already have a polished answer to.

Why *am* I running for president?

Well, the answer is pretty simple, of course. Joey. *I need to prove I have what it takes to pull off Serious and win him back,* is the most forthright answer. But I don't want to vocalize that in front of Danny. Although he knows that that's my main motivation for entering the race, he deserves a more worthwhile reason to stick around and help me pull off a win.

"Um . . . well . . . ," I mumble, licking my lips and pretending to think, but my mind is flatlining. "I guess . . . I don't know." The words slip out unintentionally.

See? *This* is why I'm out of my wheelhouse. *This* is why I'm better at painting walls solo than pretending I can be president of anything. How can I ask my friends to campaign for me when I can't even campaign for myself?

"Sorry," I say ashamedly, rubbing my temples. "I should already have an answer to that question, I know."

"Don't be sorry," Danny says, shaking his head. "That's why we're having this meeting—so that we can find an answer for you."

His remark—the most direct supportive comment he's said to me since I crashed into him near Susan's Stationary—throws me for a loop.

"Can I recommend something?" he asks.

"You never need permission to speak, dude," Camilla says, chuckling, finishing the last gulp of her latte.

"The reason you caught my eye in the cafeteria was the 'Let's Talk' sign," he says. "Er, I mean, like, caught my eye as a candidate—not like, *caught my eye*, caught my eye."

I turn even redder, noticing Trish and Camilla exchanging quick grins with one another.

"Anyway," Danny continues. "Maybe we could start there, with the table you set up with that sign. Did anything juniors mention in the cafeteria speak to you? Could anything be expanded into a bigger vision for your presidency?"

He has a great point.

Sure, the sign was intended to lure students in for their signatures, let's be real. But after Trish suggested revising the message to LET'S TALK, I sort of enjoyed connecting with juniors I'd hardly ever spoken to before. And they had lots to say.

I pull out my phone and tap into my notes app. "I wrote down what juniors told me. I bet there's a topic in here that could give us some motivation. . . ." I find the list. "Okay . . . exam anxiety . . . social media exhaustion . . . the impact of hazing in sports . . . the stresses of being second-generation . . . body image issues . . ."

"*Oof,*" Camilla breathes. "Those got heavy."

"They really did," Danny says, sucking his teeth.

"But those are the things students *actually* care about," Trish chimes in. "That's the real stuff happening behind the scenes, the quiet stuff students want their presidents to be brave enough to address." She sits up straighter on the beanbag. I can almost see the lightbulb turn on in her mind. "How about . . . mental health."

We all pause.

"All of those issues involve mental health," Trish reiterates as the rest of us silently consider it. "Exam anxiety? Body image? Social media?"

"She's got a point," Danny says, looking at me. "That's the thread connecting them together."

Camilla taps Trish's thigh supportively. "A mental health presidential platform," she says. "I dig it."

"Yeah?" I ask, glancing around, unsure. "Do you think people would take it seriously?"

"Why wouldn't they?" Danny asks.

"I don't know," I say, thinking. "Most of the time, candidates run on, like, lowering the price of prom tickets or getting new lockers in fun colors."

"Or, in Zach's case, they don't run on any ideas at all," Camilla says.

"That's why most of us get annoyed by student council kids," Trish says, before finding Danny's eyes. "No offense."

Danny shrugs. "None taken."

"Class elections are usually competitions between self-serving narcissists running on BS issues. Pushing a platform that will actually do *real* good?" Trish opens her eyes wide. "Mental health is our winning recipe, if you ask me."

I can't get over how fired up Trish is getting about all this.

I can count the times on one hand when she's been this

excited for *anything*. There was her freak-out the night that the Chicago Bulls won a big playoff game and she spilled her Coke all over poor Fudge. Then there was the time Janelle Monáe liked Trish's tweet about how important *Dirty Computer* is for queer Black girls like her, and Trish's ensuing adrenaline rush lasted an entire week.

"You two know how much I've grown through my own personal struggles," Trish says softly, glancing between me and Camilla. "This hits home."

Trish started talking to a counselor at school after her brief breakup with Camilla. It wasn't *just* the relationship woes that prompted the decision—Trish has struggled with mental health for as long as I've known her—but girlfriend struggles amplified all the other stuff she was wrestling with. Now Trish goes to therapy twice a month, and routinely notes how game-changing it's been.

"Danny!" Bao calls from behind the counter, motioning for his son's help. The line to order is ten people deep, and another soccer team is walking in with even younger and less-controlled children.

"I've got to go," Danny says, rising from the sofa and walking backward toward the counter, tying his apron as he goes. "I'm with Trish, for what it's worth. I think an agenda focused on mental health has real potential."

"Same," Camilla says, nodding emphatically. "It checks off all the boxes."

I breathe deeply. "Well, okay, campaign captain," I say. The three of us break into big smiles. "Mental health it is."

CHAPTER 12

★ ★ ★

ental health. Okay.

What can *I*—candidate for senior class president, Blaine Bowers—offer the students of Wicker West when it comes to their mental health?

Well, for starters, I know that the topic is important. I know that teenagers are stressed the hell out, like, all the time nowadays. And I know Wicker West could be doing a better job at addressing a crisis that's so obviously affecting most students walking its hallways every day. I know how loneliness feels. At least . . . I think I do? "Lonely" is the best way I can describe the evenings when Mom and Dad would work late before Aunt Starr moved in. Sure, I didn't enjoy the house feeling empty and still, but it wasn't the physical seclusion as much as the isolating thoughts that accompanied it.

And I know the complicated anxieties that social media can lure from the deepest, darkest parts of our brains too, like Maggie, Tracy, and Elle mentioned in the cafeteria. You've got to be posting *something* on *some* app, so as to not disappear from relevancy altogether. But then you're forced to scroll by an ex-boyfriend enjoying his spring break in Mexico while you're buried in blankets in the Midwest (cue the crushing weight of rejection). I guess that can feel like its own form of lonely too.

Mental health.

How can I translate such a personal topic into clear policy proposals to run on?

Maybe I can get some ideas by thinking about who I'm up against.

"Any word on what we should expect from the other six candidates' speeches?" I ask from behind my laptop, sitting cross-legged on the living room floor next to Danny.

"I agree with Danny that Zach is the most deserving of our attention," Trish says from my cell phone, which is perched against a candle in the middle of the coffee table. I told her that she didn't need to FaceTime from the Field, where Camilla is working an event, but she insisted. (Now every few minutes we spot a woolly mammoth or sarcophagus behind her in the frame.) "If we can make your candidacy a referendum on Zach's do-nothing presidency—and nail why our focus on mental health will make a difference—we'll have a shot."

I dim the lighting on my laptop screen because my eyes are beginning to burn. "I hear you, but I still feel like I should have an idea of where the others are coming from, you know? Like, Miranda Cumberbatch." I pause on her name while scrolling through a list of my opponents. "I've never exchanged two *words* with her, let alone known what she stands for."

"I heard Miranda is running on 'bringing our class together,'" Trish says with an eye roll. "No offense to Miranda, she's an angel, but that's kind of dumb."

"Yeah, Miranda is great, but that's not a message that's going to stick," Danny follows up. "There's no substance there. There's no clear contrast with Zach."

I type a note next to Miranda's name. "What about Dustin? And Melissa?"

"Don't worry about Dustin," Trish says.

"He decided to run last-minute because he thinks it'll help him score points with Lacey Binder." Danny shakes his head. "Straight dudes."

I close my eyes, trying to picture her. "Lacey who?"

"A sophomore in student council he has a crush on," Danny explains. "It doesn't matter. Dustin is not a serious contender, is the point."

"I overheard in English that Melissa's speech is awkwardly short and focused on, of all things, paving the parking lot in our school colors," Trish says.

"Seriously?" Danny lets out a sharp laugh.

"Yes," Trish says with a smirk, walking through a museum exhibit filled with what I believe are monkey skulls. "I could be wrong, but that doesn't seem like a mobilizing issue students care a whole lot about."

Trish notes that, while she hasn't heard specifics on Bryce's speech, she highly doubts a universally disdained bro like him could swing anyone in his favor. And Nancy, Danny relays, has built a reputation among council members for habitually skipping out on meetings—which is why she's failed to qualify for the ballot the other three years she's run for president.

"Our focus on mental health came about because you're

actually *listening* to students," Trish reminds me. "No other candidate is doing that."

"Especially not Zach," Danny concludes.

"Right." I sigh, finishing up some notes and feeling the weight of the world. "Okay."

We take a quick break so I can find Fudge, who I prefer to cuddle with when my brain feels like it's going to explode. He nestles up next to my thigh while we wrap up the nuts and bolts of my speech.

Trish and Danny do most of the ideation. My hand gravitates toward a pen and a pad of sticky notes, where it proceeds to illustrate a would-be mural capturing what mental health looks like to me: a big, pale brain, floating along in the troposphere. Or, as I mutter to myself after it's completed, "a mind on cloud nine."

"Huh?" Danny says.

I snap back to reality. "Oh. Nothing. Just doodling."

He smiles, nudging a can of pop my way. "How about a bit more caffeine, sleepy?"

Danny is being *way* more nice to me lately, starting with our first campaign meeting. And I can't say I hate this new version of him.

I agree to his suggestion, lifting the aluminum to my lips.

Focus, Blaine, I urge myself, pushing the mural out of consciousness. A half hour and two more mural daydream distractions later, my speech is in surprisingly good condition—no thanks to me. Who knows how it'll be perceived by the council, but I can't say we didn't try.

"I think we have the basics fleshed out, right?" I scan my five pages of notes in the Google Doc, eyes straining against the blue light. "What was the name that we all liked again, Trish?"

"The Wicker West Wellness Initiative," she answers.

"That's right," I say, nodding as I type. I read out loud the tagline we settled on just to make sure we're on the same page: "'The Wicker West Wellness Initiative . . . a comprehensive, three-pronged approach to finally start addressing mental health at our school.'"

I glance up at Danny, who's giving me a thumbs-up.

"I've been jotting down some strong one-liners we can work into your speech too," Trish says. "I'll share my thoughts with you tomorrow."

"Trish," I exhale. "I don't know what's gotten into you with all this student council stuff, but you are turning out to be the best campaign captain a future class president could hope for."

"I know," she says, puckering her lips, giving me a digital kiss. "Way better than Eve Beesbopper."

"Wait," I say. "Zach chose Eve as his campaign captain?"

Danny nods.

That figures. She's our grade's whip-smart inevitable valedictorian—the perfect person to help win an election. My chest tenses up. Eve's being on Team Zach is just one more towering hurdle I'll have to clear in order to pull this thing off.

"I've got to run," Trish says, pulling out one earbud.

"Camilla will kill me if I miss the pterodactyl unveiling." She pauses. "Or was it a brachiosaur? Either way . . . bye, guys."

"Good night."

"See ya, Trish," Danny says.

The FaceTime ends.

Then it's just me and Danny.

You'd think it'd be uncomfortable, knowing our new-found friendship (if I can even call it that yet) is based on an epic sidewalk crash involving paint cans and a broken plant holder. But it's not uncomfortable at all.

I'm weirdly at ease around him.

Crickets are chirping outside the window, a few engines purr as cars roll past our town house, and a warm spring breeze is pushing at the curtains. I close my laptop, completely drained from working whatever part of the brain is responsible for leadership skills, for the first time in my life.

Danny moves to clean up the Cheez-Its, empty pop cans, and Reese's Pieces that Aunt Starr brought out for us to indulge in during the meeting.

"No, no," I say with a yawn, motioning for him to stop. "I got it."

"Are you sure?"

I nod, picking up the bowls and cans. We rise to our feet, and he follows me into the dimly lit kitchen, where I stash the candy away in the cupboard next to the fridge and finish putting away some dishes.

Danny finds a seat at the island. "Where are your parents?" he asks, glancing around.

"Working," I say, turning to him and leaning my back against the sink.

"This late?"

"Yeah. This is normal."

"What do they do?"

"My mom's a nurse who works wild hours, and my dad's in construction and spring is always his busiest season."

"Gotcha."

"Lately it's just been me, Fudge, and my aunt Starr with the house to ourselves," I say. "What about you? I've never seen your mom working at Biggest Bean. Does she work somewhere else?"

He opens his mouth to say something, but closes it again. After a moment of weirdness, he finally gets out, "My mom died when we were in middle school."

"Oh." My stomach twists into a knot. "I'm sorry. I had no idea."

"It's okay. Cancer. What are you going to do?" He pulls his shirt collar down, exposing a small floral design in black ink on his right shoulder. "Dad just let me get this tattoo in her honor."

I push off against the sink and bend my waist across the kitchen island to take a closer look. "I love it."

"It's a peony, her favorite," he says with a small smile. He lets go of his collar, and the fabric springs back up, covering his skin once again. "She got me into plants and flowers and stuff. We used to garden together."

"Well," I say, remembering Danny's new row of succulents at Biggest Bean. "I'm sure she'd be very proud that you haven't killed your . . . 'Zebra plant' is the name, right?"

"Yes. And I'd like to think she would be."

It's strange to think that the Nguyens lost a mom and wife. They don't seem like a family grappling with grief. I don't know them *that* well, to be sure, but during my habitual trips to Biggest Bean since it opened my freshman year, Bao's been nothing but kind and bubbly—even amid the madness of screaming youth soccer squads, demanding businesspeople, and under-caffeinated parents. How could such a tragic thing have happened to such a kindhearted guy? Maybe he harbors his sadness behind his happy—like Mom says Aunt Starr tends to do.

"Anyway." He stretches his arms, long torso spanning half the kitchen (or at least it feels that way). "Sorry. I didn't mean to bum you out with all this 'my mom is dead' talk."

"You didn't bum me out," I say, shaking my head. "I'm glad you told me."

"I'm also sorry about how I acted toward you at first," he says.

I tilt my head. "How did you act toward me at first?"

"You know." He pops his shoulders up a bit, embarrassed. "I should have been nicer about the whole plant thing."

I lean on the kitchen island using my palms. "I mean, I killed your aloha—"

"Aloe *vera*—"

"I know, I know," I say. "Just kidding."

We both laugh.

"I didn't mean to harp on you about it, is all," he continues. "Sometimes my sharp edges come out around new people, especially if I like them."

Especially if he likes them?

I definitely put two and two together, but he keeps going with the flow, so I decide not to stop him. "I should have been more forgiving from the get-go," he concludes.

"You're fine," I say. "No reason to apologize."

"It's something I need to work on."

"Danny." I look at him with a grin. "Seriously, it's not a big deal."

The kitchen grows quiet. I hear the pitter-patter of Fudge moseying around on the hardwood in a room nearby and the soft sounds of an ambulance in the faraway distance.

"Anyway," I say, pretending to brush crumbs off the kitchen island. There's nothing there, but I felt the need to break the stillness of the room. "I bet your mom would've been so hyped over what Biggest Bean has become. It's, like, one of the most popular coffee shops in Chicago."

He laughs. "That distinction, I can assure you, is not accurate."

"Well, Biggest Bean aside, I'm sure she'd be happy for you, *period*," I say.

"I wish I got to come out to her before she died," he adds with a shade of regret. "You know, so that she got to know the *whole* me."

"Yeah." I pause. "I mean . . . I'd like to think that, wherever she is, she knows the whole you now. You know?"

Sometimes one look can say so much more than any string of words. And, between blinks, I can see a swirl of grief and gratitude floating in Danny's honey-colored irises. "Can I tell you something?" he asks.

I tense up, but try not to show it. "Of course."

He studies the countertop for a moment, thinking through his next words. "I'm really happy you asked me to help out with your campaign."

"Are you kidding?" I say, beaming. "Thank *you* for helping. Clearly I wouldn't be able to do this without you, Trish, and Camilla."

He turns pink. "I think you'd be just fine."

"Well, you'd be thinking wrong."

Danny leans back in his chair and sticks his hands into his pockets. "I'm stoked about the Wicker West Wellness Initiative," he says. "This stuff will really matter to students like me."

"Students like you?"

"I've had to battle through my own stuff, just like Trish has," he says. "Like I mentioned, when meeting new people . . . I've struggled with intense anxiety ever since my mom died."

"Oh yeah?"

Anxiety? Danny?

He's never *not* as cool as a cucumber (well, maybe except for when he's nearly killed by a paint cart). "Anxious" is the *last* term I'd use to describe Danny. "That's surprising."

"Why?"

"Well . . . I don't know." I tread lightly. "You always seem so calm and collected."

"On the outside, sure," he says. "There's a lot going on up here, though." He taps at his temple with a grin. "*Too* much going on, really."

I return the smile. "I get that. I'm sorry, I didn't mean to, like, assume anything about you."

He shakes his head.

"That's got to be tough," I add.

"It is. Well, sometimes. Some days, like today, I'm fine. Other days, it feels like the world is ending for no apparent reason." He laughs. "That's how my anxiety works. Weird, I know."

"Not weird at all," I say, studying my hands on the countertop because I'm not sure where else to look. "That's why we're doing this initiative, right? We all have our invisible battles. For me, lately I'm . . ." I hesitate about going there, but the words are halfway out of my mouth anyway, so I say, "I'm struggling with this breakup. It sounds so trivial—and, in the grand scheme of things, it is, really—but Joey dumping me affected how I see myself, I think?"

I wasn't even aware that that was the case before saying it out loud. But that's exactly what's happening: Joey breaking up with me—and doing it the *way* he did—steamrolled my self-confidence.

Danny presses. "How so?"

I feel my own cheeks turning pink now. "I guess it's like, Joey is the It Guy of our school." I roll my eyes. "It's stupid, yeah, but I think it was always an insecurity of mine that he's way out of my league—an insecurity that was confirmed when he ditched me for Zach." I pause to take a breath. "I'm scared this election will be an extension of that relationship, you know? Like, the votes will get counted, and I'll get trampled by a Serious Guy I had no business competing against in the first place."

Danny grins at me. "A Serious Guy?"

I shrug. "Well . . . yeah. Some guy who doesn't wander around Chicago with his paint cans, covered in acrylics."

He stands, circles the island, and leans his hip against the counter directly next to me. Even though he's sans apron, I still get a whiff of the sugary, comforting scent of the coffee shop. "You are not out of Joey's league," he says, the kindness in his eyes on full display. "If anything, it's the exact opposite."

"*Ha.* Okay."

"I'm serious." He steps even closer, his hand scooching nearer too. This energy feels like I'm being wrapped up in one of Aunt Starr's weighted blankets. "You're going to win this election, Blaine. I can feel it in my gut."

Our faces are just inches apart.

Wait. What is happening right now?

Am I about to kiss Danny?

His phone vibrates on the counter. We both jump.

"Sorry," he says, grabbing it and glancing at the screen. "Oh damn. It's my dad. I should have been home already." Before I can even compute the last thirty seconds, Danny pulls me in for a really long, much-needed, perfectly snug hug.

"Thank you for the chat," he says. "And sorry again for my sharp edges. I'll see you tomorrow."

He dashes into the living room, grabs his backpack, and vanishes out the front door in a flash.

have never been this nervous before. *Ever.* If I get through this freaking speech without projectile-vomiting all over half of Wicker West's student council, I'll consider it a victory.

"Are you nervous?" Camilla asks with a smirk, popping her bubble gum and knowing the answer.

"Not really," I lie, brushing the sweat off my forehead. "Why? Do I look nervous?"

She cringes a bit, like she wants to say no but can't in good faith insinuate that I look anything other than absolutely petrified.

Trish, Camilla, Danny, and I are in the hallway adjacent to the school auditorium, the waiting area for all seven senior class president candidates prior to our speeches. Each campaign team is separated by the length of a classroom, so no one can eavesdrop as the groups do last-minute prep. Joey and Ashtyn are the farthest away from us, talking animatedly with Zach, who—yes, I'll admit—looks pretty damn presidential in a dark gray suit and black tie. I don't look too shabby myself, in brown corduroy pants, a navy jacket, and a light blue tie Danny brought in for me to borrow.

I've been thinking about those final moments before he left my house. Like, a *lot.*

Was Danny making a move? Would he have kissed me, if his dad hadn't texted at that *exact* second? Would I have *wanted* him to kiss me?

Mr. Wells bounces over to us, clipboard in hand. His face immediately melts with concern when his eyes meet mine. "How are you feeling, Blaine?" he asks, tipping his head back to see me through the bottoms of his bifocals. "You look a bit nervous."

"Why does everyone keep saying that? I'm fine," I declare, louder than I mean to.

He jumps back.

"Sorry," I say.

"He's going to blow everyone away," Trish says in my defense. She grabs the sides of my head and turns my gaze so that I'm staring directly into her dead-serious, deep-brown eyes. "Blaine, repeat after me."

"Ah, okay?"

"I look amazing," she says.

"I look amazing," I say.

"I've prepared a fantastic speech."

"I've prepared a fantastic speech."

"And I'm going to make a terrific class president."

"And I'll probably make at least a somewhat okay class president."

"*Blaine.*"

"And I'm going to make a terrific class president."

She pats my cheeks and smiles.

"Remember: no one's expecting you to be the next

Barack out there," Camilla says, nudging my shoulder with hers. "Go easy on yourself."

"Just smile and look up from the computer every so often," Danny adds, nudging me from the other side with his shoulder too.

Trish continues, "And if you stumble over your words—"

"I know, I know, don't panic," I finish, exhaling the longest breath I've ever taken. Then I tilt my head left to right, right to left, cracking my neck.

"I've got some news for you that one might interpret as good or bad, depending on how you look at it," Mr. Wells says, checking his clipboard. "I drew names out of a hat to figure out the order of the speeches. You're going last, Blaine."

"That's good!" Trish cuts in immediately to stop my negative thoughts from churning. "You'll be the *closer*, bringing the house down."

"Agreed," Danny says optimistically, nodding with confidence.

"Yeah?" I ask, hesitant.

"Just don't sit backstage overthinking everything while the others go before you," Camilla warns. "Because then it could be *real* bad."

"Why would you even say that to him?" Trish says through a forced smile without moving her lips.

"It'll be over before you know it, Blaine." Mr. Wells taps my arm with his clipboard supportively before turning to leave.

There's a lot going through my head right now. For

starters, what in the world am I doing? Like, really, though . . . *what in the world am I doing?*

How did I ever convince myself that running for senior class president was a good idea? Is impressing Joey really worth this level of agony? I mean, sure, I think my speech is good, and, yes, I believe in our Wicker West Wellness Initiative—especially after knowing how much it means to Trish and Danny. But none of it will matter if I can't get half the student council—forty-seven of ninety-four members—to vote yes on my candidacy, putting me on the ballot. And with six other candidates raising the bar before I go out there and douse the front row in flop sweat, those odds might as well be a one-in-a-million chance.

"I need some water," I say, beelining for the drinking fountain at the other end of the hallway.

I can't hear much of what any of the other campaign teams are saying, except for when I pass Zach, Joey, and Ashtyn, who are standing nearest the drinking fountain. Leaning in for a lukewarm sip, I can't help but to eavesdrop a tad.

"Remember, avoid the 'ums' and 'ahs' between sentences," Joey presses his new boyfriend.

"And keep your eyes moving across the audience at all times," Ashtyn warns. "If you only acknowledge the same students in the front, others will notice that. It's not a good look."

"You're slouching a bit," Joey says. "Remember to stand up tall behind the mic."

I wipe the wetness from my mouth with my palm and walk back toward my team. Joey, Ashtyn, and Zach—none of whom noticed me wandering by ten seconds ago—immediately shut up as I cross their path again.

Joey refuses to make eye contact with me. Zach seems embarrassed.

Ashtyn is the only one to speak up. "Good luck, Blaine," she says flatly.

I give her a genuine smile in return. Wait a minute. . . . Why is Ashtyn back here right now giving Zach a pep talk? She's not really a good friend of his, nor is she his campaign captain. Eve is weirdly nowhere to be found.

Mr. Wells begins waving for everyone's attention at the other end of the hall. "Listen up!" he bellows. "We're about to get started. All candidates, please come stand near me in the order that you're giving your speech. All *non*-candidates, if you're a student council member, please go sit in the auditorium. Any campaign captain who is *not* in student council is allowed in the auditorium as well, but remember: you can't vote on the candidates afterward. If you're not a candidate, a student council member, or a campaign captain"—he points to the exit—"goodbye!"

Trish, Danny, and Camilla turn to me, all smiling widely.

"You're going to be great," Danny says.

"Remember." Camilla leans in. "No one's expecting Barack. Just don't pass out, and you're golden."

I sigh. "Thanks, Camilla."

Trish hands me my laptop, which has the speech downloaded and ready to go on a teleprompter app. "Knock their socks off, boo."

We share a quick group hug and disperse. My heart pounding so hard that I can feel it rattling in my throat, I join the end of the line—as the seventh of seven candidates. Zach, I notice, is going third.

"Wicker West Wellness Initiative," I practice to myself, praying it rolls off my tongue easily out there. "Wicker West Wellness Initiative . . ."

"Is everyone ready?" Mr. Wells asks us, standing at the front of our line, eyes bouncing across the candidates' faces.

We all murmur some variation of "yes."

"Good," he says. "Let's go."

He leads us through the door to the backstage of the auditorium, where it's cool, dusty, and dark. In a single file we follow Mr. Wells up to the towering, bright red curtain—the one thing standing between us and the ninety-four-person student council waiting to judge our every word, literally.

"You're up first, Miranda," he says, cracking the curtain so she can find her way to the other side.

Miranda disappears into the bright lights in front of us, and the gap in the curtain closes once again, leaving us in shadows. A moment later she begins her speech. Because of the weird acoustics of the stage, it's very difficult to hear what she's saying back here. But you know what? I don't mind. Not at all.

I don't want the others' words to get into my head.

About three minutes later the crowd starts clapping, suggesting Miranda got through her speech in one piece. A wave of jealousy blankets my body. I wish I could be in her shoes right now. I have to wait through another *five* of these before I'm up.

Mr. Wells opens the curtain again, and Dustin, the second candidate in line, follows his prompt. Judging from the applause that follows a few minutes later, Dustin's speech seems to have gone at least okay as well. Then it's Zach's turn.

I'm the most curious about what he has to say, of course, but I force myself not to try to tune in. Instead I try thinking about my pics of Fudge when he was a puppy, fantasize about the Vietnamese doughnut I want to devour at Biggest Bean after this as a treat-yo'self reward for making it through, and try to remember Aunt Starr's ridiculous knock-knock jokes—anything to distract me from what I assume is a stellar speech being spoken just a few feet in front of me.

The applause following Zach's speech is the loudest thus far.

Damn it. I expected that, but still.

Damn it.

Then it's Nancy's turn. Then Melissa's. Then Bryce's.

Then mine.

I take one last deep breath, wipe my brow, and remember what Camilla told me. *You don't have to be the next Obama,* I say to myself. *Just don't puke onstage, Blaine.*

"Last but not least," Mr. Wells whispers to me gently as the student council finishes clapping for Bryce. "You ready, Blaine?"

I smile and nod.

He peels back the curtain, and I walk through.

CHAPTER 14

★ ☆ ★

ood afternoon, Wicker West student council," I say into the microphone, voice trembling. A quick burst of feedback sends a shock through the cavernous auditorium, but I trudge on like it didn't happen. "Thanks for letting me be here with you today. I'm Blaine Bowers, junior running for senior class president."

I glance up from the words of my speech slowly scrolling on my laptop. The stage lights are way more intense than I expected, and I can't identify a single silhouette of the hundred or so people staring at me.

Just keep swimming.

I place my hands on the podium next to my computer.

"I know that many of you don't know who I am," I read on. "I'm not a current student council member, nor am I one of our star athletes. I don't have a standout GPA, and I'm certainly no Mr. Popular. A few of you may recognize me as the kid who paints murals around the neighborhood, and that's about it." I pause, clearing my throat. "So, why would a kid like me want to run for senior class president? Well, I think we have a crisis on our hands in our school. A mental health crisis."

A group of girls giggles somewhere.

What's so funny?

Then someone immediately shushes them. The auditorium falls silent again—but the distraction is enough to screw with my rhythm.

"A few, um—a few days ago, I—" I stammer a bit and have to hit pause on the teleprompter so as to not lose my spot. *Just breathe, Blaine,* I think. *Just freaking breathe.* I hit enter so the words keep scrolling.

"A few days ago I set out a sign at lunch that read 'Let's Talk' in order to connect with fellow juniors about the school issues they care about," I say. "To my surprise, I was absolutely blown away by the responses I got. Juniors weren't complaining to me about the cafeteria's new macaroni and cheese recipe, or how terribly the refs blew it in the district football match against Naperville East last fall—although they'd have every right to vent about either of those things. No, juniors overwhelmingly opened up about issues involving mental health."

I take a breath and remind myself, yet again, to go slow. I practiced this a hundred times in my mirror last night. I know I can say it in under three minutes without rushing.

"Cyberbullying. The exhausting pressures of social media. Body image insecurities. Increasing anxiety over ever-important exams," I carry on. "Almost every single time someone opened up to me, it somehow related to an internal struggle. It's way past due for the current junior class— and *all* the students at Wicker West High—to have leaders who will commit to making student mental health a priority.

"That's why, should I be fortunate enough to become

next year's senior class president, I will work with the rest of the senior class leadership and the broader student council to implement what I'm calling the Wicker West Wellness Initiative—a comprehensive, three-pronged approach to finally start addressing mental health at our school. Through additional fundraising and the reallocation of wasted class resources, I will lead the way in implementing three programs that will help all seniors succeed."

I glance up.

Now that my eyes are more used to the bright lights, I can start to see the specific faces in front of me. I spot Joey and Ashtyn in the first row, just a few seats away from Dustin and Melissa. They're expressionless, but I assume that all four of them are hoping I trip over my shoelaces and nose-dive off the stage. Thank God I see Trish and Danny next, a few rows back. Although they're draped in more darkness, being farther away from the stage lights, I can spot subtle smiles on their faces. That immediately puts me more at ease.

If they're smiling, I can't be doing *that* poorly.

"First I will establish the Senior Space," I continue. "The Senior Space will be a quiet, softly lit area that our class can use during lunch periods to take a break from the chaos of the day. We can decide on an exact location together, but we'll have plenty of options. Since the marching band got a new storage facility for their instruments and their old room is vacant, I think it'd make the perfect spot. I'll aim to include cots, should students choose to take catnaps. There will be soothing videos playing on a projector, if students want to meditate or simply zone out in peace. And there will be no talking or phone usage allowed. You can unplug in more ways than one."

I breathe more easily, finding my pace and hitting my stride.

"Secondly, I'll set up Senior Chat—an anonymous email service that will be run by a group of student volunteers. If you need someone to talk to, we will be there. And if your issue requires a mental health professional, we can connect you with the expert care you deserve. We'll be all ears, all the time."

"And lastly," I say, my pulse slowing down, now that I'm in the home stretch, "I will host Senior Sundays. At the end of each weekend, I and/or the other members of the senior class leadership will go live from our official class Instagram account and talk about the anxieties and challenges facing us in the week ahead. Ideally, viewers can ask questions, express their own thoughts, and be candid about what they're experiencing in the comments. Down the road, I hope others will be able to host Senior Sundays too, creating a space where our class can bravely share, de-stress, and have a digital destination that's safe and supportive.

"I'm not naive," I note, looking up at the crowd. "I know that the Wicker West Wellness Initiative won't solve all mental health challenges for our soon-to-be senior class or the larger student body. But I do think it'll help create a culture where students can prioritize self-care, speak up when they need support, and connect with others in meaningful ways.

"If I'm fortunate enough to become next year's senior class president," I say, standing up straighter, "you can count on me, Blaine Bowers, to put students first. Thank you for your time, Wicker West student council. Have a terrific afternoon."

I step back from the podium and nod.

The applause begins. It's not overwhelming, but I don't think it's too terrible, either. It sounds . . . pretty much like the applause everyone else got, I think?

Except for Zach.

I step down the stairs on the side of the stage, and take a seat next to Trish and Danny. I don't have a clue as to how much my words resonated with the student council. (I could have just gotten pure pity applause, after all.) But at least it's over.

"You did amazing," Trish whispers as I settle into the seat next to her.

Danny reaches around her back and taps my shoulder. "I agree," he says softly.

"Really?" I ask, my cheeks still hot from the glow of the stage lights. "You're not just saying that?"

They both shake their heads adamantly.

"Why did people laugh, though?" I ask.

Danny shrugs while Trish rolls her eyes. "Don't worry about that. It was nothing," she says. "I may be biased, but I think your speech was the best."

"*Our* speech," I correct her.

Mr. Wells takes the stage. "Thank you, candidates! Amazing speeches, with incredible ideas for the future of our school." He starts a final round of applause, and the student council follows suit. "Now, if you're a member of the council, please exit through the main auditorium doors behind you. At the table outside, you can vote for whichever candidates you believe should be on the ballot. As a reminder, you must vote for, at a minimum, two—but you can vote for all seven if you'd like. Please let me know if you have any questions. Go forth!"

Everyone begins moseying toward the exit. We follow the crowd, as Danny needs to cast his votes and Camilla is waiting outside in the hallway. A few people nod and share smiles with me on our way out. A couple of kids that I've never met before tell me that I did a good job. Hey, maybe Trish and Danny aren't lying.

Maybe I *can* make it onto this freaking ballot.

I say I need to use the bathroom, and peel away from the group of student council members and candidates congregating in the hallway. But mostly I need a minute to myself to relish in the sweet relief of avoiding a worst-case scenario onstage.

No one else is in the bathroom, fortunately. I lean my forehead against a mirror, hands gripping either side of the ceramic sink extending from the wall. I exhale, long and hard, letting the anxiety of the day escape from my body. *I did it,* I congratulate myself, grinning.

I freaking did it.

A urinal flushes on the other side of the stalls, out of view.

I jolt, straighten my back, and begin washing my hands, so as to not look like a total doofus lost in my own my reflection.

I catch a glimpse of the person in the mirror, walking my way. It's Joey.

Those nerves I just let out? They all come roaring back in exactly one nanosecond.

"Hey," he says, approaching. There are many sinks he could use, but he walks all the way to the one right next to mine.

Soap dispenses onto his palm.

"How's it going?" I ask, trying to play it cool.

"Good," he says.

We both scrub our hands beneath the bathroom's unforgiving fluorescent lights.

I want to seize the moment and turn over a new leaf. Start a new chapter. Leave the horrors of Grey Kettle behind and tell him—right now, on the now-rare occasion when I have him all to myself—that I *can* be Serious. That I *can* be the guy for him.

But before I can gather my thoughts and spit it out, he's drying his hands, tossing the paper towel into the trash bin, and on his way.

"See you later," I say, sending him a subtle smile.

He turns back to me, hand resting on the bathroom door handle. "You did well up there, Blaine," he says with a congratulatory nod. "Impressive speech. Especially for a rookie."

And he's gone.

I turn off my faucet and stare back at my reflection, feeling my heart drumming against my insides.

CHAPTER 15

Trish, Camilla, and Danny are over for brinner tonight in honor of the fact that I survived my speech without projectile-vomiting all over Wicker West's student council. I'm not getting too excited, though. My speech went better than I expected it to, but it's still a numbers game, as Danny noted. Five other people also had solid speeches, judging by the applause I heard after each one. And the other candidate seemingly knocked it out of the park.

As much as I'd love to let loose, all this premature jubilation will likely blow up in my face in a matter of days. Heck, maybe even *hours*, depending on how long it takes Mr. Wells to tally the council members' votes. Aunt Starr is never one to pass on a win when one comes along, though, and tonight, victory means an especially decadent brinner of extra-cheesy prosciutto frittatas.

Aunt Starr, in an oversized bright orange sweater and matching sweatpants, is dancing in front of the stove to a song by the Weeknd playing on Camilla's playlist.

"I wish all of you were twenty-one so you could partake with me," she says, bobbing her head to the beat while pouring herself a glass of white wine. Multitasking proves too difficult, and half of it splashes across the countertop.

"You *could* be the cool aunt and let us have a glass?" Danny says with a smirk, looking handsome tonight in a red flannel shirt and backward black baseball cap. "We wouldn't tell anyone."

"Aren't you sixteen, Danny?" Aunt Starr exclaims, tearing off a row of paper towels to clean up her spill. "You're a baby! You're all babies! Stick with water until you're thirty. Trust me."

Trish is in campaign captain mode after my speech, scrolling through the #WWSeniorSpeeches hashtag on Twitter, and scouring any video content that council members shared on Instagram and TikTok. "Any post I'm seeing from the auditorium that includes you is a positive one."

"How many posts are there about me?" I ask, hopeful.

"Um . . ." She does a quick count, scrolling with one hand and adjusting the drawstrings of her hoodie with the other. "Three."

"How many are about Zach?"

She pauses. "A few more."

I give her a look.

"A couple dozen," she clarifies.

I anxiously bite my lower lip.

Not that social media buzz directly correlates with support, but it's seeming increasingly likely that Zach's a shoo-in for the ballot. Broad appeal among council members? Check. Resounding applause after his speech? Check. Adoring supporters who are willing to make campaign-style TikTok videos for him? Check. I'm oh-for-three on those fronts.

But I know that I *did* earn the respect of at least a handful of council members who appreciated my speech. And, even more important, Joey was impressed.

That has to put me in the running.

Hopefully.

"I thought Miranda's bit on uniting our class was solid in a *kumbaya* way," Danny opines like a CNN pundit, helping Aunt Starr crack a massive amount of eggs into a big bowl near the stove. "And Bryce did a surprisingly good job with the line about how inconsistently our class tardy policies are enforced. But in terms of overall substance?" He turns to me. "Yours was a homerun."

"Danny, you're right about Zach's name recognition too," Trish adds. "His speech was all about himself, filled with a bunch of feel-good platitudes. It lacked real depth. It lacked vision."

"Believe me," Danny says, "plenty of people in student council can see through Zach's BS. Not all of them—maybe not even most of them—but people are looking for an alternative to Zach-*ism*. I think you filled that role nicely, Blaine."

"You swear our initiative didn't come across as strange?" I ask.

"Not at all," Danny says.

"Stop it with that nonsense." Trish sets down her phone, knowing where my insecurity is rooted. "Those tiny giggles at the beginning came from weird little freshmen who were probably laughing about something unrelated anyway."

"People laughed at your speech? Whose butt am I kicking

tonight?" Aunt Starr asks, rummaging around on the refrigerator door. She finds what she's searching for and returns to the stove, where Danny is flipping a pan of sautéed veggies like a boss. "Whoa!" she exclaims, jaw dropped. "We've got Bobby Flay in the house."

"His dad owns Biggest Bean, Aunt Starr," I say. "He definitely knows his way around a kitchen."

Aunt Starr nods, impressed. She drops a handful of crumbled cheese into her egg mixture. "Are you planning on taking over the family business someday?"

Danny pauses. "Um . . . maybe? I don't know yet."

"Well," Aunt Starr says, deciding another handful of cheese is appropriate, "the good news is, you don't have to know yet. That's the best part of being sixteen. Sure, you can't get liquored up on a weeknight like your aunt Starr." She takes a sip of her wine. "But you also have some time before you've got to make those kinds of big life decisions."

Danny agrees with a thoughtful nod.

"What would you do if you didn't take over Biggest Bean?" Trish asks him.

He turns to her, oily spatula in hand. "I've never told anyone this, but I think I'd want to start my own plant nursery," he says. "I love working with plants and getting my hands dirty. It helps with my anxiety. And it reminds me of my mom."

Aunt Starr clutches her chest, as if it's the most adorable thing she's ever heard.

"Why are we the first people you've told this to?" Camilla

says, rounding the island to check out the progress happening at the stove. "You're not embarrassed, are you? Because owning your own nursery would be badass."

"Saying it out loud makes it feel more real, I guess," he says. "It's scary."

"Why's that?" Aunt Starr asks.

He thinks for a second. "I saw firsthand how hard it was for my dad to start a new business. Do you know how many people doubted he could do it? His friends told him that Chicagoans go to Uptown when they want Vietnamese food and bubble tea—that there's no appetite for Biggest Bean's *Asian offerings* in this neighborhood. But my dad worked his ass off and proved them wrong, and this year our Bánh Tiêu began outselling our chocolate chip cookies, and our—" He pauses, takes a breath, and lets a smile creep into his cheeks. "Sorry, I get worked up talking about it. But my point is, while I respect my dad for what he's accomplished, I also don't want to sign myself up for a lifetime of stress."

"Well, I say, go big or go home," Camilla advises, nudging his shoulder lovingly. "One day I'll discover an entirely new dinosaur species while digging in Argentina, and you'll be the owner of a very successful plant nursery chain throughout the Midwest." She pops a runaway piece of cheese into her mouth. "It's fate."

They exchange smiles.

Aunt Starr starts explaining the last steps of the frittatas to Danny and Camilla. I'm about to join them at the stove, but Trish grabs my arm at the island before I can wander

ROBBIE COUCH

over. "Hey," she says quietly, looking up from her phone at
me. "Did you see the message from Mr. Wells?"

Oh my God. Is this it?

Do we know whose speeches made the cut?

I pull out my phone and tap into my Gmail. *(Minor)*
Senior Class Presidency Election Update! the subject line reads.
The message has been sent to all seven candidates and their
campaign captains, I notice.

"Ashtyn's taking Eve Beesbopper's place as Zach's campaign captain?" I say, reading the email. I look up to Trish.
"That's weird."

"Right?" Trish says.

This seems like an odd move for Zach. Eve is his most
obvious choice for campaign captain. Did she step down?
Did they have a falling-out? Was she fired? And what's inspiring Ashtyn to take her place?

"I don't know," Trish mutters, giving me a look. "This
sounds fishy."

CHAPTER 16

The next morning, I should be focused on my water-color painting in art—who knew capturing the Lean-ing Tower of Pisa's actual lean could be so difficult?—but my mind keeps wandering back to Ashtyn's suspicious new role on Zach's team.

It just doesn't make sense.

Sure, she's a student council veteran who's in the know on just about everything related to Wicker West, and yeah, she understands the demands of an election better than just about anybody else. But she and Zach have never been friends. Like, not even a little bit!

Something's up.

Focus, Blaine, I tell myself, trying to mix the right shades for the lawn in front of the tower. *This tourist trap isn't going to paint itself.*

There's a knock on the doorframe.

"Ms. Green?" Mr. Wells asks, popping his head in. "Can I borrow Blaine Bowers?"

The humming of the room dies down at once.

"Of course," Ms. Green says, her gray eyes zeroing in on me in the back of the classroom. Every student turns too, knowing that Mr. Wells is here to relay my electoral fate.

Even with a performance that Joey himself found

impressive, I'm not being naive about all of this; I know the odds are still against me. Seven speech-givers would never make the cut onto a class election ballot. It's usually three or four; five candidates, tops, as Danny noted last night over frittatas. The idea that forty-seven of those faceless, fidgeting, laughing silhouettes scattered throughout the auditorium would think I deserve to be on the ballot? I'm no statistician, but I know an underdog when I see one.

I walk down the aisle of desks to the exit, feeling the intense gaze of the entire classroom with each step. I wish Mr. Wells had just delivered the news to me last night in a follow-up email after the one he sent about Ashtyn, instead of this dramatic ordeal.

I follow Mr. Wells into the deserted hallway. He stops and turns, ready to deliver the council vote totals, as I lean against a row of lockers. "Hi, Blaine," he says, glancing down at the same clipboard he had before our speeches. "How are you feeling after yesterday?"

I think. "I guess I feel okay?" I say, not entirely sure myself. "I think I did an all right job up there."

"I think you did *fantastic*," he says emphatically, dropping the clipboard to his side, eyes looking especially googly behind the bifocals. "Truly remarkable."

Uh-oh. This isn't good.

Because he's doing the thing where teachers are overly nice to you about something right before relaying terrible news. I'm having déjà vu. It's like the time Mrs. Julliard took me aside in algebra and began complimenting my shoes *seconds* before telling me that my mom had called the school to tell me that Fudge had been rushed to the vet. (He ended up being fine, but the bowl of grapes he'd devoured was not.)

Rip off the Band-Aid, I think. Let's get this over with.

Mr. Wells scratches his beard. "This year's student council voted pretty tough when it came to the speeches," he says, striking a somber tone. "They had a very high bar, apparently."

Here it comes. "Oh yeah?"

"Yeah. Only two students in your class passed the forty-seven-vote threshold."

"Dang." That's even more cutthroat than I'd imagined.

Zach and Miranda, I bet. Or maybe Zach and Bryce? Zach and Melissa isn't out of the question either—I could see an outsider like her taking on the role of dark horse.

"It's always difficult to guess how the council will respond to the speeches, I've come to learn from being adviser for the past decade," he says. "But this year was particularly unpredictable."

"It's okay, Mr. Wells," I tell him softly, leaning in and grinning. "You don't have to do this."

He looks confused. "Do what?"

"You know, do the whole . . ." I'm not sure how to say it, so I lift my hands into the air and make my fingers dance around—as if I'm a circus performer, or something. I stop, realizing he looks even more confused than before. "You don't have to talk me up and be all nice, I guess is what I'm saying."

"Blaine—"

"I'm a big kid. I can take it."

"Well, yes, I know you are, but—"

"I know I didn't get forty-seven votes."

"You're right," Mr. Wells interjects. "You got fifty-nine."

I freeze.

His lips spread into a smile.

"Are you serious?" I say, gobsmacked.

"Yes, Blaine," he says, doing the thing again where he taps me on the arm with his clipboard. "Congratulations. You've made it onto the ballot."

My jaw completely unhinges for a solid three seconds before I realize what's happening and cover my mouth with my hands. "I—what? Are you sure?" I murmur through my palms. "Should there be a recount?"

He laughs. "Yes, I am sure. And no, there is no reason to have a recount."

My heart begins racing.

"I got fifty-nine votes?"

"You got fifty-nine votes."

"I'll be on the ballot?" I'm repeating what he's already said, I know, but I'm at a loss for new words.

He nods, clearly amused.

Holy crap. Holy, holy, *holy crap.*

"Who's the other person?" I say, dropping my hands from my mouth.

"Zach."

I knew it would be. But it still doesn't stop a shiver from

rippling down my spine. It's me and Zach. David and a student council Goliath, more or less.

"How many votes did he get?" I ask. "Wait, you probably can't tell me."

Mr. Wells shakes his head.

"That makes sense."

"You still have the election packet I gave you when you signed up to run, right?" he says, getting serious. "All the information on next steps is in there. The debate is next week—twenty minutes, in front of the whole school—and I highly suggest you prepare." He says it like preparing for a debate is just a thing everyone knows how to do.

I smile and nod, head still spinning like wheels on a speeding car.

"But for now, celebrate." He gives me a wink and starts to walk off. "You deserve it, Blaine."

Oh my God. Oh. My. *God.*

Fifty-nine votes. I'll be on the ballot. I'll be on the *freaking ballot* for senior class president against Zach Chesterton.

Melissa isn't the dark horse in this race. *I* am.

CHAPTER 17

H aving friends that believe in you can be a double-edged sword.

Trish, Camilla, and Danny are not surprised in the slightest to learn I made it onto the ballot, having genuinely thought I had a great shot after my speech. It's flattering, but it leads to my inevitable disappointment after their anticlimactic reactions. Trish drops a "Told ya so," Danny mutters "Nice!" before dashing off to second period, and Camilla gives me a weak thumbs-up. (Like I said, double-edged sword.) Aunt Starr is there to make up for their blasé responses, though, screaming through the telephone in pure euphoria as if she's just won the $100 million jackpot.

Her excitement reminds me that I still need to tell her about the Field Museum job. Running for president has taken up so much space in my head that there's little room to remember anything else. I promise myself I'll do it when I get home later.

The rest of the school day flies by in a happy blur before I dash off to Biggest Bean after last period. An especially determined Trish and I are huddled together in our corner of the coffee shop, reading through the election packet Mr. Wells gave me when I first signed up to run. Before, I only skimmed it. But now I'm going through line by line, eyes glued to each page, like every word needs to be memorized. I really need to know how all of this works, seeing as I'm actually on the ballot now.

I'm actually on the ballot now. It still hasn't sunk in yet.

"Election Day is going to be bananas," Trish says, reading her own packet. She made copies of mine after school in the office. "'Students across grade levels will vote at the beginning of their first periods on Friday, April 22, for the following year's class treasurers, secretaries, vice presidents, and presidents,'" Trish reads, sipping her chai latte between sentences. "'Campaign captains representing each candidate must collect ballots from homerooms during the last half of the hour, in conjunction with the campaign captains representing opposing candidates, to ensure that there is no cheating.'" She drops the packet and looks up at me, face squished in revulsion. "In other words, I have to go around collecting ballots with freaking Ashtyn?"

I shrug apologetically. "I owe you one?"

She shakes her head. "You owe me a lot more than *one* after this election comes and goes."

Danny jogs out from behind the counter and collapses onto the sofa across from me and Trish on the beanbags. A puff of powdered sugar clouds the air when he lands, and I notice a much-thicker-than-usual coat of pastry toppings on him from the neck down too; it must be a hectic shift.

"Where's Camilla?" he asks Trish.

"Internship," she answers, looking at his apron with a grin. "Crazy day of catering?"

"More like crazy *month* of catering," he breathes, sitting upright and chugging his cup of water.

"At least it's good for business?" I say optimistically.

"Maybe?" he says, tilting his head in thought. "If only my dad paid me by the calories burned and not the hours worked." He glances at our packets. "How's debate prep going?"

My stomach drops, just hearing the word "debate." "Oh, is that what we're supposed to be doing?" I ask innocently.

"He's been putting it off since we got here," Trish says, calling me out on my procrastination. "I agreed to run through the packet first. And *then* we will move on to debate prep." She says it more like a threat than a command.

"Can you blame me for feeling the weight of impending dread?" I ask. "I am notoriously bad at debating! You know this, Trish. Every time I get into it with Aunt Starr over who's the best *Drag Race* queen, she ends up changing my mind."

"Zach is a good debater, I won't lie," Danny admits. "He was born to be onstage, in that conventional-politician kind of way. But people saw the authenticity in your speech, right? That should give you hope. Stick with your message—don't worry about being the perfect, polished candidate—and you'll break through."

He shakes his baseball cap to get the extra powdered sugar off and sends me a smile through the haze of white floating between us.

"Well, we have some time to prepare," Trish says, flipping the page in the packet. "We'll nail down all the fine print for our Wicker West Wellness Initiative, map out how we plan to pay for every last penny with our class funds—*without* raising the cost of prom tickets—and make sure Zach has nothing to ding us on."

Trish pushes on with debate talk, but I'm distracted by the horror that just walked in.

Zach.

Damn it.

"Oh no," I mutter, interrupting Trish and nodding his way.

"Speak of the devil," Trish says.

My pulse starts racing. Now that I know it's the two of us on the ballot, just *seeing* Zach's face sparks a fight-or-flight response. He unzips his steel-blue bomber jacket and flings his brown computer bag over one shoulder, staring up at the big chalkboard menu hanging near Danny's row of succulents. I don't think he's spotted us yet.

"Should I go say hi?" I ask.

"*Hi?*" Trish gapes. "Why the heck would you go say hi?"

"I don't know!" I retort, getting nervous. "It's the nice thing to do?"

Her glare suggests that I should know better. "Blaine. He's the competition. Like, he was the competition before, but now he's *really* the competition."

"You're right, you're right," I say.

Trish clears her throat. "As I was saying . . . ," she continues.

"Be right back," I say, jumping up and heading in Zach's direction.

"Blaine!" I hear Trish hissing after me.

He doesn't notice me until I'm standing just a few feet away. "Hey, Zach," I say with a hesitant smile and a wave. "How's it going?"

"Oh," he says, surprised. "Good. You?"

"Good, good. Grabbing a drink on your way home from school?"

"Lemon pound cake for my dad."

"Nice. I'm sitting over there"—I point toward our corner—"with my campaign team."

Trish and Danny, peeking over in our direction, immediately look away, pretending to be busy.

Zach smirks. "You, ah . . . you got something on your . . ." He nods at my chest.

I glance down.

Shoot.

The powdered sugar Danny shook off has inconveniently settled into a very visible layer on my dark T-shirt, like light snowfall on black pavement. "Whoops," I say, brushing it away with a forced laugh, feeling my cheeks get rosy. "Thanks."

"No problem." He looks back up at the menu—as if to tell me he's over our conversation.

"Listen, Zach," I say, more nervous than I should be. "I know things between us didn't exactly, er, get off on the right foot, I guess you could say."

He waits a moment before looking in my direction again. "I think that's a fair statement."

"I know the whole Joey thing is a bit awkward for us, but now that we're both on the ballot, I just . . ." I'm not even sure what I want to say. "I guess, just . . . Good luck." I give him a genuine smile and a nod.

He looks at me suspiciously.

Things feel a bit contentious.

"I mean it," I say to fill the void. "I respect that you've been in student council for a long time, and I hope we can both run a good race and leave it all on the court. Er, on the debate stage. Or whatever." I stick my hand out in front of him. "How does that sound?"

He looks down at it for a second before deciding my skin isn't poisonous, and completes his end of the shake. "Okay."

It gets quiet.

I'm not sure what else to say, and I'm pretty sure Zach hates the fact that we're breathing the same air right now, so I turn to leave. "Well, have a nice—"

"You gave a good speech, by the way," he says in a rush.

I rotate back.

"It's not every day that first-time candidates deliver up there, but you did," he continues, uncharacteristically timid. He's turning pink now too. *I'm actually making Zach Chesterton blush?* "Your mental health initiative shows real promise."

I rock back and forth on my heels awkwardly. "Thank you. I appreciate you saying that."

"You're welcome."

The conversation flatlines again. I'm about to leave for good this time, but then Ashtyn's mischievous face pops into my consciousness.

"Can I ask you something?" I say.

He zips up his jacket with a nod.

"Why'd you replace Eve with Ashtyn as your campaign captain?"

He stares at me.

I stare back.

"You're really asking me that?" he follows up.

What, is that an offensive thing to inquire about? "I don't mean to pry," I say. "It's not like I'm, you know, *digging* for dirt or something. I'm only curious."

He glances around Biggest Bean before taking a step closer toward me. "That's sort of an inappropriate question for a candidate to ask another candidate, don't you think?"

I pause. "I mean . . . no? Campaign captains are public knowledge. The position change was announced in an email from Mr. Wells. Like I said, I'm just curious—"

"I wouldn't ask you about your choice of campaign captain. Why are you pressing me about mine?"

"I'm not *pressing* you," I laugh, taking a step back to give us space.

"What is it, then?"

"Zach, c'mon."

"Why are you so curious about Ashtyn?"

"Because I don't think you should trust her."

Welp.

I didn't plan on going *there* in this conversation, but here we are.

He smirks. "I shouldn't *trust* her, huh?"

"No," I reply. "I don't think you should. After being with

Joey for a year, I know her way better than you do."

"What are you implying?"

I hesitate, deciding how candidly I should answer. "Well, I guess I'm saying that she's a bit slimy," I blurt. "Not to mention, she's loyal to Joey, and Joey alone. If you care about the integrity of your campaign, and I believe you do, I wouldn't have Ashtyn on board."

I may butt heads with Zach—and he may be in office solely to help with his college prospects—but taking on a shady character like Ashtyn still feels like it's beneath him.

He stares. Neither of us is blinking.

"I'm telling you this as your friendly competition who wants us both to run good, clean campaigns," I say, breaking the silence. "I don't mean to ruffle feathers."

His face collapses into a smile—a knowing, maniacal, pretty much terrifying smile. "How about this, Mr. Mental Health," he says, brushing off some remaining powdered sugar from my shoulder. "You run your campaign, and I'll run mine. Okay?"

"Okay, but I didn't mean for this to get weird, Zach, I swear—"

He's already halfway out the door, though.

"Hey, what about your dad's lemon pound cake?" I call after him as the door jingles to a close.

CHAPTER 18

★ ☆ ★

'm pacing my bedroom in circles, pad of paper and pen in hand, thinking through all the attacks Zach may launch at me during the debate—both political *and* personal. Now that I've apparently pissed him off by asking about his campaign captain swap, I have no doubt that Zach will be out for blood on the gymnasium floor. I've got to be prepared.

I feel eyes on me from the foot of my bed. It's Fudge, ears perked, staring into my soul.

"What?" I ask him.

His tail starts wagging.

"Do you have any debate prep advice?" I stick my clenched fist in front of his face, offering him an imaginary microphone to speak into.

He barks.

"Is that a yes or a no?"

He pops up onto his four legs, thrilled to be getting some attention.

"Okay, I know, I know," I tell him, grabbing his leash. "Time for a walk."

We head downstairs and pass by the living room, where Aunt Starr is in an all-pink athleisure outfit, attempting to do sit-ups like the fitness YouTuber on the TV. "Where are you going?" she asks breathlessly over her workout playlist.

"Taking Fudge for a walk. I need to clear my head. It might be a long one."

"Okay! In that case," she says, pausing to catch her breath, "can you pick up some doughnuts at Stan's? I've been craving one. Only if you're headed that way anyway, though."

The Wicker Park Stan's is definitely a hike—and one that leads into a more congested, pretentious part of town—but Fudge could certainly use the fresh air, and so could I. "Yeah, no problem."

"Yes! One Maple Long John, please! Do you have money?"

"Yeah."

"Good," she says. "Because I don't."

"Oh!" I gasp, remembering the Field Museum job.

"What?" she asks, startled.

I pause.

Is now the best time to tell her? If I do, she'll have many questions about the position and rope me into an hourlong discussion about the details. And I really need this walk right now.

"Never mind," I say, deciding I'll give her the business card when I return. "Just remembered some homework that needs to get done. Bye!" I pop in my earbuds, turn on some Lil Nas X, and slip out the front door with Fudge on his leash.

The sky is bright blue and empty of clouds. Every few steps I inhale a different smell from either a blossoming garden or a restaurant firing up its grill. I try to soak in this

Chicago spring bliss, hoping it will aid in washing away the stress of this upcoming debate.

And this effort to win back Joey.

I miss him. I really, truly, deeply miss him. Sure, he and I are different in a myriad of ways, and what he did at Grey Kettle is still inexcusable—there's no question about it. But the nerves I felt in my chest when I saw him in the bathroom? And the way he looked at me, smiling, and said I was *impressive* behind the podium? It all has to count for something.

Wait. Oh my God.

There he is.

I pull out my earbuds, feeling every one of my appendages freezing up in shock. Is this a mirage?

Joey's one block ahead of me, standing outside the Fat Banana wearing his favorite aviator sunglasses and a black leather jacket. His mom and dad are next to him, dressed to the nines, as usual.

And so is freaking Zach.

I glance down at my outfit: old shorts dotted with specks of red paint from the slices of pizza I created on the exterior of Reno's restaurant last summer, sandals that are falling apart, and a crummy cutoff T-shirt. Not exactly the type of look I want to be wearing to show the Olivers what their son is missing. To them, I might as well have climbed out of a dumpster.

None of them has seen me, I don't think, so I could make a run for it and pretend I was never here. Yes. That's what I'll do. Book it the hell home and hope Aunt Starr isn't upset about the lack of doughnuts upon my return. What good could possibly come from a sidewalk encounter with the guy who just dumped me, his parents, and his new boyfriend— who happens to also be fired up to crush me in a class election?

I rotate on my heels and attempt to melt away into the distance unnoticed, but Fudge spots Joey at exactly the worst moment and starts barking up a storm.

"Blaine?" I hear Joey call after me.

I turn back slowly. "Oh, hey!" My jaw drops in fake, pleasant surprise. I cross the street and approach their group, with Fudge trotting at my side happily, completely unaware of the chaos he just caused. "How's it going?"

"Fine," Joey answers.

Zach's wearing the most disingenuous smile I've ever seen on a face as he plays with his silver wristwatch. "We're about to grab food at the Fat Banana," he says. "What are you up to?"

"Taking Fudge here on a walk. It's such a nice day out." I turn to Joey's parents. "Hey, Mr. and Mrs. Oliver."

But they are *not* having it.

Mr. Oliver nods at me but completely avoids eye contact. Mrs. Oliver clears her throat and exhales, rocking back and forth in her white high heels. "Blaine," she says, as if having to acknowledge my existence just ruined her day.

The conversation falls flat, and I struggle with what to say next, seeing as I've clearly been designated the awful fifth wheel.

The tension is immediately unbearable.

"Hey, can we chat?" Joey interjects. It's not a friendly

request—more like an urgent demand—and he grabs my elbow and ushers me around the corner of the Fat Banana before I can respond.

"Wow, so your parents really *do* hate my guts, huh?" I ask, laughing a bit to ease the discomfort. "Despite what you told me at Grey Kettle, it sure seems like that's the case."

He holds a finger over his mouth, urging me to speak softly. "It's . . . I don't know."

He doesn't *know?* What the hell is that supposed to mean? This interaction feels light-years away from the flirtatious energy I felt in the bathroom after the speeches. That person is gone—the one in front of me now feels like Grey Kettle Joey all over again.

"On our anniversary, you said that they still liked me and that I shouldn't take the breakup personally," I press on as Joey remains silent. "But that's not true, is it? They despise me, and you really are letting them dictate your dating life. Dictate your *entire* life, actually—"

"Yes, okay?" he hisses. "My parents told me to dump you. Are you happy now?"

I take a step back. "Well, damn. Okay."

So he takes a step closer. "Blaine. Please don't be like this."

"Be like what?"

"Don't get all riled up over nothing."

I squint at him, my mouth hanging ajar. "Riled up over *nothing?* Joey, you're basically confirming that your parents think I'm a loser, and that you, like . . . more or less agree with them."

"You're being ridiculous."

"And *you're* gaslighting me."

"Gaslighting?" His face drops into a vicious grin. "What, you think you can throw around psych terms, now that you're the *champion* for mental health?" he mocks.

Fudge is sniffing Joey's pant legs, hoping for a scratch. I tug him back toward me. "You were all about my wellness initiative when I saw you in the bathroom after my speech," I snap. "What changed?"

"I was trying to be nice, Blaine," he says, all serious again. "I felt bad for you."

"Why?"

"Because I didn't think you had a shot at making it onto the ballot, truth be told. And I'm shocked you did."

My blood pressure skyrockets. "Screw you, Joey."

He stands in front of me so I can't leave.

"Get out of my way—"

"Let's just cut the BS," he says. "It's obvious you're running to get revenge on me, or to impress me, or accomplish *something* concerning me. The whole school sees through it. It's time you stop being foolish and pull the plug, babe."

Stop being *foolish?*

Pull the plug, *babe?*

I'm about to explode. "I swear to God, Joey," I mutter through gritted teeth, "if you call me 'babe' one more time . . ."

"Blaine—"

I plow into the side of his body and don't look back as Fudge skips along at my side.

CHAPTER 19

★ ★ ★

I t's been difficult to concentrate on anything other than Joey mocking me outside the Fat Banana.

It's time you stop being foolish, he said.

Pull the plug, babe, he hissed.

I start to piece together a better, more scathing retort than the one I said in the moment, but Camilla's raised voice brings me back to earth.

A.k.a., Mr. Wells's nearly empty classroom during our debate prep.

"Blaine Bowers has *zero* years of student council experience!" she yells from behind the makeshift podium we constructed out of textbooks and tissue boxes. "Why should soon-to-be seniors trust someone who's never even been in student government, let alone held a leadership position before?"

I clear my throat, trying to throw myself back into my performance.

"I don't see my inexperience as a weakness. I see it as a strength," I say, subtly swiping away the sweat collecting on my chin. "We need new ideas and new leadership at Wicker West—leadership that cares about mental health."

"Nice!" Danny, sitting on a desk, interjects from the first row of Mr. Wells's classroom. Our practice debate comes to a screeching halt. "Oops, didn't mean to blunt your momentum."

I laugh, flattered.

"That was a great example of pivoting—flipping an attack on its head and transitioning into a talking point," he says. "Zach's going to ambush you tomorrow, I'm sure, so be prepared to pivot."

"Agree with all of that, but one important note," Trish adds from the chair next to Danny, glancing down at the notes in her lap. "Refrain from saying the word 'inexperience' as it relates to you."

"Why?"

"You don't want to remind students that you're . . . well, inexperienced," she says, chewing the end of her pen. "You know?"

I rub my temples. "I thought you said it was a strength?"

"I mean, it is in a certain sense," she explains. "But the word itself carries a negative connotation." She puts on a fake, cheery face, straightening the collar of her turtleneck sweater. "You're shaking up the status quo, Blaine! You're bringing new ideas to the presidency! You're not, however"—her face drops into dreariness—"an inexperienced newbie who's going to ruin prom and mess up planning our graduation because you're an amateur. See the difference?"

"Okay," I say, my mind officially melting into mush after nearly two hours of this kind of tedious back-and-forth. "I think so."

"Instead of inadvertently promoting one of Zach's main arguments against you, use another word that turns a negative into a positive," Trish says, expanding on her thought when she notices that I'm struggling to keep up. "Say that you're, like . . . an *outsider* or *a new kind of leader.*"

"A *reformer*," Camilla adds.

"Yes!" Trish points at her. "There you go. You're all the good things a candidate like Zach can't be."

"You're the anti-Zach," Danny says.

I nod, looking down at my binder to make a note to myself. It's already covered in a million other half-baked thoughts referencing debate tips from Trish. I find a space in the bottom left-hand corner to jot down, *Don't say "inexperienced"—new kind of leader, outsider, reformer.* Then my mind begins to wander. In the remaining white space on the page, I start doodling Ms. Ritewood's mural; its rings, its starry background, its eyelashes, and—

"Blaine?" Danny says. I look up from my doodle to find all three of them staring at me with varying degrees of worry.

"What?"

I mean, I know *what.* They all think I'm crumbling under the pressure, I bet—especially after my run-in with Joey. And you know what? Maybe I am.

Maybe being mocked as *foolish* by the guy I thought I loved rattled me more than I'd care to admit, okay? There's so much to keep in mind too—so many potential attacks Zach could fire at me. I pissed him off last week at Biggest Bean for asking about Ashtyn, then poured gasoline on the already-roaring fire outside the Fat Banana. Zach is going to come at me. And come at me *hard.*

"You seem stressed," Trish says.

Camilla cuts to the chase. "I would say more like panicked." She leans on her faux podium, nearly toppling it over before catching the first textbook to drop.

"I'm not panicked." I force a laugh, trying to hide my panic. I drop the pen onto my doodling. "I'm just a tiny bit, kinda-sorta overwhelmed."

"That's okay," Camilla says. "This is all overwhelming."

"It doesn't help that you're being a very good Zach," I say to her. "So villainous, so cruel. It's like I'm debating the real thing."

She shrugs with a smirk. "Maybe I should go into acting, not science."

"Look," Trish says, leaning forward in her chair, elbows pressed against the desk. "We're all brand-new to this student council stuff—well, except you." She glances at Danny. "I've never run a campaign before. You've never run for office, let alone senior class president. It's okay to embrace the fact that, yes, we're in over our heads."

"Is this supposed to be making me feel better?" I cringe.

"*But,*" she carries on, "look at where we are. Look at how far we've come."

"You beat out five other candidates," Camilla squeals.

"And you made it onto the damn ballot," Trish exclaims.

"You're proving that your candidacy isn't just about Joey," Danny says.

The room falls silent.

"What?" he asks after no one chimes in. "Don't let his words outside the Fat Banana get into your head, Blaine," he continues. "That's what he wants. He wants you to buckle. He wants you to feel *foolish*. He *doesn't*, however, want you focused on your own ideas and your mental health platform. Because that's how you'll beat Zach."

"He's right." Trish finds my eyes and lowers her voice. "Because, okay, maybe the whole school *did* think you were running because Joey broke up with you, and—let's face it—they weren't wrong," she says. "But that was then. You gave an amazing speech highlighting great ideas that justify your place on that ballot, Blaine. No one's thinking it's all about Joey anymore."

"Agree, one thousand percent," Camilla says.

I hope Trish is right. I hope students perceive my candidacy as legitimate, even if I'm not so sure myself.

But what if she's wrong?

"Well." I clear my throat, looking at Danny. "You're right. I want to win this thing, and it has nothing to do with Joey anymore."

Trish grins. "All right, let's do it, then," she says, flipping the page of her notes.

We carry on for another twenty minutes—during ten of which Trish patiently explains to me what a "straw man argument" is—before Danny has to bounce to help cover a coworker's shift and Camilla heads off to the museum to gather data on the diets of saber-toothed tigers. Trish and I stay behind a tad longer to address a few remaining vulnerabilities on the wellness initiative and clean up the mess we made in Mr. Wells's classroom.

"This was your best session," Trish says to me, stacking a couple of chairs. "By far."

"Really?" I ask, deconstructing my and Camilla's teetering Kleenex-box podiums. "I'm not sure I believe you."

"You're going to nail it." She sighs, closes her eyes, and holds a hand over her chest. "And I'm going to feel like your proud mama when it happens."

I laugh, placing a geometry book back on Mr. Wells's desk. I accidentally bump a pencil, which falls into the nook between the table and wall. "Oops," I mutter, reaching down to retrieve it.

I gasp.

Oh my God. There they are.

The ballots are stacked and organized in a box that Mr. Wells was clearly trying to hide from view. Each individual race is printed on colored sheets not much bigger than driver's licenses; our grade's races are on orange. My eyes scan several of the stacks before finding the ones for the senior class presidency.

"Trish!" I whisper-yell, urging her to come, my heart pounding through my chest. "Look!"

She rushes over, and we take it in together.

SENIOR CLASS PRESIDENT

BLAINE BOWERS

ZACH CHESTERSON

It does not seem real.

"Holy cow," she says.

"Right?"

"Holy. Cow."

"I know!"

The classroom door swings open.

Trish and I immediately jump back from the desk.

"Oh," Kim the custodian says, holding a broom, surprised to see us. "I didn't know anyone was using this classroom tonight."

"Sorry, Kim," I say quickly, sounding guilty. Very, very guilty. "We're almost done."

"I can do this room tomorrow. Take your time," Kim says, moving to leave. She stops in the doorway. "You two okay?"

We both nod intensely, forced smiles plastered across our faces.

"Yep," I say.

"Uh-huh," Trish confirms.

Kim backs out slowly and shuts the door behind her.

I exhale, snag the pencil off the ground, and place it back on the desk.

"What's Mr. Wells leaving the ballots lying around for, anyway?" I say, scrambling to grab my things.

"Yeah, that's stupid."

"Why would he even *print* the ballots before Election Day, with the chance that a candidate could find them?"

"I—"

"That seems pretty reckless. He should've printed them the morning of, and then like, locked them away in a safe until it's time to vote."

"Blaine."

"Like, Mr. Wells definitely needs to—"

"*Blaine.*" Trish reaches out and grabs my shoulders, staring directly into my eyes. "Are you okay?"

I bite into my cheek anxiously. "Yes? I think so?"

"We did nothing wrong. We just happened to see the ballots. It's not a big deal. Why are you getting worked up?"

"I don't know."

"Breathe. Just . . . *breathe.*" She shakes me a little and smiles. "It sounds like you could use a break in our Senior Space right about now."

"Right?" I rub my eyes, trying to stop the tornado of nervous thoughts from spinning out of control.

Like, am I going to blow this whole campaign on the debate stage tomorrow?

Will Ms. Ritewood hate me forever if I don't finish her mural?

Is Aunt Starr going to freak when she finds out that I keep forgetting to tell her about the Field Museum job?

"Hey." Trish nudges me lovingly with her elbow—a move that's grown to feel like a hug. "Seriously. Are you all right?"

"I'm worked up, is all," I say. "I still want to go over all your debate notes tonight, and—"

"No. Don't."

"Don't . . . do what?"

"Don't go over your notes tonight. We've had three prep sessions. You're ready."

"You think?"

She nods. "Your mind needs a break. Just try to get some sleep."

I scoff and roll my eyes with a grin. "Yeah . . . sleep. Like that will happen."

"For real," she emphasizes, opening her eyes wide. "Just go home. Relax. Practice what you're about to preach tomorrow and prioritize some self-care. Watch *Big Brother* with Aunt Starr and Fudge."

"Have you ever watched *Big Brother* with Aunt Starr?" I ask. "That is *not* a relaxing experience."

"You know what I mean," she says. "Don't be a candidate tonight. Just be Blaine."

Just be Blaine?

That's not as simple as it sounds.

CHAPTER 20

Debate day.

It's here.

I'm standing in front of my closet, trying to blink myself awake and figure out what the heck to wear. Story of my life, right?

Keep it simple, Trish advised yesterday. That way, students will be listening to the words coming out of my mouth, not distracted by my shirt or shoes. This falls under Debating 101, apparently.

Simple. Okay.

Seems *simple* enough. But it's not.

I hardly got a wink of sleep last night. Maybe an hour or so, but not nearly enough to feel like a real person. The anxiety about the debate contributed to my insomnia, of course—the endless rules, Trish's phrases to avoid, and half a dozen talking points bouncing around in my mind like in a rumbling washing machine. But I was tossing and turning also due to guilt; how I've avoided Ms. Ritewood and her half-done mural, my selfish reluctance to tell Aunt Starr about her dream job—which, I've decided, I might as well not even bring up now, seeing as the opportunity is probably gone for good.

And then there's Danny's observation yesterday.

Your candidacy isn't just about Joey, he said. And he's right. It isn't—especially after Grey Kettle Joey resurfaced outside the Fat Banana, proving, once and for all, that we are officially over.

But then, what *is* my candidacy about?

I believe in our Wicker West Wellness Initiative. Truly I do. But still. Something's missing. Something about all of this feels off.

Honestly? I wish more than anything else that I were picking out which old, raggedy shorts to wear before starting a new mural, instead of choosing a debate outfit.

"Hey, doll."

I jump, clutching my chest. A startled Fudge lets out a bark from atop my bed.

"I'm sorry!" Aunt Starr says from my bedroom doorway, mug of coffee in one hand, sesame seed bagel in the other. "I didn't mean to scare you."

"It's okay," I say, looking back into the abyss of my closet.

She slides into my bedroom in her yellow duckling slippers. "Nervous?"

"Understatement."

She falls onto my bed next to Fudge, who sniffs at her bagel enviously. "What's on your mind?"

I turn to her. "You mean besides the fact that I'm about to go stand onstage next to the school's Mr. Golden Boy, where I will definitely look like an amateur?"

"Yes, I *do* mean besides that," she says without missing a beat. "Something else is gnawing at you. I can tell."

How does she know? How is Aunt Starr *so good* at reading between my lines?

I sigh, unsure where to begin with my tornado of thoughts. "I had a mini *aha* moment yesterday, I think."

"And?"

"And I realized I'm not running to show Joey I can be a Serious Guy anymore. I mean, how pathetic would I have to be to *still* want him after what went down outside the Fat Banana?"

"I hear that," she says. "But running for a reason other than to win back your ex is . . . not necessarily a bad thing, Blaine." She holds up her hands defensively. "Although, yes, I admit I was probably the loudest voice in your ear telling you to do just that."

I laugh.

"But really, though," she says, wrapping herself tighter in her bathrobe. "It sounds like now you're running for yourself and for your well-being thing."

"The wellness initiative," I clarify.

"Right, your wellness initiative."

I turn back to my closet. "The initiative is important, but I still feel like . . . I don't know . . ."

"What?"

"Like, I don't have a good reason for students to pick *me*. Of all the other juniors, why should I be our class president? The mental health stuff is mostly Trish's and Danny's doing, honestly. And if I'm not even sure why anyone should vote for me, how can I go out there and tell everyone else to do just that? You know?"

Aunt Starr nods, staring at Fudge. The city is quiet for a few moments outside my window—no airplanes flying to or from O'Hare, no honking cars, just a lulling stretch of morning calm—before Aunt Starr stands and slides over to me, in front of the closet. She tears off a chunk of her bagel, which is smothered in cream cheese, and hands it over. "Do you want my advice? Because it's okay if you don't."

"I do. I definitely, *definitely* do."

She leans her elbow against my shoulder, looking at me in the mirror. "Most of the things in life worth doing are scary and confusing," she says. "At least at first."

I nod.

"Maybe you don't know why you're running, and that's okay," she continues. "But clearly there are students—*plenty* of them—who think you'd make an excellent president. Maybe give it your best shot today for them, and the answer will come to you later." She plops the last bit of bagel into her mouth and ruffles my hair, turning to leave. "And if you want another piece of advice . . ."

"Always."

"I think the outfit you wore to Grey Kettle would make the *perfect* outfit for a debate." She winks at me before disappearing out the doorway.

"Really?"

"Just my two cents!" she yells from down the hall.

I turn back to my closet with a grin and spot the now infamous shirt—the one I've been avoiding in my closet because of that night. The white-and-yellow-checkered button-up.

She's not wrong. It *is* a great shirt. And I do look good in it.

I take it off the hanger, along with the corduroy pants, suspenders, and bow tie. Trish may kill me—this look is a lot of things, and simple is not one of them—but it's the first wardrobe idea that's actually made me smile all morning.

A few minutes later I dash down the stairs and through the foyer. "Thanks, Aunt Starr!"

From her corner of the sofa she spots me in the outfit. "Yes!" she yells through a mouthful of cereal.

I walk to school with extra pep in my step. Lizzo singing "feelin' good as hell" in my ears is an instant adrenaline rush, but I mostly need to book it because the debate is during first period. Can you imagine how pissed Trish would be if I missed my own opening statement?

The nerves kick in again once I'm at school.

"Good luck today, Blaine!" Carly Eggman says as she walks by, giving me a thumbs-up.

"Rooting for you," Bobby Wilson says a moment later, providing a fist to pound.

This is really happening. I'm about to debate Zach. Well, if Trish doesn't murder me over my outfit choice first. I tap her on the shoulder as she closes her locker, and she turns to me.

We both stare.

"Well?" I ask, sucking my teeth. "I know it's not simple, but—"

"No, it's not," she interrupts, looking me up and down. Her face falls into a smile. "And I love it."

I let out the biggest sigh of relief. "I was thinking you'd hate it."

She looks at me like I've lost my mind. "This look exudes *you*. That's all that matters."

I check out her outfit. "Oh my *God*, you look amazing too."

"Yeah?" She takes a step back and does a twirl.

She's got on a forest-green pantsuit, golden raindrop earrings, and purply-red lipstick that brings the whole look together flawlessly.

"You look beautiful, captain," I say, shaking my head in disbelief. "*You* should be the one going up there today."

Trish shrugs bashfully before abruptly shifting gears. "No time to get into a compliment war. Let's head to the gym."

"Where's Danny and Camilla, though?" I ask, glancing around.

"It's just candidates and campaign captains allowed in the waiting area, for one," Trish explains, briskly walking down the hall as I struggle to keep up. "But also, I know you. And I know you'd get more nervous seeing them beforehand." She glances at me with a sparkle in her eye, lowering her voice. "Especially Danny."

"What? Nah."

"Blaine . . ."

Okay, she's absolutely right. "Whatever," I mutter.

"I asked them to keep their distance before the debate. Don't hate me. Part of my responsibility as a campaign captain is making sure you are as ready as you can possibly be before prime time." She digs in her bag and pulls out a Biggest Bean chocolate chip cookie and a card. It's a good-luck note with little, handwritten messages from Danny and Camilla inside. "They wanted you to have this."

I nearly start tearing up.

As instructed, we find Mr. Wells, all the candidates who are debating today, and their corresponding campaign captains gathered in the hallway behind the gym, which has been closed off and reserved for the student council. I can already hear the murmuring white noise as the student body crowd grows larger in the bleachers on the other side of the wall.

It's a terrifying sound.

"Everybody here?" Mr. Wells asks, glancing around, clipboard in hand.

I take a deep breath and think for about the millionth time how the next hour is going to go down.

Other than for president, no class leadership race requires a debate, and as the election packet explained, next year's freshman class chooses its leaders in the fall, seeing as they're eighth graders scattered across area middle schools at the moment. So that means the debates happening are between candidates representing the rising sophomore, rising junior, and rising senior classes.

In order for all the classes to get done during the first-hour time frame, each class has a different debate length too. Rising sophomores will only go at it for twelve minutes, which is barely enough time for their opening statements and, like, one or two questions from Mr. Wells. (I'm so, *so* jealous of the freshmen right now.) Rising juniors get sixteen minutes. Then there's me and Zach; we'll be up there, one-on-one, for a whole twenty minutes. One thousand, two hundred seconds. (Yes, I did the math last night when I couldn't sleep.)

Twenty minutes might as well be eternity.

Mr. Wells calls over the freshman candidates and their campaign captains. I know I shouldn't feel this way, but realizing that I don't look quite as petrified as the rising sophomores—one of whom is *literally* trembling—makes me feel a tad bit better. After he's done fielding questions, Mr. Wells leads them through the gym doors, like a guard leading soon-to-be vanquished warriors into the Colosseum.

For the brief three seconds the gym doors are open, the white noise coming from the assembled student body turns into an overwhelming roar. Then the doors slam shut again. My stomach does somersaults.

About twelve minutes pass. Judging from the loud applause, their debate's finished.

Mr. Wells pops back into the hallway and calls over the rising juniors for the same talk, and then they all disappear into the gym together.

Then it's just me, Trish, Zach, and Ashtyn.

"Awkward" doesn't even *begin* to describe it.

Time grinds to a halt. I just want to get this over with, honestly. I'll do my best for the students who believe in my candidacy and the wellness initiative, like Aunt Starr suggested this morning, and then I'll be able to sit back and let Election Day happen tomorrow.

I wish I could fast-forward my life about an hour.

Trish pulls me farther away from Zach so that we're out of earshot and starts listing off final things to keep in mind. But I'm basically a useless pile of tangled nerve endings right now, and it's all going in one ear and out the other.

"Zach looks great, doesn't he?" I say between questions from Trish, glancing down the hall at him, in a burgundy suit jacket with a cream-colored tie. "I saw the same look on a mannequin at William's Outfitters." His hair's been meticulously styled to look messy—but, like, hot messy, not disheveled messy—and his belt buckle has a . . . Wait, is that a . . . ?

"His belt buckle is designed in the shape of a *wizard*?" I gasp. "As in, our school mascot?"

Trish's jaw drops, and she cranks her head to look.

"That's it," I say. "He's got a freaking wizard belt. I'm toast."

"Stop it," she says, turning back to me. "That belt is *so* extra. And no one will even see it. It's stupid."

Doors open at the end of the hallway, and Joey emerges.

"What the hell?" Trish mutters, disgusted. "It's only supposed to be candidates and campaign captains back here."

Joey approaches Zach and gives him a peck on the lips before noticing me. His face drops. "Seriously?" he shouts over.

I try to play dumb, glancing around. "Are you talking to me?"

He scoffs, "Your shirt? Your suspenders?" He points at it. "Your whole outfit?"

"What's going on?" Ashtyn asks Zach.

Zach shrugs, looking confused.

"Why would you wear that?" Joey glares, walking over to us.

"Why would I wear what?" I say, examining my outfit. "Clothes from my own closet?"

"You know what you're doing." He stops a few feet in front of me. "Blaine, c'mon," he whispers—as if it's torturous to see me in this outfit. "Are you doing this just to hurt me?"

Trish steps between us. "You shouldn't be here, Joey," she says. "Only candidates and campaign captains are supposed to—"

"Yeah, I know the rules," he spits. "I *made* the damn rules."

"Well, then," she hisses back, unintimidated. "You should know better than anyone else why you need to leave."

The hallway falls quiet.

"What's going on, babe?" Zach asks from down the hall.

"It's nothing," Joey says, turning and walking back to his boyfriend. "Blaine's just trying to get into my—*your*—head. Don't let him."

A moment later, the gym doors swing open and Mr. Wells comes bouncing in. "Why are you here, Joey?" he asks.

"Sorry, Mr. Wells," Joey says with a phony smile, handing Zach a torn piece of notebook paper. "Zach just forgot a page of his debate notes, and I wanted to bring it to him, is all. I'm leaving!"

Zach takes it with a smile and pecks his boyfriend one last time before Joey disappears down the hallway.

"And then there were two," Mr. Wells says, gesturing for the four of us to come closer and form a circle around him.

Deep breaths, Blaine. Deep, deep breaths.

Trish, standing at my side, pats my lower back.

"The rules were outlined in your election packet, but just to make sure everyone is on the same page, here's what you two can expect," Mr. Wells says, eyes darting between me and Zach. "The debate will be twenty minutes in total. A coin toss will determine who goes first for your two-minute opening statements. You'll each get a two-minute closing argument as well. Before your closing arguments, we'll take a quick, one-minute recess so you can chat with your campaign captains and regroup. Make sense?"

Before either of us can reply, he carries on.

"For the other twelve minutes of debate time between your opening statements and closing arguments, I will be asking questions that were submitted by council members for each of you. Do not interrupt the other candidate while it's their turn to answer. Got it? And if a candidate directly attacks another candidate, the candidate on the receiving end of the attack will have a chance to respond. Are we clear?" He takes a deep breath, winded from doing the same monologue for a third time. "Okay, let's go."

Mr. Wells opens the gym doors. The thunderous, humming echoes of Wicker West's student body nearly send me running in the opposite direction.

"You ready, boo?" Trish asks, smiling.

"No," I say. "Not at all."

Mr. Wells leads me and Zach into the gym. It doesn't feel real.

None of this feels real.

The bleachers—reaching all the way up to the rafters on every side of the court—are completely packed with students. Joey and the other class leaders are crammed into a first row to my left, but beyond that, I can't pick out a single recognizable face in the crowd. It's all just a blur of various skin tones and hair dyes.

I wish I knew where Danny was sitting.

Kim the custodian and a freshman council member are dragging a podium used during the previous debate off to the side. Now there's just two podiums left under the nearest basketball hoop, separated by ten feet of hardwood. The one on the right has a name tag signifying I should stand behind it. A large desk with a long, white tablecloth covering it is centered near the free-throw line, where Mr. Wells takes a seat. He nods at us, confirming we're about to begin.

"Hey," Zach says, stopping me before I can step behind my podium.

I turn to him.

"Good luck, Blaine," he says, holding out a hand to shake.

I do. "Thanks. Same to you."

He's smiling really wide. "And really, truly . . . *thank you.*"

I stare. "For what?"

Our hands still clasped, he pulls himself in, puts his lips an inch from my ear. "For leaving your debate notes in Mr. Wells's classroom last night for us."

My mouth turns dry. He must see the color draining from my face. "You didn't know we had the room reserved right after you, did you?"

That's what Joey just dropped off for Zach.

My debate prep notes.

"Gentlemen," Mr. Wells says into the microphone on his desk. His voice booms throughout the gym. "Please head to your podiums and we can get started."

Zach slips his hand out of mine and floats away.

I head to my podium too, now trembling worse than any of the freshmen.

CHAPTER 21

★ ☆ ★

E veryone, settle down," Mr. Wells says sternly into the mic. "I know we're nearing the end here, but let's keep it together for one more debate."

Smile, Trish advised me. *Every second you're behind that podium, smile.*

So I do. It's so painfully forced that my cheek muscles are legit shaking in order to keep my lips raised and spread. But better to suffer through a forced facial expression than to start crying on a debate stage.

Zach has my notes. It's the only thing I can think about.

"Our final debate is between juniors Blaine Bowers and Zach Chesterton, who are competing to be next year's senior class president," Mr. Wells says after the crowd quiets down. "Before we get started, let's give them both a round of applause for making it this far in a hard-fought election, shall we?"

Half-hearted claps fill the air.

"Each candidate will be given two minutes for their opening statements," Mr. Wells continues. "We will now do a coin toss to determine who goes first. Blaine, because your last name comes first alphabetically, would you like to choose heads or tails?"

"Um," I say, and my voice echoes off the walls. It startles me.

Keep it together, Blaine. "Tails."

Mr. Wells flips the quarter. "Heads. Zach, would you like to go first or second?"

"First, please, Mr. Wells," he says in the most butt-kissing tone ever.

I want to roll my eyes, but I just keep smiling.

"Okay, then," Mr. Wells says. "Your time starts in three, two, one . . ." He points at Zach.

"Hi, students of Wicker West High School," Zach begins. "I'm Zach Chesterton, junior class president. I'm running for senior class president, and I think I'd be an excellent choice. Let me explain why."

His voice is clear, confident, and the perfect volume for the space. It sounds like he's done this a dozen times before.

"To my fellow juniors: I've been your class president the past three years. Throughout that time, we've been through a lot together. The ups . . . like when our class won the bake-off freshman year, raising thousands of dollars for the children's hospital . . . and the downs . . . like when our homecoming float got a flat tire during the parade last year and we nearly didn't make it to the football game. But we did, and we still won first place!" He lets out a totally fake but admittedly charming laugh.

A chunk of the audience whistles and claps in support.

"You know me by now," Zach continues, striking a more serious tone. "You know that I've visited each extracurricular club during a meeting to show my support. You know that I've attended at least one game played by every single sports team so that I could root for our Wicker West Wizards. You know that I care deeply about this school, about its students, about the class of 2023." He stops to take a deep breath and shift his tone. "I'm guessing most of you, however, do not know who Blaine Bowers is."

Here. We. Go.

Don't get flustered by his attacks, I remember Danny warning me yesterday.

It's proving to be more challenging when it's actually Zach in front of two thousand students, and not Camilla standing behind a tower of Kleenex boxes, but I try to keep smiling.

"Blaine Bowers has never been in student council before, let alone run for elected office," Zach says. "He's never been involved in any extracurricular club or sports team more than one semester. The records show that Blaine joined art club freshman year—but dropped out shortly after."

Oh my God. He dug through my whole school history?

"He tried photography when we were sophomores," Zach continues. "But made it just one week."

Breathe, Blaine. Just breathe.

"Blaine Bowers has shown Wicker West High that he's good at one thing, and one thing only . . . quitting."

The gym falls silent. I can feel my heartbeat pounding in my fingertips.

But I act as though I can't hear a single word.

"Now, I bet Blaine will come out here today and try to spin his complete lack of experience in student government as if it's a positive. He'll claim that he'll be a *new kind of leader*, an *outsider*—the *reformer* you've all been waiting for." Zach shakes his head. "That's how politicians operate. They hope you'll be easily tricked."

Holy crap.

"Fellow juniors, I beg you . . . don't be fooled," Zach concludes. "With prom, graduation, and all the other critical events that are on the line senior year, do you really want to hand over those responsibilities to a rookie? A *quitter*? Someone who woke up one morning and decided to run for office for, I can only assume, an ego-driven—and maybe even *vindictive*—reason involving an interpersonal relationship?" He pauses to glance at me. "Or do you want *me* as your senior class president—a tried and tested leader who's had your back since day one?"

He smiles wide, gazing across the stands.

"Class of 2023. You *know* me. You *trust* me. You know that, together, we'll make our senior year one we can cherish forever. Tomorrow morning, please vote for your champion, Zach Chesterton." He pauses again. "Go, Wizards!"

The crowd erupts.

For a solid ten seconds, the entire gym is filled with applause. And with every single passing second, I feel my soul slowly leaving my body.

What the hell am I going to say now?

Seriously. The beginning of my opening statement focuses on throwing out the status quo so we can make my mental health initiative a reality! It focuses on me being the *reformer* that'll shake up the system! Zach just demolished my entire argument.

I glance back at Trish, who's watching near the doors, mortified.

Mr. Wells leans into his mic again. "Thank you, Mr. Chesterton. Blaine?" He looks up at me. "You'll have two minutes starting in three, two, one . . ."

"Hey, Wicker West," I say nervously. Unlike Zach's voice, mine sounds horrendous ricocheting around this open, humid space like nails on a chalkboard. I look down at my notes. "Um . . . So I'm Blaine Bowers, senior running for— *whoops*, that's not right." I laugh.

Crickets.

The whole gym is freaking crickets.

"I'm Blaine Bowers—*junior* running for senior class president."

This is already a disaster.

I glance back down at my notes again. The first five lines will sound totally different, now that Zach preemptively defined my "reformer" status as a political ploy. I skim farther to find a different place to start instead, but the clock's ticking and no sentence is jumping out as a good spot. . . .

Screw it. I'll wing it.

I look up.

Every eyeball is on me. It feels like a million pounds weighing down against my chest.

"So, ah . . . yeah," I say, struggling to articulate anything sensical. "I'm Blaine Bowers, and I'm running for senior class pres—"

"You already said that!" someone yells from the upper bleachers.

A few people start laughing.

"Hey!" Mr. Wells bellows into the microphone, staring up into the stands where the heckler's voice came from. "That will not be tolerated!" He glares menacingly into the crowd for a moment longer before turning back to me. "Go ahead, Blaine."

"Well, you're, ah . . . you're not wrong." I laugh in the direction of the heckler. "I know I already said that. Sorry, everyone. I'm a bit . . ." I fiddle with my notes. "I lost my place here."

Where do I start talking about our wellness initiative? If I can just get into a groove talking about that, maybe I can turn this thing around.

I see Joey. He's looking on as if I'm a car crash he can't turn away from.

Stop being foolish, he warned outside the Fat Banana.

Maybe he had a point.

I flip the page and keep scanning, determined to find the first line introducing the wellness initiative, but a bead of sweat drops into my eyeball, blinding me. I blink it away as fast as I can, but by the time I can actually see clearly again, I have no idea how much time I've lost. Thirty seconds?

A minute?

Is my time about to run out?

"Let me just say this," I finally get out, imagining sand in an hourglass trickling between bulbs. "I *also* care deeply about this school. I love Wicker West. Like, a whole lot. And as your president, I will fight every single day to make it a better place."

Please let this be a nightmare.

Please, dear God, let this be a nightmare I wake up from any second now.

The gym is quiet. No one's clapping.

"Is that it, Blaine?" Mr. Wells asks softly, checking his watch.

"Yep," I say, smiling and nodding. I lean in closer to my mic. "Thank you—" A blast of feedback rips through the gym, and everyone jumps back in pain. "Oof, sorry! I, um—" I lean back. "Thank you, Wicker West."

Mr. Wells, probably embarrassed for me, starts clapping loudly into his mic as a way to get everyone to follow suit. A small chunk of students gives me a round of pity applause that quickly dies out.

That could not have gone worse.

"Blaine, the first question is for you," Mr. Wells continues, quickly moving on.

"Oh." I clear my throat, surprised. "Okay."

"You've never been in student council before," Mr. Wells reads off a sticky note. "What about your skills set or background make you qualified to be senior class president?"

"Well," I say, sighing into the mic, my mind racing. I know Trish prepped me for this exact question—probably ten times. "Let's see here. Even though I've never been in council, I think I can be a leader. Er, let me rephrase that. I *know* I can be a leader. I, uh . . . I just need the opportunity to prove myself, I guess?"

I gulp.

Sensing I'm finished, Mr. Wells moves on. "Thank you, Blaine. Zach." He turns away from me, reading from another sticky note. "You've been class president for three years now. What would you tell students who are hungry for a change in leadership?"

"I would empathize with them, first and foremost," Zach answers immediately, clearly prepared for the question. "I know how it can feel, seeing the same faces up here year after year. But behind closed doors, away from the bright lights of a debate stage, most students want someone that they know can get the job done—not someone who will quit when the going gets tough. They want a real, trusted leader who knows what it takes to succeed. I know I can be that leader because I've *been* that leader."

The crowd cheers.

This is a train wreck. A full-blown, horror-show train wreck.

Mr. Wells asks each of us two more questions before the one-minute recess, but my mind is pure goop responding to both. Words just fumble out of my mouth, and then Zach completely bulldozes over them. His opening statement totally threw me, and I haven't recovered since. I *can't* recover.

I stumble off the hardwood after Mr. Wells dismisses us. Trish guides me into the side hallway.

"Hey, hey, look at me," she says, knowing I'm spiraling. "It wasn't that bad."

"Trish." I'm almost in tears. "That was . . . *horrible.*"

"No, it wasn't."

"He found my debate prep notes!" I say, glancing down the hallway to make sure Zach and Ashtyn can't hear me.

She sighs. "I figured."

"After you encouraged me to get some rest instead of preparing at home last night, I totally spaced and forgot them in Mr. Wells's classroom."

Trish retracts her head, irked. "Are you saying that this is my fault?"

"No, *no*," I say, closing my eyes, regretting how I worded that. "Not at all. I'm just . . ." I cover my face with my hands. "It's *so* intense out there, Trish."

"I know."

"I don't think I can go back out there, honestly."

She rips my hands off my face and stares into my eyes. I've never seen her this determined before. "You're going back out there, Blaine."

"But—"

"You need to finish strong. You owe it to all the council members who voted you onto the ballot after your speech, and you owe it to yourself." There's fire burning in her eyes. "Don't let them think you'll quit this, too."

"Blaine? Zach?" Mr. Wells says, head popping out from the gym. "Let's go. Closing arguments."

"But *really*, I don't think I can," I say as Trish pulls me back down the hallway. I can feel the tears collecting behind my eyes. I've let everyone down. Trish. Camilla. Aunt Starr. Danny.

Trish nudges me back through the gym doors. *"Go."*

Zach and I take our places behind our respective podiums again, the restless student body anxiously buzzing to get this over with. It has probably been just as painful to watch this debate as it has been to be part of it. (If you can even call it a debate.)

"Because Zach chose to go first for the opening statements, now you get to choose if you'd like to go first or second with your closing argument, Blaine," Mr. Wells says.

I clear my throat. "I'll go last."

"Great," he says. "Zach, it's all yours in three, two, one . . ."

"Thank you, Mr. Wells," Zach begins. "And thank *you*, students of Wicker West High."

Zach goes into his now-familiar spiel about *experience* and *trust* and *blah-blah-blah,* as I spot Joey in the first row again, watching his new boyfriend. He looks so smug too, just sitting there, taking in the Serious Guy of his dreams as Zach slays the apparently very overrated competition.

You know what? Screw Joey Oliver.

If only I could spot . . .

Danny.

There he is. A few rows back. He's sitting with Camilla.

And they're wearing matching shirts that read GO, BLAINE! on them.

My heart melts.

All of it. Every last ventricle, vein, and artery. *Gone.*

My eye leaks a single tear, I'm so overwhelmed by the sight of my own, tiny cheering section. I wipe it away real fast and swallow hard to avoid crying another. Danny sees that I spot him and smiles.

I've got this. . . .

The crowd cheers, signaling that Zach has finished his closing argument. After the applause subsides, Mr. Wells addresses me for the final word of the debates. "Blaine?" he asks, visibly nervous for me. "You ready?"

I exhale and nod.

"Three, two, one . . ." Mr. Wells points.

I glance back at Danny one more time. His eyes—even from this far away—are so comforting. My breath steadies for the first time all morning.

"Hi, everyone," I say, pausing to look around at all the bleachers with a smile. "Okay, let's face it." I sigh. "I absolutely bombed this thing."

You could hear a pin drop.

"I mean, you can laugh, if you want to. I'll probably laugh later—once I'm done crying. Needless to say, this went really, *really* badly for me. Way worse than the worst-case scenarios I had envisioned in my head."

Several people *do* laugh, and that makes me feel better.

"Clearly I'm not a polished politician," I continue. "Out here, in front of you all, I feel completely overwhelmed. I'm way out of my wheelhouse, and miles away from my comfort zone. Give me a paintbrush and a blank brick wall, and I'm good. But put me behind a podium, and I apparently can't string a sentence together. I'm certainly no Zach Chesterton," I say, looking at him with a smile. He doesn't know how to respond to that. "And I don't mean that as an insult. Zach, you did a great job today. And you deserve a lot of props."

I pause to take a deep breath.

"I'm really disappointed in myself right now. I have a cool mental health initiative I wanted to talk about, but my nerves got the best of me. My amazing campaign captain, Trish"—I point at her behind me—"and my friends Danny and Camilla"—I nod at them in the stands—"all worked so hard in helping me plan it out. I won't have enough time now to dig into the details, and that's a huge bummer."

I take a second to swallow.

"Future seniors, I'm telling you right now that I will not be a perfect president. Clearly I need help with public speaking." Laughter, more than before, rumbles throughout the gym. "And, I mean, Zach is . . . right. I *am* a newbie at all of this. I'll mess up. I'll be on a learning curve. But one thing I *can* promise you?" I remember one of the slam-dunk talking points that I rehearsed with Trish. "I'll be your president for the right reasons."

I shift my weight behind the podium, hitting my stride.

"Unlike most class presidents, I'm not running to pad my résumé for college or to climb the social ladder at Wicker West. No. I want to be a *solutions* president—one who doesn't just win homecoming float competitions but one who will fight to make your experience at this school better. More fulfilling, more rewarding, more connected, more *happy*."

I take one last big breath, feeling a quiet tension building in the crowd.

"So, no, I'm not the *safest* choice, I guess, if you want a president who gives good speeches or has, like, a 10.0 GPA. That's not me. But if you're looking for a president who *actually* cares about improving things around here? Vote Blaine Bowers for president of the class of 2023."

There's a second of silence before the gym goes freaking nuts. Students rise to their feet. It's a legitimate standing ovation.

Me. *A standing ovation.*

The feeling is so intense, my knees almost buckle as I try to absorb the moment. "Thank you, juniors!" I yell into the mic over the applause. "And *go, Wizards!*"

Danny is beaming and Camilla is whistling, her thumb and pointer finger pressed between her lips. I walk over to Zach's podium and stretch out my hand for a shake, before shuffling off the hardwood, buzzing like a bumblebee.

Trish gives me a celebratory nudge with her elbow before we collapse into the most gratifying hug I've ever experienced.

"You did it," she breathes into my ear.

CHAPTER 22

The rest of the day is a blur. I get a bunch of smiles in the hallways, a few shout-outs from teachers at the beginning of classes, and, maybe most unbelievably, a congratulations from a crossing guard outside school, someone I've never even seen before, let alone have a rapport with. Apparently he caught wind of my closing argument too.

"Hey, the debate kid!" he shouts. "Great job today!"

"Thanks?" I reply, completely shocked, hustling through the intersection.

Everyone is busy with family stuff after school—even Aunt Starr is out of the house for the first time in days, grabbing happy hour drinks with an old colleague—so I have the place completely to myself.

After the chaos of this morning? It's a welcome relief.

I strip off my bow tie, unbutton my shirt, and fling my shoes into the corner before crashing down onto my bed with a sigh. Fudge, never one to pass on a moment to snuggle, plants his chin on my chest, begging for a head rub.

I did it.

I survived the debate. Sure, the first 90 percent was a chaotic disaster usually only seen in anxiety-induced nightmares. But spotting Danny in his GO, BLAINE! shirt?

It made all the difference in the world.

I space out and stare straight up, feeling the stress of the day washing away. The eggshell ceiling transforms into the mural outside Susan's Stationery for a brief moment before Ms. Ritewood's Saturn face evolves into Danny's.

I imagine how I'd bring him to life in mural form. His alluring eyes, rounded lips, buzzed jet-black hair.

"Blaine," Mural Danny says, pink lips popping into life. "Do you want to go to Cabo with me?"

I nod enthusiastically.

"Blaine?" he says again.

Blaine?

"Blaine?" Aunt Starr's animated face comes into view. She pokes at my side. I sit up in bed, feeling intensely embarrassed about the dream.

Fortunately, Aunt Starr is way too distracted to notice how awkward I'm being. "Hello?" she says, poking my side even harder. "How did it go?" She's going to combust if she doesn't get an answer.

After I shake off my catnap, I relay everything from that morning—how Zach found my notes; how I totally melted away into a blob of goo for most of the debate; how Danny and Camilla wore GO, BLAINE! shirts; how my closing argument potentially, just maybe, kept me in the running.

"I am so impressed by my nephew," she says, leaning in for a hug. "Even if you bombed the whole damn thing, you still got up there, and you *did it*. Do you know how cool that is?"

I feel myself getting red. "Thanks."

"Whatever happens tomorrow, I'm proud of you," Aunt Starr says, standing to leave. "Text your mom and dad back, by the way. They've been bugging me, asking if I've heard anything from you."

I remember that I didn't respond to texts they sent me earlier.

"I will," I say, a bit reluctantly. "Weren't they supposed to be home by dinner tonight?"

Aunt Starr glances back from the doorway. "Your mom covered for a sick coworker, and your dad apparently had a site visit go awry." She frowns, knowing as well as I do that the circumstances are irrelevant. "I know, it stinks." She smiles sadly. "Love you."

I sleep surprisingly well that night. Probably because my brain has exhausted itself of things to stress out about over the past few weeks, and all there is left to do now is wait for the junior class to vote.

I wake up the next morning, ready to go.

Election Day. It's actually here.

I shower, put on a colorful outfit that feels like me, and head down to grab a light breakfast. Just as I'm popping the last slice of apple with peanut butter into my mouth, there's a knock at the front door. I feel a burst of butterflies; it must be Danny. He told me yesterday that he would try to drop by on his walk to school so we could go together.

That's a first.

"Hey," I say, opening the front door and joining him on the porch.

"Hi." Danny's in a nice, pin-striped T-shirt and cutoff denim shorts, standing beneath a small olive-green umbrella to avoid the drizzle.

Even before the debate, I had an inkling that I'm falling for him. But seeing him in the stands yesterday solidified it— and then my Danny mural dream made it *abundantly* clear.

I'm crushing on Danny.

I'm crushing hard-core.

"No 'Go, Blaine!' shirt today?" I smirk.

He rocks his head back and forth. "I thought, maybe two days in a row would be overkill?"

We head down the sidewalk toward the high school. "Thank you for wearing it. For real," I say.

"You're welcome," he says, shifting the umbrella in his hands so that I'm entirely covered, leaving his right arm exposed to the rain. "The first three quarters of the debate were a little tough."

"Understatement of the year," I cut in with a laugh.

"But your closing argument *more* than made up for it."

"Here." I lean in closer to him so that the umbrella can keep both of us dry. "That's better."

Our sides are brushing up against one another with each step. It's not even that big a deal, but my whole body starts tingling. He's not stepping away to avoid the friction, and I sure as hell am not either. I glance his way out of the corner of my eye, and he does the same.

"My prediction remains, by the way," he says. "You're going to beat Zach Chesterton today."

We part ways once we get to the school because our first periods are at opposite ends of the building. I walk through a slew of fist bumps and supportive nods from juniors who are pumped up about yesterday's debate. Dmitry Harrison shouts that I'm "the comeback kid" in front of a bunch of fellow cross-country runners, and it legitimately cracks me up. I hope he's right.

I catch up to Trish walking to her first period.

"There you are," she says, a twinkle in her eye. "How we doing?"

"Fine," I say, even though my insides feel like they're in the first seat of a roller coaster.

She doesn't believe me, of course.

"Okay," I admit. "Obviously, I'm nervous."

"There we go. Let it out."

"But I just had a really nice walk to school with Danny, and he made me a bit more Zen."

She gasps. "A romantic walk in the rain?"

I smirk, shrugging.

Her face goes from silly to serious, which I've learned reflects her transition into campaign captain mode. "You're good on how this will go, right?" she asks for the dozenth time since yesterday.

"Yep."

"We'll both cast our votes in first period. Ms. Green should know you're on the ballot, and let you leave for the auditorium as soon as you vote, but if she gives you any trouble—"

"Text you, and you'll come to my rescue. I know, I know."

We get to the end of the hallway. Trish's first period is to the right; Ms. Green's classroom is on the left.

"Deep breaths," Trish says for the both of us.

"Deep, *deep* breaths," I concur, floating away into art class.

As soon as the bell rings, Ms. Green urges us to quiet down and take our seats. My stomach is in a perpetual state of dropping, more or less, as I crane my neck to see the stacks of ballots waiting on her desk. My art class has freshmen, sophomores, and juniors in it, so there are ballots printed on three different colors, as I saw in Mr. Wells's classroom the last night of debate prep. Part of me is jealous of the seniors, as they sit back and watch the rest of the school stress out over who wins and loses today. But not Joey; he's just as invested as Zach is or I am in who his successor will be, I'm sure.

Ms. Green wastes no time getting down to business. Once everyone is seated, she passes out four ballots to each student for the different races within their class—president, VP, secretary, and treasurer. The races for the rising sophomores are printed on blue, the races for the rising juniors are on yellow, and the races for the rising seniors are on orange.

"Good luck, Blaine," Ms. Green whispers with a smile, placing four orange sheets on my desk. It feels even weirder seeing it this time around, now that it's actually Election Day.

SENIOR CLASS PRESIDENT

BLAINE BOWERS

ZACH CHESTERSON

Being in a classroom that's voting for student council elections when your name is on the ballot has to be one of the most surreal experiences ever. It's like there's a huge elephant in the room and *you're the huge elephant in the room.*

For the other offices, I select the candidates that I think I could work best with. Then I pause, inhale slowly, put a check mark in the box next to my name, and breathe out.

There.

It's done.

I quietly head up to the front, hand off my ballots to Ms. Green, and leave for the auditorium. When I walk in, it's just as intense and awkward as I imagined.

The seats are entirely empty, but all the candidates and campaign captains for the various races across grade levels are congregating onstage. Mr. Wells is among them, answering questions and pointing off in different directions using his clipboard.

I walk up the side stairs, legs feeling like complete Jell-O, and see that there are various signs taped to the curtains around the perimeter of the stage that designate where each candidate should stand. Trish is in a corner with the other rising-senior candidates and their campaign captains, Zach and Ashtyn included. I'm not interested in wishing the two of them good luck, and—judging by the fact that they're very intentionally avoiding eye contact with me—it seems like we're all on the same page.

"How did it feel voting for yourself?" Trish asks as I approach.

"Weird AF."

A few minutes later, after everyone has arrived, Mr. Wells gets our attention at the edge of the stage. "Thank you all for being a part of this year's student council elections," he announces, big bifocal eyes scanning the sea of students before him. "We had terrific candidates, and I'm confident next year's leaders will continue to raise the bar when it comes to student government at WWHS."

He leads us in a few seconds of self-congratulatory applause.

"Now, here's how this will work—and please pay attention because it will *not* be fun if people mess this up!" He stops to wait for a few giggly freshmen to zip it. "Campaign captains, in a moment you'll group up with the other campaign captain or captains who represent candidates in your race." Mr. Wells points down to the first row of seats in the auditorium, which are filled with huge paper grocery bags. "Together you will select one of those bags, and then, in unison, you will retrieve the ballots for your specific race and *your specific race only* from the entire school. Yes, separating ballots into individual races makes the collection process a bit more hectic, but it speeds up the counting process tenfold. As long as something doesn't go horrifically awry, like with the class of 2017's race for treasurer"—he shivers in dread at the memory—"we should know all the winners across grade levels later this morning."

He takes a deep breath.

"Keep in mind there are four wings of the school: Mathematics, Sciences, Creative Arts, and Social Studies. Please make sure you visit *every* classroom in *every* wing before you return to the auditorium. Any questions?"

No hands go up.

"All right, then. Campaign captains, go forth."

In a show of stressful solidarity, Trish nudges me with her elbow before syncing up with Ashtyn and walking down the side stairs of the stage. Together they select a bag and disappear through the doors. In under a minute, the number of students in the auditorium is cut in half, and the stage takes on a much more serious and pressurized energy.

Zach, in a rust-colored suit jacket and floral T-shirt, rocks back and forth on his heels next to me. "Blaine," he finally says, acknowledging my presence.

"Zach." I nod back at him.

And then we both go back to being uncomfortable.

With nothing else to distract me from my nervous thoughts, and with time seemingly standing still, I decide to walk myself through the rough vote tally needed for me to win. This certainly won't help with my anxiety—which is sufficiently reaching the level of "about to have a heart attack"—but whatever. I rack my brain trying to recall the figures Trish laid out for us during our second debate prep.

After doing her research, Trish told me that the current junior class is 553 students. History shows that the vast majority of the 553 will vote, Danny explained to us. But, seeing as a few will opt out and others may be sick and miss class, we should expect around 500 votes to be cast for senior class president.

That means, with just two candidates on the ballot, I'll likely need to be in the ballpark of 250 votes to have a shot at winning.

Finally the campaign captains start trickling back into the auditorium with their big paper bags of ballots. Trish and Ashtyn appear with theirs, and my blood pressure skyrockets to the moon. Zach, pale and sweaty, looks visibly shaken. It's the first time I've seen him like this.

The votes are cast. The campaign is done. The bag in their hands holds the winner of the senior class presidency.

Trish and Ashtyn are each given a pad of paper and pens by Mr. Wells, and return to me and Zach in the far corner of the stage.

"Are you boys ready?" Trish asks, setting the bag down on the wooden stage.

I swallow hard and nod at her. "Let's do this."

CHAPTER 23

The four of us sit cross-legged circling the bag. Trish pulls the first ballot out and lays it on the stage floor. We all look at it anxiously.

"Zach," she says aloud.

My heart sinks.

Knock it off, Blaine, I think. *It's one damn vote.*

Both Trish and Ashtyn mark it on their respective pads of paper.

Ashtyn pulls out another. "Blaine," she reads.

Yes!

Okay. I need to calm the heck down.

This is a marathon, not a sprint.

The auditorium gets quieter and quieter as more teams dive into their counts. You could cut the tension in the stale, cool auditorium air with a butter knife. At one point I stand to stretch and pace a little because it's too much. Seriously.

Too much.

I peer over at Trish's pad of paper, but it's all in tally marks and too difficult to know who's ahead from a quick glance. From the number of times I've heard them say either "Blaine" or "Zach," I'd say we're . . . about fifty-fifty? But we have to be nearing a hundred votes by now. After listening to our names that many times, it's easy to be off.

"Wait," Ashtyn says between ballots. "Should we pause and count up our current totals, just to make sure they're the same?"

"Yes!" I squeal.

Trish, Zach, and Ashtyn stare at me.

I clear my throat. "I think that'd be a good idea, yes."

Trish and Ashtyn both lean closer to their papers.

"I have . . . ," Trish says, looking back up at us, "Zach, forty-seven, Blaine, forty-four."

Ashtyn nods, confirming the same. "Yep."

Holy crap. It's really freaking close.

Right now, it's anyone's game.

I glance at Zach, whose face has stopped being pumped with blood. He catches my eye, but looks away quickly.

Trish and Ashtyn go back to counting.

I go get a drink at the water fountain backstage, where I then continue to pace. At one point I do a freaking cartwheel next to a pile of fake tumbleweed that the drama department used in *The Grapes of Wrath*, just to let out some of my nervous energy.

When I return, the pile of counted ballots is a lot taller.

"Hey, so, how about another pause to make sure you both have the same numbers again?" I ask, my voice an octave higher due to nerves.

Trish and Ashtyn look at each other, agreeing that that's a good idea.

This time it takes them a lot more time to count.

"I have . . . ," Ashtyn says, finishing up, "Zach at one hundred sixty-two, Blaine at one hundred thirty-nine."

BLAINE FOR THE WIN

A chill runs down my spine.

Damn it. I'm falling behind.

I look to Trish, actually *hoping* there's a discrepancy.

But she nods. "Same."

Shoot.

Shoot, shoot, shoot.

"I'm going to get more water!" I announce loudly to the other three, as if any of them care.

This time I stay and pace for a while, knowing it won't be good for me or Trish if I stand around her, hovering like a vulture.

A lot of thoughts start racing through my mind.

What if I lose?

But, oh my God, *what if I win?*

Is Joey nervous right now, wondering who's going to be his successor?

On a scale of one to infinity, how pissed off is Ms. Ritewood with me right now?

Does Danny like me as much as I like him?

My phone buzzes. I legit gasp, startled, and look down at a text message.

DO YOU KNOW ANYTHING YET???? Aunt Starr wrote.

No . . . , I text back with a smiley face that's sweating.

No matter what, LOVE U, she replies with pink hearts. SO PROUD OF U.

I sigh, my heart pounding against my ribs.

The dread is almost overwhelming, but I need to go back in there. . . .

I walk up to Trish, noticing that the pile of counted ballots is getting unruly at this point.

This time it's Zach who speaks up. "Another count?" he asks. I notice there's more color in his cheeks and confidence in his voice—no doubt due to his growing margin.

Trish and Ashtyn both pause to tally up where things stand, and their silence hits me like a bag of bricks.

Because this could be it.

Like, this could seal the deal.

Judging by where the vote figures are, Zach could be at the two-hundred mark. And if he's grown his margin even further since the last tally, the gap will probably be too large for me to make up at this point. If I haven't shrunk the margin, and shrunk it considerably, the race is all but over.

I mean, we're in the fourth quarter now.

I'd need a miracle.

"Okay . . . ," Trish says, staring at her paper.

My chest tightens.

"I have . . . Zach, two hundred and one, and Blaine . . ." Trish looks up. "One hundred seventy-two."

My gut drops.

"Ditto," Ashtyn says, hardly able to contain her glee.

I glance at Zach, who's biting his lower lip with a grin, knowing where this is headed. He's a stone's throw away from the two-fifty mark. I'm toast.

But then there's Trish.

I expect her to look just as devastated as I feel, but she . . . doesn't? As Ashtyn turns toward Zach to giggle about their inevitable victory, Trish pops her eyes open at me. She knows something I don't, it seems, insinuating that I should hold out hope.

But what could that something possibly be?

What is she seeing that I'm not? "I'll be over there," I announce, rubbing my temples, completely overwhelmed. "I'm going to just, like . . . I don't know. I need to move my legs. Will one of you signal me when you're done counting?"

I don't wait for a response. I bounce, heading down the side stage stairs, and begin pacing the far aisle of the auditorium.

Every minute or so I hear a squeal onstage coming from one of the candidates or campaign captains in a different race who has realized they've won. Most of the other races have been called by now. We're one of the last ones to finish.

"You holding up okay?" Mr. Wells asks me, a bit concerned, as he walks by.

"Yep," I reply, trying to pull off calm.

But I am *so* not calm. I am anything but calm.

Finally I'm put out of my misery. Because I hear it.

I hear the bad news.

It comes in the form of Ashtyn's shouts of joy and Zach's laughter. I look up to the stage, and my heart sinks. The two of them are embraced in a smiley hug, jumping up and down.

Trish is sitting cross-legged on the floor next to them, chin dropped in sorrow.

Why did she give me that look? Why did she still have

hope when the math so clearly told us that I had a next-to-nothing chance of a comeback?

Gutted, I slowly make my way up the stairs and cross the stage.

"Hey," I say to Trish.

She looks up at me, eyes watery. "Zach, two hundred eighty-six," she says. "Blaine, two hundred twenty-three."

CHAPTER 24

The past few weeks flash through my head.

The nightmare at Grey Kettle. The euphoria of reaching fifty signatures. My run-in with Joey outside the Fat Banana. Making the ballot. Totally bombing my debate performance before ending it on a high note. And now, losing to Zach.

And losing by not a tiny amount.

What an absolute roller-coaster ride—one that just ended in a devastating crash.

Trish links arms with me as we walk up to Mr. Wells with Ashtyn and Zach to turn in the ballots and report our totals. Mr. Wells marks his clipboard, congratulates Zach with a pat on the shoulder, and gives me a handshake.

"Tough race," he whispers, leaning in. "You did a great job, Blaine."

Trish and I are basically like zombies walking to our second periods, as the emotional letdown—an entire month in the making—washes over us.

Word spreads fast that Zach won, and I'm inundated with condolences from friends, and comments from complete strangers with hot takes about what went down and why. Someone in second period already caught wind of the vote totals and relays to me that I lost to Zach 56 to 44 percent—a "surprisingly lopsided" defeat, as they phrase it, before apologizing for the insensitivity. A girl I've never even spoken to in third period explains to me, unprompted, that I could have closed the gap if I'd worked harder to win over the True Crime Club vote.

Yes, the *True Crime Club* vote.

"Just a thought," she says smugly, turning back to her calculator.

Both Danny and Camilla hear the news before I even get the chance to text them. At lunch they wrap me up in hugs and attempt to distract me from the loss with funny memes over potato chips and chocolate milks. After that strategy fails to put a genuine smile on my face, they resort to telling me how great a candidate I was. I'm not sure I believe it.

It's strange. Now that the race is over, the question that was gnawing at me—the morning before the debate—is back in full force, rotating like a record player in my brain. If it really wasn't about stealing Joey back, why *did* I want to become senior class president?

And if there's no good reason, why am I so bummed that I lost?

It's the fact that I let my team down, I realize.

Danny sacrificed his breaks at work to give me the student council insight I never would have gotten without him. Camilla spent the only evenings she had off from the Field being a damn good villainous Zach Chesterton during our debate preps. And Trish? I've never seen her more passionate about anything in her *life* than our Wicker West Wellness Initiative. It was her baby.

Then there's Ms. Ritewood. What does she think of me now? Not to mention the handful of other store owners whose messages I've been putting off, in pursuit of Serious Guy status—a recognition I've clearly failed to attain? Have I ruined those connections for good? Should I even write those people back?

Even though the only thing I want to do is go home and sulk-watch *The Great British Bake Off* with Fudge in bed, Trish decides we should go to Biggest Bean after school with Danny and Camilla. After a few minutes of pushing back, I finally comply.

We snag our corner. I drop into a beanbag next to Camilla, while Danny and Trish take the sofa.

"Here," Camilla says, handing me the last bite of her marble cake. "Sugar heals all wounds."

"Thanks," I say, shaking my head. "I'm okay, though. Not hungry."

"Suit yourself." She pops the rest of it into her mouth.

"You can still sign up to be a student council member, like I am," Danny says, shrugging. He looks at Trish and Camilla too. "You should all sign up."

"I don't mean to sound like a jerk," I reply, "but can we . . . maybe not talk about student council stuff right now?"

Danny nods.

"It's just," I say, knowing I sounded like a jerk, "I don't want to think about the race."

"I get it," Danny says. "Enough election talk."

Apparently no one has much to say outside of election

talk, though, as the four of us sit there, staring into space. Biggest Bean is dark and drafty, reflecting the storm clouds outside. A few businesspeople pop in, order black coffees, and disappear into the rain again, but beyond that, the store floor is quiet and still.

My phone buzzes with an incoming text.

Shoot. Aunt Starr. I completely forgot to send her an election results update. And now that I've lost, I'm dreading sharing the news.

I open the text message, assuming it's a panicked follow-up begging to know the outcome, but instead it reads, Hey, doll, what is this? along with a picture of the Field Museum business card. Across the top, Camilla's handwriting clearly reads, *Cool gig for your aunt!*

Damn it.

Damn it, damn it, *damn it.*

I bet Aunt Starr spotted the card on my dresser after getting Fudge from my bedroom for a walk.

"What's wrong?" Danny asks, seeing the mild terror spreading across my face.

I stand and begin floating toward the community bulletin boards on the other side of Biggest Bean. "I need to call my aunt real quick. She's trying to add a streaming service to our TV or something and needs some help. Be right back."

Once I'm safely out of Camilla's earshot, I hit the call button and lift the phone to my ear, a nauseating sense of regret filling up my insides.

"Hey!" Aunt Starr bellows on the other end of the line.

"Hi," I reply.

"Well?" she demands.

Wait. Does she somehow already know that I've been withholding this job opportunity from her for weeks?

I freeze up.

"Doll, don't leave me hanging," she says, and sighs, exasperated. "How did the election go?"

Oh.

Duh.

The election. She's asking about the stupid freaking dumb election results.

"The election was, ah . . ." I gulp. "I'll . . . tell you all about it when I get home a bit later."

"Oh. Okay." She can hear the defeat in my voice, of course, and chooses not to pry. "Well, remember that I love you and you're amazing, no matter what happened. Okay?"

The faucet filling my insides with regret grows a whole lot larger as the phone line falls silent. I clear my throat. "About that business card, though!" I exclaim, trying to inject some excitement into the call. "It's for you! Camilla got you an interview."

"An interview? At the Field? Holy crap. What's the gig?"

"Director of events for kids' programs, or something like that."

She gasps. "What?"

"Yeah."

"For real?"

"Yes. It sounds fantastic."

She takes a moment to breathe. "Okay, what do I need to do, what do I need to do . . . ?" I can practically hear her mind creating a checklist. "I can send him my résumé today! He'd want it before the interview, right? I mean, I can send it right *now*, in fact. And should I send a cover letter with it? Does Camilla know if he'd like one? Never mind, I'll send my cover letter. It can't hurt. And also—"

"Hold on *just* one second." I gulp. "You might want to check online and make sure the job is still open."

There's a pause. "What do you mean?"

"Well . . ." I cringe to myself. "Camilla told me a few days ago that you should email her boss."

"Okay . . . ?"

"I mean . . ." I cringe even harder, closing my eyes. "More than a few days ago."

"When?"

I think. "You know the night you made us bacon-and-egg sandwiches for brinner?"

"Yeah?"

"That day."

"Oh," she says. "Gotcha."

Ugh. I hate this feeling.

I. Hate. This. Feeling.

"Aunt Starr," I say, searching for excuses. "I'm so sorry I didn't tell you about it earlier."

"It's okay," she says. But you can tell by the way she says it that it's *not okay*.

"It slipped my mind," I continue. "I've been wrapped up

in the election stuff and everything else. I just . . . I blanked. I feel awful."

"It's okay, Blaine," she repeats gently. "Really, it is."

But I can tell that *really*, it's not.

"I'm going to check if it's still up on their job board," she says. "I'll see you tonight, all right?"

"Are you angry with me?" I ask.

Silence.

Gut-wrenching silence.

Fudge barks somewhere in the distance.

"Of course not," she answers. "I could never be angry with you. I'll see you later."

She hangs up.

I lay my forehead against the bulletin board and close my eyes, feeling shame oozing out of every pore.

Aunt Starr has never been disappointed in me. Not like this, at least. We bicker over *Drag Race* performances and brinner ingredients sometimes, but we never get upset with each other over serious stuff—stuff like maybe ruining your unemployed aunt's chances at getting her dream job.

I return to Trish, Camilla, and Danny a minute later.

"Everything cool?" Camilla asks.

All three of them are staring at me. They have to know something's up.

I don't feel like talking about it right now, so I bolster my white lie instead. "Just tech issues with the TV and Wi-Fi. No big deal."

Camilla and Danny spin off into their own conversation

about how Biggest Bean makes those Vietnamese doughnuts that come with sesame seeds on top. I try to listen and chime in here and there, but it's incredibly difficult to do with not one but *two* dark storm clouds hovering above my head. I got creamed in the presidential race *and* I hurt Aunt Starr, in the same twenty-four hours.

When it rains, it really does pour.

"Those vote totals don't make sense," Trish mutters out of nowhere, staring at the coffee table in a trance.

Danny and Camilla shut up about the doughnuts.

The three of us turn to her, waiting for a follow-up thought. But she doesn't say anything.

"What?" Danny prods. "How so?"

"I keep going over them in my head, and I . . ." Trish trails off. "I don't know. It feels sketchy to me."

"Blaine wants to forget about the election right now," Camilla urges. "Okay, babe?"

"It just doesn't feel right," Trish continues. "Ashtyn and I went around to the four wings of the school, and—"

"Trish," I interject. "I promise, we can talk about this tomorrow—or, preferably, a decade from now—but please, not today? Not right now?"

Trish sinks back into the sofa and falls silent.

Danny laughs a little, I think to de-escalate the friction. "Blaine, she's just trying to help."

"I know," I say, wishing I'd never even come to Biggest Bean today. "But I don't want the help right now."

Trish, clearly upset, stands and heads for the bathroom.

Camilla sighs and follows after her. "Be right back."

Then it's just me and Danny.

"You should probably go apologize to her," he suggests.

"Why would I?"

His eyes grow big in surprise—as if I should know why I'm in the wrong. "You were pretty rude to her just then."

I shake my head, letting out an agitated laugh.

He scrunches his face. "Why are you acting like this all of a sudden?"

"Acting like what?"

"You were mean to Trish, and now you're being a jerk to me, too," he says. "It's not like you."

"I said I didn't want to talk about the election, okay?" I snap, feeling my throat narrow. All the emotions from the past month's roller coaster, topped off by the shame of Aunt Starr finding the business card, are bubbling up to the surface.

"Me, Trish, Camilla—we've been nothing but supportive of you this whole campaign," Danny says. "I think you owe it to us to, like . . ."

"What?"

"To not be a total dick."

"You don't know the whole story," I retort softly.

I wish he did, though.

I wish he knew how disappointed I am in myself for letting him, Trish, and Camilla down; how angry I am that Joey was right all along in thinking no one had a shot at dethroning Zach; how gutting it is to have Aunt Starr feel as though I forgot about something that's important to her.

But if I go there—if I explain all that—I know that I'll melt into a puddle of tears.

"What's the *whole story*, then?" Danny asks.

"You've been in council for a while," I answer. "But you don't know what it's like to lose a big race, Danny."

"I *do* know what it's like to lose something important to you," he says. "It sucks. But you should remember that you're not the only one feeling the loss right now."

"I'm the only one whose name was on that ballot," I snap back. "I'm the one who lost this election."

My eyes find his, and he's staring, unblinking, like he doesn't recognize the person sitting across from him.

"You know how much this campaign meant to Trish," he notes. "She's grieving too, Blaine. You're her best friend. How can you not see that?"

I gulp down a tear. "Well, maybe I wouldn't be, as you called it, *acting like a total dick*, if I had friends who were honest with me instead of filling my head with lies about me *actually* having a shot at beating Zach."

"Filling your head with lies?" He looks totally lost. "What are you talking about?"

"At my house, when we were writing my speech," I barrel onward, "you told me you *knew* I was going to win this election."

"So . . . you're upset that I believed in you?"

"And this morning, on our walk under the umbrella, you said basically the same thing: that you expected me to win."

He shakes his head, bewildered.

"I'm angry you helped push me into a race that I never should have entered in the first place," I say, certain I don't even mean it. "It's embarrassing."

"Pushed you into this race?" His jaw is hanging in shock. "Seriously? *You* were the one who entered solely to win Joey back. Remember? You even admitted it to me! You were hardly *pushed*." I don't say anything. Because if I do, my eyes will explode, covering Biggest Bean in tears.

He stands and moves toward the counter. "My shift starts soon—I have to go."

I am the worst. The absolute, bottom-of-the-barrel, scum-of-the-planet worst.

I grab my coat and bag, and take off toward the door.

Bao, bringing in a stack of baking sheets from outside, holds it open for me as I walk out. "Hey, Blaine."

I need to hold it together.

Hold it together, Blaine.

"Hi, Bao." I'm fighting so hard to not break into a million pieces.

"Look," he says softly, rain pitter-pattering on the awning above us. "Danny texted me earlier about the election results. I'm sorry, bud."

"Thank you. It's okay."

"I know how hard you all worked for it. A loss like that can sting."

"Yeah."

"Between me and you?" He glances around to make sure

no one can hear us. "It was great seeing Danny get excited about something again. He'd kill me if he knew I was telling you this, but"—Bao drops his voice lower—"he couldn't stop talking about you and the election at home. It was neat seeing him get fired up." He smiles big. "Hey, even if you lost, you still lit up something special in him—and I'm sure a lot of other students too. That matters."

His words might as well be a knife plunging through my chest.

"Thanks, Bao," is all I can get out before I jog off, surrendering to the rain.

CHAPTER 25

Welp, this isn't how I planned to spend the day after the election. Fudge is curled up against my back in bed. I'm completely smothered in blankets except for my face and outstretched arm, which is scrolling through Instagram like a zombie, mindlessly liking pics of ice cream, puppies, and Jonathan Van Ness.

I wish our Wicker West Wellness Initiative was a real thing, because I'd be taking advantage of it right about now, sending off anonymous emails asking for advice via the Senior Chat service and spending next week's lunches finding my Zen in the Senior Space.

I force myself to close Instagram after seeing the same risotto recipe video for the fourth time, and open my email instead. There's another message awaiting me from Ms. Ritewood. A lump forms in my throat. The subject line reads, *I have an update about my mural, Blaine!* but I'm so paralyzed with dread that I drop the phone onto the mattress without even opening her email. I can read it tomorrow. Or next week. Or never.

I know I need to get out of this bed. I know I need to take a shower, put on real clothes, and at least try to be a real human today. But those are the last things I want to do.

It's not even losing that I'm upset about—it's how

terribly I *handled* losing. I felt ashamed and frustrated for letting down Trish, Danny, and Camilla, and then—in a brutally ironic twist—I took out that shame and frustration on the people who deserved it the least. I may not be able to win an election, but I could teach a freaking master class on how to lose one. And hey, while I'm at it, sign me up to instruct Being a Terrible Nephew 101, as well.

Barely thirty seconds go by before my fingers get antsy without something to scroll, so I snatch my phone up again and retreat to Instagram.

The *exact* image I do not need to be seeing right now is the first one that appears.

A post from Joey, shared mere seconds ago. He's standing on a boat, floating down the Chicago River, arm snug around Zach. They're both beaming in the sunshine like they've won the lottery, the glittery skyline towering behind them.

Surprised the bf with a morning Chicago Architecture Tour boat ride after his big win yesterday!!! the caption reads, along with the hashtag #SeniorClassPresidents.

"You've *got* to be kidding me," I sigh, tossing my phone to the floor.

"Are we really doing this again?"

I jump. Fudge barks.

It's Trish, standing in the doorway, holding two iced drinks. "I'm having déjà vu, Blaine." She pauses, listening to the song humming along softly in the background. "Is *Folklore* the only thing you ever listen to?"

"Taylor Swift gets me."

She rolls her eyes.

I sit up in bed and make room for her. She sits, crosses her legs, and exhales, taking in my disheveled room like it's the week of spring break all over again.

The silence begins to feel heavy, so I dive right into what needs to be said. "Trish," I begin, swallowing hard and sitting up a bit straighter. "I am so, *so* sorry about my foul mood at Biggest Bean yesterday—"

"Nope, I'm not here to do that," she says, thrusting the mocha drink into my hands. "I'm not here for an apology. We can take care of that some other day."

I take a sip, sort of confused. "Do you . . . wanna watch *The Great British Bake Off* with me, then?"

"I'm here to talk business, and time is of the essence. Didn't you hear me yesterday? The vote totals don't make sense."

"Oh right. I forgot you brought that up."

"Someone messed with the ballots."

I close my eyes, dreading where this conversation is headed.

It's been obvious that, once the wellness initiative got off the ground, Trish was more committed to this race than I was. But leaning into some conspiracy theories to rationalize my failure? That's next-level.

"Trish." I open my eyes again, speaking slowly. "Zach got more votes than I did. That's how elections work."

"Blaine," she replies. "If you patronize me like that again, I'm taking your headphones and never giving them back."

She pulls a piece of paper out of her purse and tosses it into my face.

I flip it to see the contents. "A map of the school." I look up at her. "Thanks?"

"Look at the Creative Arts classes, doofus." She points to the upper left-hand side, where the classrooms are highlighted. Trish listed out the names of the courses taught in that area of the school.

"Okay?"

"Think about those classes."

"They're . . . Creative Arts classes." I am so confused right now. "What am I not getting?"

"Band, music theory, creative writing, drama, photography, art, and a bunch more. Who's in those electives?"

I think. "Well, not too many future finance majors. Artsier people, like me."

She nods. "Do you think a bunch of artsy people would be fans of Zach Chesterton?"

"Probably not, no."

She takes the school map back from me. "You'd assume you would win those classes, and win them by a lot, right?"

"I never thought about it, but sure. Yeah."

"I didn't want to tell you this because I didn't want to sound . . ." She pauses sheepishly. "Overeager. But in the week leading up to the election, I went around surveying juniors on who they were thinking about supporting in the race—you or Zach. I didn't, like, write down their responses or anything. I just wanted to get a general feel of which wings of the school were your strong areas and your weak areas, in case we wanted to put up posters in wings where you could use the boost."

"Wow," I say, grinning a bit. "'Overeager' is one way of putting it."

"Shut up. I was a damn good campaign captain. Anyway." She sucks from her straw. "Sure, it was just anecdotal evidence, but from what I gathered, you should have dominated the Creative Arts wing, Blaine. Like, big-time. Those students were itching to abandon Zach, and they were willing to give you a shot."

"I mean, cool, I guess?"

"I would say, out of every five people I asked, four were either firmly in your camp or leaning your way. That's eighty freaking percent, dude. The other wings were way closer to fifty-fifty, but not Creative Arts."

"What are you saying?" I ask, sitting up straighter and patting Fudge's head.

"Ashtyn and I collected votes from the Creative Arts wing *first*, meaning all of those classes' ballots were at the bottom of our bag." She looks at me like I should be getting it by now. "*Meaning that* the last bunch of votes we counted should have been disproportionately in your favor. You should have won the vast, *vast* majority of them."

Wait a minute.

"*Ohh,*" I say. "*That's* why you gave me that look toward the end of the vote-counting session—because you thought I still had a shot at a last-minute comeback."

"Yes." She exhales in relief. "Finally you get what I'm saying."

"I don't know, Trish."

"What do you mean, *you don't know?*"

I shrug. "It's a solid theory, but it feels like a stretch."

"Blaine." Her jaw drops. "Zach *grew* his margin in the last hundred-plus votes we counted—votes that would have mostly been those artsy juniors." She shakes her head. "Doesn't that seem odd?"

I *really* don't want to do this right now.

Losing to Zach—and losing to him by a not-very-close margin—was embarrassing enough. Can you imagine if I went to school on Monday demanding that Mr. Wells give me a recount, based on a conspiracy theory built on nothing but unreliable research done by my own campaign captain? They'd send me home, thinking I'd gone delirious.

"Can this wait?" I say, unsure how to deal with this.

She gapes. "Wait until *when?*"

"I don't know."

"You don't believe me?"

"It's not a matter of *believing* you. It's just—" I stop to think. "I'm not sure what we could even do at this point."

"Ask Mr. Wells? Confront Zach? Demand to see the ballots again and look for anything suspicious?" She stands up abruptly. "I mean, those are three ideas, just off the top of my head."

"Demand to see the ballots again? I love you, Trish, but do you hear yourself?"

She grabs her purse and storms off.

"Hold up!" I call after her, feeling like I've just made everything worse. "I really am sorry about the way I acted at Biggest Bean yesterday!"

She stops at the door. "As your best friend, I wanted you to win," she says. "But honestly? I wanted the wellness initiative to become a reality even more. Because I know it'd truly make a difference." She gulps. "I think you've been too selfish to see its potential, Blaine."

"Trish—"

She walks out.

CHAPTER 26

★ ★ ★

Monday arrives after a long weekend of me barely getting out of bed. I want to skip—*so badly*—but Mom
and Dad are "putting our foot down," as they say.

"Just get through the day, kiddo," Mom says,
giving me a kiss on the head as I crunch on my sugary cereal
at the kitchen island. She disappears out the door in her
scrubs. A minute later Dad pauses the phone call he's on to
whisper, "You got this," and rushes out too.

Aunt Starr floats into the kitchen in her bathrobe, carrying a bowl of sliced grapefruit. "Hi," she says.

"Hey," I say.

All weekend we both tried to act like everything was
normal—as if I hadn't just crushed her feelings by derailing
an amazing career opportunity. But it's tough acting unaf-
fected; neither of us is great at ignoring elephants in rooms.
Especially when the elephants involve one another.

"Any updates on the Field job?" I ask, trying to sound
optimistic.

She drops her bowl into the sink and turns to me, one
hand on her hip. "Well, no response yet. I only emailed the
guy Friday afternoon, though, so chances are, he hasn't even
read my message yet." She crosses her fingers. "Let's hope I'll
get good news soon."

I lift my hand, crossing my fingers too. "For sure."

She begins to mosey off.

"Aunt Starr," I say.

She stops and turns.

"I really am sorry I didn't tell you about the job sooner," I emphasize. "I feel awful about the whole thing."

She shakes her head, a smile spreading across her face. "Blaine. I promise you, I understand. You've got a lot on your plate now. Don't worry about it."

She leaves, Fudge following in her footsteps.

But I *am* worried about it. And I *do* feel awful.

I finish up breakfast and take off to school. Three days ago this walk felt so different, when I was nestled under Danny's umbrella, hopeful that I could soon become the senior class president-elect. But now all I can ruminate on is how selfish I've been since deciding to enter this freaking race.

I was so focused on winning, I failed to see how much the wellness initiative genuinely meant to Trish. I was so determined to win Joey back, I didn't think twice about how selfless Danny was in devoting his energy to our campaign. And I was so hell-bent on keeping Aunt Starr all to myself that I may have squashed the coolest job opportunity she's ever gotten.

"Hey," I say, approaching Trish at her locker.

"Hey." From her tone, she clearly wants nothing to do with me.

"I'm sorry." I push my thumbs between my backpack straps and chest, rocking back and forth awkwardly. "I've been an idiot—"

"It's cool," she says quickly, closing her locker and zooming off.

It is *not*, in fact, cool.

I scramble to keep up with her. "Can we talk about it?"

"I'm not sure there's much to talk about."

"I . . . kind of feel like there's a *lot* to talk about?"

"Can this wait?" She slices me open, firing back the same line I said to rebuke her rigged-ballot theory. She turns the corner and successfully flees, leaving me gasping for a response like an out-of-water fish.

Just like with Aunt Starr, it's exceedingly rare that Trish would be genuinely upset with me. But *unlike* with Aunt Starr, when it does happen, Trish is certainly unafraid to let it be known.

Danny's locker is on my way to art, so I decide to drop by and see if he's around, hoping I can repair at least one tattered friendship this morning. But from a few classrooms away, I see that he's chatting with a student council friend; I don't want to interrupt with my apology.

Today's a day that's simply destined to suck.

At lunch only Camilla is sitting at our go-to table in the cafeteria. I'm not sure if she's officially on Team Trish at this point, so I approach with caution. She greets me with a smile, though. I can't describe how comforting it is to still have at least one friend who doesn't despise my guts.

"So," I say with a sigh, sitting down across from her with my square slice of pepperoni pizza. "You're not upset with me?"

"I could *never* be upset with you," she says, sipping her green tea. "Wait, that's not true. Of course I could. But I'm not right now."

"She's avoiding me, isn't she?" I ask, glancing around the cafeteria for Trish.

"She's making up a quiz."

"Have you seen Danny?"

Camilla shakes her head with a slight frown. "Him, I can't say."

"Camilla, I was an asshole at Biggest Bean." I don't want to waste another breath that doesn't include an apology. "I was pissed about losing and took it out on you three. I'm sorry."

She holds her fist up for a light bump.

I tap it gently.

"Yeah, you were an asshole," she says. "But I get it. Friday was terrible."

"You don't even know about the other horrible part of that day," I admit, feeling my face get warm. "My asshole self forgot to tell Aunt Starr about the job at the Field that you recommended. She found the business card while we were at Biggest Bean."

Camilla's face drops. "Dude!"

"I know."

"I told my boss to look out for her email!"

"I'm sorry."

"That's *my* butt on the line too."

"I know, *I know.*" My stomach swirls with guilt. "I messed up. I'm the worst. I'm sorry."

She pauses to reel in her frustration with me. "Well, she still emailed him, right?"

"Yeah."

She lets out an enormous sigh that draws stares from the table next to us. "Good. I know they're still looking for candidates, so she *should* be in the clear."

"Wait, really?" Relief rises in my chest. "Are you sure?"

"Yes. They've struggled to find a qualified person who's the right fit. They'll eat up Aunt Starr, though. I just know it." She takes a swig of her tea. "Can I ask you something?"

"Of course."

"Did you *forget* to tell her about the job, or did you, you know . . ." She tilts her head at me, like I should know.

"Huh?"

"Did you intentionally not tell her?"

My heartbeat speeds up. "Why would I do that?"

She tilts her head even more. "Blaine . . . c'mon."

I squint at her, studying her face.

She does the same back at me.

I'm *exposed.*

"Fine," I breathe. "How'd you know?"

"You're more transparent than you think." She nudges my tray playfully. "It's understandable. I get why you wouldn't want Aunt Starr to get a job. It means she's got to move out. And she's, like, the best roommate imaginable."

"Right?"

"She cooks incredible brinners, she's hilarious, and she's everyone's number one cheerleader." Camilla lays out the argument in such a matter-of-fact way. "I'd be devastated to see her leave too."

It's like a warm hug, hearing Camilla validate my feelings. Because, sure, it was incredibly selfish of me to hide the job from Aunt Starr. There's no denying that. But I did it because she means so much to me. I did it because I'm afraid of losing her.

Maybe I should tell Aunt Starr all of this too.

"Is she hurt that you didn't tell her?" Camilla asks.

"Yeah, I think so," I say.

"Just explain to her why you did what you did," Camilla says, like it's so easy. "She might still be upset, but at least she'll understand."

"True. Trish, on the other hand . . ." I puff out my cheeks and exhale slowly. "Your girlfriend has made it abundantly clear that she is *not* happy with me."

"And rightly so," Camilla adds, popping up an eyebrow.

"Agreed."

"Don't worry." She tears a corner off my pizza. "She just needs some space."

"I underestimated how important the mental health initiative was to her, I think," I say. "I knew she was fired up, but I didn't realize how invested she became."

"Yep." She shoves the pizza into her mouth. "Trish is an ankylosaurus."

"A what now?"

She takes a moment to chew. "An ankylosaurus. A type of dinosaur that was covered in armored plates. A predator's worst nightmare." She pauses to think. "Imagine, like, a massive dino version of a turtle. That's basically an ankylosaurus."

"Trish is a giant turtle?" I arch my brow at her. "Not sure she'd be too thrilled about that characterization, Camilla."

"Eh, I say it to her face all the time." She tears another piece of my pizza off. "She's guarded, is what I mean. She carries around a shield wherever she goes. As her best friend, you, of all people, know that."

"Yeah."

"That's why it took her a while to open up about her depression and talk to a counselor," she says. "She's always real with us about silly, trivial things, for sure."

"Definitely."

"But the tough stuff? The vulnerable stuff? It takes time with her. And I think that's what happened with the campaign." She dunks the pizza into a cup of marinara on my tray. "*I* knew how personal the wellness initiative was for her, but I don't think it was as obvious to you, seeing as you got caught up in winning."

"True."

Trish has a tough exterior and holds a lot in. But when you *do* pierce that outer armor and scratch the turtle inside, it's much easier to see why the puncture hurt so badly—and what you did to cause it.

Camilla just straight up takes the rest of my slice. "But don't fret too much, Blaine," she says, chewing through a mouthful of cheese. "The ankylosaurus just needs time."

CHAPTER 27

I get home from school knowing what I need to do. I climb the steps to the guest bedroom and, after a few taps on the door, push my way in.

A freaking tornado swept through here, apparently.

Mountains of Aunt Starr's clothes are scattered across the floor, lopsided towers of disorganized books are on the verge of collapsing, and a ball of bent hangers—so contorted they look more like barbed wire—lies atop the bed. She's only been staying with us for a matter of months, but from the story this scene tells, a stranger might guess my thirty-seven-year-old aunt is gutting her childhood bedroom for the first time.

"Hey," she says, spotting me. "How was school?"

"Eh," I say, walking in and sitting on the floor across from her. "Let's just say I survived, and leave it at that."

"There you go. Glass half-full. Can you hand me that?" She points to a teal box perched on a pile of bras behind me. I reach back to get it and glance inside to find no fewer than thirty different nail polish colors. "Thank you," she says, taking it and promptly dumping its contents into a bigger box of chaos.

"What's going on in here?" I ask, glancing around.

She pauses to take in the upheaval too. "I figure, I'm

moving out of here sooner or later, whether it's next week or in six months." She blows her bangs out of her face. "Might as well start getting organized."

I nod in agreement, nearly certain I'm responsible for this.

She's extra antsy to pack up and get out of here, all thanks to me.

"Aunt Starr, I—"

She holds up a finger. "Before you apologize *again*—because I know that's what you were about to do," she says, grinning, "you should know that the museum gave me a call."

"Really?"

"Yes. And I have an interview this week." Her grin grows into a smile. "Crisis averted."

I exhale, leaning over onto a pile of comforters. "You have no idea how scared I was that I ruined this for you. I'm so sorry—"

"Blaine." She plops a hand on the side of my face for a moment. "No. More. Apologizing. Okay?"

"Okay. Sorry—*er*, I mean . . . okay."

"We all forget things sometimes, doll. We're all human."

Aunt Starr goes back to sorting nail polish. The room gets quiet.

It's now or never. I need to be honest about what happened or I'll never forgive myself.

"Aunt Starr," I say hesitantly. "Would you kill me if I told you that, technically, I didn't forget to tell you about the job?"

She tosses a container of nail polish into the trash before

giving me a look. "You're saying you chose not to tell me about it?"

I cringe at her, unsure how she'll respond.

"Yeah," she says, pursing her lips. "I figured."

I gasp.

She lets out a laugh.

"Wait, you can see me doing something like that?" I ask, offended.

She laughs even harder. "Isn't that exactly what you're confessing to doing, though?"

Yes. Of course it is. But I want her to be *surprised* that I'm capable of doing something that selfish. *Surprised* that I can be an asshole.

"Can I guess why you didn't want me to get the job?" she asks.

I nod.

"I'd say it's because you didn't want me to move out?"

I nod again.

"Because if I move out, that means you'll have more evenings alone? And we'll see each other less? And I'll get busy, and you'll get busy, and life will get in the way? And we'll have fewer brinners, and we won't be able to veg out with snacks and watch movies every weekend?"

I feel a tear forming in my eye. "Maybe it's something like that."

"Yeah," she says. "Me too."

Fudge comes pitter-pattering into the room and, after taking a lap around the floor in front of us, crashes down into an empty space between piles of books. He rests his head on the carpet and lets out a long sigh, probably sensing that Aunt Starr's days here are numbered.

"Believe it or not, the few months I got to spend here with you were some of the best months of my life," she says.

I roll my eyes with a grin. "Okay."

"I mean it."

"You don't have to say that just to make me feel better."

"I'm not, Blaine. I've loved every minute that I got to hang out with you." She looks to a sleeping Fudge. "And you too."

I nestle my head deeper into the plush comforter. "It's not like I wanted you to be unemployed forever," I clarify. "I just, I knew that you'd be moving out after you got a job. And with Mom and Dad being gone so often . . ." I shrug. "It's been nice having you around, is all."

She swallows hard, thinking over her words. "Well." She pauses again. "First of all, I know it's frustrating when they're not around much, but try to be patient with your mom and dad, okay? For me? You're their number one priority—even if it's difficult to see sometimes." She takes a breath. "And secondly, it's been nice having you around too. *Really* nice."

I start turning red.

"Sure, I've had my dark moments since getting laid off," she continues, examining the label on an old, blackened candle. "Unemployment is no joke. I've felt like a big, broke loser more days than not." She pauses. "But you were my bright spot, Blaine."

I don't know what to say.

"And you know what?" she continues. "Now that I think about it, listening to you kids talk about your well-being thing—"

"Wellness initiative."

"Right, your wellness initiative . . ." She trails off in thought, lips folding into her mouth. "It reminded me to breathe deep. To go easy on myself. To be grateful for all the things I couldn't live without—like *you*." She ruffles my hair, before letting out a sigh. "You know what I mean?"

I absolutely do.

"I've got to start a new chapter, though," she says, picking up another candle for examination. "I can't hide away in my sister's guest room forever, living vicariously through my teenage nephew and his friends." She smiles. "As fun as it's been to feel sixteen again, I—"

I sit up and lean forward, pulling her in for a hug.

I needed one today.

I think she's caught off guard, because she doesn't react for a second. But then I feel the softness of her bathrobe reaching around my back and holding tight.

"You're going to be okay without me, Blaine," she whispers. "You're going to be *way* more than okay. You're going to shine."

"All my friends hate me, though," I say, feeling a tear leak from my eye. "Well, besides Camilla. But Danny and Trish do."

"Stop it," she scolds. "They don't hate you." We pull apart, and it's comforting to see that her eyes are watery too. "Friend-ships are kind of like . . ." She thinks on the fly. "Gardens. You've got to nurture them. A plant might wilt, but that just means you need to give it a bit more water and sunshine. Give Trish and Danny extra TLC, and things will work themselves out."

"Yeah."

If only I could dump a bucket of water onto my friends to make everything okay again.

Wait a minute.

"Oh my God," I gasp.

Aunt Starr jumps. "What?"

"I've got to go."

She tilts her head at me, confused.

I stand and dash off. "Love you!"

"Okay, but be careful, whatever it is you're doing!" she shouts as I speed down the stairs, two steps at a time. "And I love you too, doll!"

I slip on my shoes and run out the door, hating myself for not thinking of this sooner. A few minutes later I sneak up to the glass storefront of Biggest Bean and peek inside. It's pretty dead in there. Danny is nowhere in sight, but his dad is manning the register.

I slip in.

"Hey, Bao," I whisper, tiptoeing toward the counter. "Is Danny around?"

"Hi, Blaine," he says, unloading a tray of brownies before looking at me suspiciously. "Mondays are quiet, so I gave him the night off. Why are you whispering?"

"This may sound weird, but—" I glance around to be 150 percent sure Danny's not hiding nearby. "Do you have a picture of Ms. Nguyen that I can borrow?"

"A picture of Ms. Nguyen?" he asks, convinced he misheard.

"Yes."

"My wife?"

I nod.

Bao crinkles his face, skeptical. "Can I ask what for?"

I lean over the counter nervously and relay my plan, hoping it doesn't sound bonkers said aloud. "What do you think?" I ask hesitantly.

He stares at Danny's row of new succulents near the window, expressionless.

Shoot. Maybe I overstepped. Even though I've been visiting Biggest Bean for years, I wouldn't say I'm *close* with Bao. Our relationship mostly hinges on friendly hellos and mocha latte orders. Did I go too far?

He turns away from the succulents, a sparkle in his eye. "I love that idea. Let's do it."

A big smile creeps across my face. "Are you sure?"

"Absolutely."

Bao disappears into the kitchen, leaving me tingling from head to toe. He re-emerges a moment later and hands me a photo of his wife.

Ms. Nguyen, probably about thirty years old in the pic, is bursting with life. Her mouth, slightly ajar, is captured in the middle of a hearty laugh. There must have been a breeze, too, as a portion of her long, black hair is floating behind her; she's using her right hand to steady the bowler hat atop her head.

I see the same kindness in her eyes that I see in Danny's.

"She was beautiful," I say, smiling at the photo.

"She sure was," Bao recalls. "It's my favorite photo of her. I keep it above my desk."

The image frames Ms. Nguyen's torso as she sits on what I imagine are porch steps, but the blurry background is much less important. Her face is crisp and clear, with every subtle line and curve of her skin radiating joy.

"Will it work?" Bao asks.

My brain is firing on all cylinders, imagining the potential. "Is it cool if I make a copy of this? It's so much easier to have a physical photo to reference."

"Yes, of course. When can you get started?"

I think. "How about . . . now?"

He rubs his palms together, excited. "Fantastic."

I stare at the brownies for a second, trying to gather my thoughts. "Do you think it's possible for you to get Danny to drop by in a couple of hours? That way I can show him what I'm thinking in person."

Bao nods.

"Cool," I say, a surge of inspiration twirling inside me—a splash of fervor I haven't felt since working at Susan's Stationery weeks ago. "I'll be right back."

I race to the office supply store down the block to make a copy of the photo, then sprint home as fast as I can. Aunt

Starr, taking a break from her organizing with a jar of peanut butter, screeches in surprise as I tear through the house and head to Dad's shed in the backyard. I fling open the doors, and the smell hits me hard—the smell I didn't realize I was missing until this moment: sawdust, pine, and the subtle scent of moss.

The smell that means a new mural project is underway.

I want to pick up each individual gallon of paint sitting against the wall and give it a hug. "I've missed you guys," I say to them, fully aware that I'm greeting inanimate acrylics.

I glance around at all my supplies—buckets, brushes, paint rollers, crates, drop cloths, and so much more—wondering why in the world I convinced myself that becoming Joey's version of a Serious Guy trumped the pure bliss of this.

Then I pick out the items I need for today—tape, sketch pad and pencils, tape measure, ruler, and small stepladder—and haul them through the house.

"What on earth is going on?" Aunt Starr asks, a spoon of peanut butter in her hand, as Fudge barks for a lick at her feet.

"I have a mural idea for Biggest Bean."

Her eyes pop wide open. "Hell. *Yes.*"

I drop everything into my cart in the front yard and trek back to the coffee shop, where I park my stuff on the side of the building and look up at the expansive brick wall in front of me.

First things first: I figure out what proportions I want

the mural to be, as well as its exact placement on the wall. Because Ms. Nguyen's photo is vertical, I decide that the total design should be eight feet tall by six feet wide. Working with a photograph actually makes my job much easier at this stage, as I easily trace Ms. Nguyen's outline onto a separate sheet of paper.

Then I lightly mark up the drawing with an eight-by-six-inch grid—the dimensions of which I'll replicate on the wall. Since each inch on my tracing equals one foot of mural, I can keep things perfectly proportioned as I translate the image from paper to brick. Using my stepladder, I tape off the outline where the mural will go, to give me a better idea if its size works well with the space. I think it does.

I take a step back to visualize the soon-to-be mural in its entirety—and panic a bit.

I'm assuming Danny will appreciate this. But what if he doesn't? What if the mural backfires? I'd been under the impression that Joey liked my work the entire time we were together, until he confirmed at Grey Kettle, in *no* uncertain terms, that he'd never been a fan of my unserious side hustle.

Danny dubbed me the "mural kid," after all. Will he think my work is a big joke?

"How about a treat, Blaine?" It's Bao, walking toward me with a snickerdoodle cookie and cup of ice water. "On the house."

"I will never say no to that," I say, taking it and nearly swallowing it all in one delicious bite.

"Danny just arrived in the kitchen," he says.

"Oh."

"Should I send him out?"

"Yeah." I gulp down my nerves.

He smiles, disappearing back into the café.

A minute later I hear the jingle of Biggest Bean's front door, and Danny turns the corner into view. He's in a gray hoodie, basketball shorts, and bright white sneakers. Overwhelmingly cute. As always.

"Uh . . ." He glances at me and the stepladder, completely disoriented. "My dad said you wanted to show me something?"

I step closer toward him. "Yeah." I point up at the wall, where the tape is outlining the rectangle where the mural would be. "If you're okay with it, I'd love to paint a photo of your mom." I hold up the image that Bao gave me. "This one."

He looks between the photo and the wall, but doesn't say anything.

"I'd leave out the background in the pic, though, because it's kind of boring and out of focus anyway," I say, examining the photo in my hand. "But I was thinking, maybe, I could fill in the space behind her with a bright floral design instead."

Still not a word.

So I keep talking. "It'd be her, laughing in the foreground, and then all of these colorful flowers and plants sprouting up around her. You can help me pick out which ones, if you'd like."

His eyes are darting around the expanse of bricks in front of us while his silence continues to kill me.

"You told me you two gardened together, so I thought . . . I don't know, I thought that would be a cool way to remember her?" I carry on. "And your dad said there's enough room against this wall under the mural for you to try growing your own garden too—only if you want to, of course."

He opens his mouth like he's going to say something.

But then shuts it again.

"And I, uh . . ." I attempt to fill the void, because apparently he's not going to. "I'm really sorry about Friday, Danny. I was in a terrible mood because of the election, and I took it out on you and Trish, and I shouldn't have. I know how much you cared about the campaign, and I was such a—"

"Look, Blaine," he interjects, dropping his chin to his chest. "I think I've been sending you the wrong message."

I tense up.

He takes a step closer. "I got caught up in the whirlwind of the campaign, and my emotions got the best of me. I think I implied that I wanted us to be more than . . ."

"Friends?"

"Well, yeah."

My heart sinks. "Okay."

"Does that make sense?"

It doesn't. Not at all. Not one bit.

Zilch.

"Yeah," I say. "I guess."

"I came out just last year," he says. "I've never dated a guy before. It's all just—it's a lot of confusing thoughts, having to walk that fine line between friends and more than friends. You know?"

I gulp. "Sure."

He stuffs his hands into his pockets awkwardly, glancing around the empty lot. "I need some time and space, is all. I'm sorry."

I laugh to brush off the discomfort. "Don't stress it. This mural was my way of saying sorry about Friday. That's all. You have nothing to apologize to me for."

"Are you sure?"

I brighten my eyes and nod, hopefully at least a little bit convincingly. "Of course."

He remains still, and so do I.

"So . . ." He kicks at the grass under his sneakers before pointing behind him. "I'm going to go inside." He starts backing away toward the door to Biggest Bean as the awkward silence crushes my soul. "You don't need my permission to do the mural."

I grin uncomfortably. "I know I don't need your *permission*."

"My dad likes the idea," he says, nearing the corner of the building. "So feel free to go for it."

"Okay . . . ?"

"I'll see you at school, Blaine."

And he's gone. I lean against the bricks, completely deflated. My worst-case scenario came true. Danny, just like Joey, doesn't want anything to do with my murals. He doesn't want anything to do with me. I wanted to do this project

ROBBIE COUCH

because I thought it would mean something special to the Nguyens. I thought it'd mean something special to Danny.

Oh how horribly I miscalculated the entire plan.

I stand back up and am walking over to collect my things for the night, when a car screeches to a halt in front of the café, shattering the neighborhood's silence.

I jump and turn to see Trish emerge from the passenger-side door. "There you are," she sighs, her eyes finding mine. From the look on her face, I can tell something has gone wrong. "Why haven't you texted me back? We've been looking for you."

We?

I glance down at my phone and see missed notifications. "Sorry," I say. "I've been a bit distracted. Is everything all right?" Then I realize why that car looks familiar: it's Zach's. He pops up on the driver's side.

Now I know that something has gone *very* wrong.

CHAPTER 28

What's going on?" I ask, sweat forming on my palms.

"Can you come with us?" Trish says, a dire tone in her voice.

Come with *us?*

Why does it sound like those two are on a team?

I look at my items scattered across the ground near the wall of Biggest Bean. The fact that Trish isn't excitedly asking me about what's clearly evidence of my mural planning—that's further proof that something's gone badly awry. "I have my stuff with me, though—"

"Can you leave it here?" Zach asks. He looks just as stone-faced as Trish. "This is important."

I gape at him—at his audacity to be so demanding. What do I owe Zach Freaking Chesterton? Certainly not my patience.

"*No,*" I snap back. "I can't leave all my stuff just sitting out here, waiting to be stolen."

"Blaine, please," Trish says with the smallest hint of desperation. "We've got to hurry. Can we get it later?"

I hesitate.

Although I hate bending the knee to Zach, I also know how badly I've hurt Trish. I don't want to give her another reason to hate me right now.

I step closer toward the car, Bao's snickerdoodle cookie doing somersaults in my middle. "Can someone tell me what's going on first?"

"We're meeting Mr. Wells at school." Trish pauses, eyes widening, before lowering her voice. "And we're going to talk about *election results.*"

"Election results?" I repeat, looking at Zach.

His eyes move away from mine—as if he's ashamed.

"Yes, Blaine," Trish emphasizes slowly. "Election. *Results.* Now will you get in?"

I do. Zach floors it, and we take off toward WWHS.

Neither of them are saying a word. Trish still seems angry with me.

"So, about these results," I press, glancing between Zach's eyes in the rearview mirror and the side of Trish's face in the front.

"Remember when I told you my theory about the ballots?" Trish says, eyes still straight ahead.

"Yeah?"

"Well, turns out I knew what I was talking about."

"Huh?"

"Won't it be easier just to show him?" Zach suggests. His eyes dart up to the rearview mirror, meeting mine. "Before we get to the school, I want to say that I'm sorry about what happened at the debate, Blaine."

I'm so confused.

So, *so* confused.

"The debate?" is all that comes falling out of my mouth.

Zach's attention moves between the road and me in the mirror. "How I used your debate prep notes?"

"Oh."

"Yeah. Honestly, I didn't want to after we found them in Mr. Wells's classroom, but Ashtyn and Joey overruled me. I should have pushed back harder."

I look to Trish, who's holding in a million things to say, I'm sure. But she keeps her attention on the moving brownstone porches outside the window.

Am I being pranked right now?

Zach parallel parks outside Wicker West. It's now late enough into the evening that hardly any students are around.

Except there's Joey and Ashtyn. Waiting outside the main entrance together. If someone doesn't tell me what's going on—and *soon*—my head is going to explode.

Joey squints over at our car, perplexed.

Zach takes a deep breath and steps outside. Trish finally acknowledges my existence again, glancing backward and giving me a foreboding look—the one that I've grown to learn translates roughly to *You'd better hold on for dear life*—before following after him. I think I might be sick.

"Babe?" Joey says slowly to Zach, eyebrows furrowed, as the three of us approach him and Ashtyn. "We got your text to meet us here. Is everything okay—"

"Mr. Wells is expecting us," Zach says, cutting him off and breezing his way through the doors without a pause. "Let's go."

Joey and Ashtyn both glare at me, clearly just as confused

as I am about what this is all about. Zach and Trish beeline for the main office as the rest of us follow.

This afternoon has been one big, messy emotional whiplash. In a matter of hours I've gone from crying into Aunt Starr's shoulder, to buzzing with excitement alongside Bao over the mural, to discovering that Danny wants absolutely nothing to do with me, to *this*?

Zach leads us into the office, where the secretary scowls silently. We head down a narrow hallway toward the school's security room—an area I've never been in before—which is *not* helping with the all-consuming dread that's been building inside me.

"The security room?" I whisper at Trish.

Her expression suggests I haven't seen anything yet.

"Shut the door behind you, Ashtyn," Mr. Wells orders as we enter, sounding absolutely, positively, 100 percent pissed off. The irate look in his eyes—magnified through the bifocals—sends chills down my spine. I've never seen him like this. "Have a seat, everyone."

Principal Spice, a six-foot-five giant of a human who always looks confused, is leaning against the wall next to Mr. Wells, confirming my worst suspicions. Whatever went awry with the election results, his presence means it's now officially above Mr. Wells's pay grade.

All my insides are in knots.

There's one long, empty table surrounded by chairs in the middle of the gray room, which has no windows, posters, or anything on the walls inviting you to feel anything other than utter terror. Mr. Wells is standing in front of a row of TV screens that depict security footage throughout the school's hallways.

"Zach, would you like to speak first?" Principal Spice asks, once we're all seated in front of him and Mr. Wells.

"I'll let Trish," Zach answers. "She deserves the credit. We should hear it from her."

I swallow hard.

Did I do something awful without realizing it? Did I break a campaign rule, fill out my ballot wrong, or somehow accidentally cheat? I begin racking my brain, going line by line through the election packet, trying to remember each stipulation and what I could have done to inadvertently break it.

Trish clears her throat gently and turns to face the four of us sitting around the table. "I had a suspicion on Friday that the ballots weren't accurate," she says. "Blaine can back me up on that."

I nod in support.

"As I told him, it seemed odd that Zach won the last batch of votes we counted at the bottom of our bag," she continues. "Ashtyn and I had gone to the Creative Arts wing *first* to collect ballots, which means we would have counted those ballots last. And I knew, based on my own anecdotal research—and honestly, just using, like, common sense—that those voters were supporting Blaine by a big margin." She looks to Zach, as if to hand him the baton.

"So," Zach begins, turning red. He's staring at the table,

looking so angry, I fear he might flip it over at any second. "Trish came to me this morning to ask what I thought about her suspicion. At first I thought she was just being a sore loser, hell-bent on overturning the results." He pauses. "But then I started thinking."

Zach stands, folds his arms across his chest, and starts pacing the floor between Principal Spice and Mr. Wells like an anxious dog.

The tension building around us is downright suffocating.

I think I'm going to break a rib, my heart is pounding so hard.

"One benefit of being in student council as long as I've been—and running in as many races as I have—is that I've developed a keen awareness of political momentum. After Blaine's speech, I had a feeling he'd get on the ballot and become a real threat." He stops walking, shaking his head. "No, I knew he was *already* a real threat. And honestly? After his closing argument at the debate, I believed *I* was the real underdog. That's why a fifty-six to forty-four percent win, although hardly a landslide, didn't feel right." He looks up at Joey and Ashtyn, pure rage emanating from him. "So, after giving Trish's idea some thought, I used my access as an office aide and asked Principal Spice if I could check the security camera footage from first period on Friday, when the ballots were being cast and collected."

I glance over at Joey and Ashtyn—who are both *whiter than ghosts.*

Oh my God. What the heck did they do?

"Can we roll the tape, Principal Spice?" Zach says, nodding at him.

Principal Spice takes a long, loud sip out of his coffee mug before leaning over and hitting play on the laptop that controls the security footage.

The hallway is completely empty, except for the occasional student walking by or briefly stopping at their locker. But nothing out of the ordinary. I glance around the room; every eye is glued to the screen as if we're watching the part in a horror film when an especially grotesque plot point is imminent.

"These classes are in the Sciences wing," Principal Spice notes, "which, I learned from Trish, were the very last classes to have their ballots collected from you two."

Trish inhales sharply and holds her breath.

So I know it's coming.

In the far corner of the screen, Trish appears next to Ashtyn, who's carrying the bag used to collect ballots. They walk down the hallway, approaching a drinking fountain. It's the kind that's built into the wall, creating a small, hidden space beneath the fountain that's out of view. Ashtyn stops abruptly to bend down and take a sip. As Trish briefly looks away, waiting for Ashtyn to finish, there's a blur beneath the fountain that disappears as quickly as it popped onto the screen.

My entire body freezes up.

"And there it is," Trish says. Principal Spice rewinds the footage to that precise moment. With the screen paused, it's much easier to see what happened.

There's an identical bag in *each* of Ashtyn's hands.

She's dropping one off and taking the other.

"Holy—" I stop myself. "Crap."

Joey buries his face in his hands.

Ashtyn is staring at the footage, not blinking, seemingly in a state of shock.

"Oh, but wait," Zach says. "There's more."

Principal Spice hits play again. Ashtyn leaves the bag—presumably the one with the *real* ballots in them—under the fountain, and walks off carrying the other alongside Trish.

Principal Spice hits fast-forward for a moment.

Joey appears on-screen.

My heart sinks into my toes.

With no one else in the hallway, Joey approaches the fountain and takes a sip, reaching under to grab the bag with the legitimate ballots inside. He walks to the nearest garbage can, *trashes the bag*, and nonchalantly strolls off, as if he didn't just rig an election.

"You've *got* to be kidding me," I mutter, jaw fully on the ground.

Trish bends toward me. "I told you," she says.

"It's not what it looks like," Joey argues, rising from his seat. "I swear."

"Don't even bother," Zach says, visibly shaking. "It's all on camera, Joey."

"But . . ." Joey looks between the security footage and Zach. A dark red rash—the one I know he gets when he's nervous—is spreading across his neck. "I can explain."

"Okay, Mr. Oliver," Principal Spice says, nodding at him. "Go ahead, then. Explain. Because this certainly looks like Ashtyn switched out the real ballots for forged ones, and you were her accomplice."

"Or, more likely, she was his," Trish adds.

Desperate to defend himself, Joey starts opening and closing his mouth like he's a suffocating salmon. "How would we have gotten forged ballots, though?"

"Simple," Trish interjects. "We saw the printed ballots near Mr. Wells's desk during debate prep."

"He could have stolen them during one of their prep sessions," I say softly to myself in a state of shock—but the whole room hears me. "It'd be easy to make more copies on orange paper and replace the ones he'd stolen."

"And to think I was trying to avoid having a stressful election week by printing all the ballots ahead of time," Mr. Wells grumbles to Principal Spice, shaking his head. "Never doing that again."

Joey is redder than a ripe tomato. "Why would I do this? Why would I care enough to interfere with the class election *below* me?" He lets out a forced, sharp laugh—as if it's ludicrous to suggest such a thing.

"You didn't do it to help me win, that's for sure," Zach says, irate. "It was about you. It's *always* about you, Joey."

"Me?" He looks around at the rest of us desperately—as if Trish and I, of all people, would be giving him backup in this situation. "How is this about *me*?"

"You couldn't live with your ex-boyfriend beating your

current boyfriend and becoming your successor, could you?"
Zach snaps. "That would be beyond embarrassing for *Joey
Oliver, senior class president*," he mocks. "So instead of just letting the election play out, you convinced me to replace Eve
with Ashtyn as my campaign captain because you sensed that
Blaine could be a real threat. That way, the two of you could
pull this whole scheme off."

"No," he says. "That's not—"

"Joey," Ashtyn interrupts, the blood completely drained
from her face. "It's over."

"But I—"

"Just stop!" she shouts, finally peeling her eyes away from
the security footage to look up at him. "It's on camera. We
got caught. Please . . . ," she begs him. "Just shut the hell up
before you get us into even more trouble."

The room grows quiet, but the absurdity of this moment
is buzzing loudly between my ears.

Joey and Ashtyn cheated. They forged *hundreds* of fake
votes to ensure a Zach victory. All because of Joey's ego?
All because Joey couldn't stand the fact that he could be
replaced *by me?*

"Needless to say, I'm incredibly disappointed in you
two," Principal Spice says to Joey and Ashtyn, sounding like
a heartbroken parent. "Your actions are unbecoming to any
Wicker West student, let alone leaders in the student council.
I'd like to discuss disciplinary steps in my office and contact
your parents." He takes another long slurp from his mug
while gesturing toward the doorway. Joey and Ashtyn, com-

pletely demoralized, leave the room. "I'll let you take it from here, Warren," Principal Spice says to Mr. Wells.

Once they're gone, Mr. Wells lets out the longest, most exasperated sigh I've ever heard escape a human mouth. He strokes his beard in thought for a few moments. "Trish," he says softly, staring at the aged, orange carpet. "Will you wait outside? I need to speak with the candidates."

Trish stands and, on her way out, squeezes my arm lightly to show she still has my back. I let out a mental sigh of relief.

That felt nice.

"So," Mr. Wells says after the door closes and it's just the three of us. "How are we feeling, guys?"

Zach takes a seat again, arms still folded tightly across his chest. "Angry."

Mr. Wells nods. "Fair."

"Sad," Zach adds.

"Valid."

"Hurt," Zach continues.

"I get that," Mr. Wells says.

"Embarrassed." Zach turns to me, looking more miserable than I've ever seen him before. "I'm so sorry, Blaine."

I don't know what to say.

"They planned all of that behind my back," he continues. "I'm competitive, but I never would have cheated to win. You believe me, right?"

I nod.

I know he's telling the truth now for the same reason I tried warning him about Ashtyn at Biggest Bean; Zach, although at times insufferable, is someone who respects the rules.

Ashtyn does not.

And I now know that, clearly, neither does Joey.

"I should have listened to you about Ashtyn," Zach says. He turns away, lowering his voice. "I never should have started dating Joey to begin with," he mutters.

"Here's the deal," Mr. Wells says. "As you probably could have guessed, we do not know who won the election fair and square. It's unfortunate, but those are the cards we've been dealt at this time."

"Can we see if the ballots are still in that Sciences wing garbage can?" I ask.

"We looked," Zach says. "A custodian already dumped it."

"And even if they *were* still there, picking through trashed ballots is no way to declare a reliable race. So here's what I propose." Mr. Wells twiddles his thumbs in thought. "We announce to the council and broader student body that there has been an unfortunate mishap with the ballots, and we need to do a redo election for the senior class president race. How does that sound?"

Mr. Wells looks at Zach.

Zach, staring at the table, completely deflated, shrugs. "Sure. I guess I'm fine with that."

Then Mr. Wells looks at me. "What about you, Blaine?"

What *do* I want?

It's difficult to know how I'm feeling about anything right now. It's like I've been flailing on an emotional roller coaster all day that's just screeched to a halt, and now the amusement park worker is asking if I want to ride again.

But I don't. I don't want to ride again, I realize.

I want off.

I want off this ride right fucking now.

"No," I say flatly.

"No?" Mr. Wells asks, confused.

Zach peeks up at me curiously.

"No," I repeat, more confidently now. "I don't want a redo race. I don't want to be senior class president."

laine." Mr. Wells, exhausted, forces a smile. "I know it's been a long campaign, and it's understandable that you'd be overwhelmed learning all of this."

"No, that's not it," I say, defiant. "I'm telling you, Mr. Wells. I don't want to be class president."

"Why not?" Zach asks, perplexed. "You may have earned more votes than I did. You could have already beat me."

"I don't care," I say. "I don't—wait a minute."

I think about Trish, Danny, and Camilla. How much time they invested in my campaign. How much they cared about the wellness initiative. How much they believed in me. If I drop out of the race now, I'm dropping out on them.

"Can I meet with my campaign captain real quick?" I ask.

"Of course," Mr. Wells says.

I leave the freaky security footage room; head back down the narrow, winding hallway; and spot Trish waiting in the main office. Joey and Ashtyn are nowhere to be found, but there's nothing I could care less about right now than where they slithered off to.

Trish is waiting with bated breath, anxious to hear updates.

"Can we talk?" I ask.

She glances around awkwardly. "Right here?"

"Oh." I realize the secretary is still sitting there, scowling at us. "Hi, Ms. Hamilton."

"The supply closet is open, if you two want some privacy," she says, reluctantly helpful.

"We spent way too many years in a closet and don't want to go back in now," I say, trying to crack a joke.

Neither Ms. Hamilton nor Trish are in the mood for it.

I clear my throat. "The supply closet will work great, thanks."

I lead the way in and close the door behind us. It's suffocatingly cramped in here, with a surplus of blank poster board, gargantuan boxes of markers, and massive rolls of colored paper pushing me and Trish absurdly close. I make a mental note for the next time I'm running low on supplies in art class.

"I do *not* like this," Trish says, our noses nearly touching.

"Trish—" I sigh, accidentally right into her face.

"Oof," she says, cringing at the smell of my breath. "Did you have something with cinnamon?"

"Bao gave me a snickerdoodle cookie, but listen." I sigh again, this time slightly to my right. "First, I'm sorry. You were absolutely, totally, one hundred million percent right about the ballots and I should have listened to you."

"You mean to tell me I actually *knew* what I was *talking* about?"

I let her have this one. "Yes."

She nods. "Great. And?"

"And . . . I decided I don't want to be senior class president."

"What?"

"Mr. Wells proposed doing a redo election. But I don't want to be on the ballot."

She squints, struggling to comprehend the bomb I just dropped.

My guilt kicks in. "But here's the thing! I know how much work you've put into our wellness initiative, so I'm committed to running, if you want me to. I'll still be on the redo ballot, for you, and Camilla, and Danny. And if I win, you three can be the ones steering the ship of my presidency—but, like, from behind the scenes."

"So you want us putting in all the work you'll get credit for publicly?" Her left eyebrow arches upward.

I bite my lower lip. "Well, when you put it like that . . ."

"What are you even talking about?" Her face twists in confusion. "What's with this last-minute change of heart?"

I pause, trying to turn my epiphany into a coherent thought. "Something clicked when Mr. Wells asked if I agreed to a redo race. I *don't* want to be in the redo race. That sounds absolutely awful. Like, I'd rather relive my date at Grey Kettle ten more times than have to be on the ballot again." I pause to take a breath. "The past few days I've been asking myself why I wanted to run. Because if it's no longer about proving I can be a Serious Guy to Joey, then what is it? Why do I want to be senior class president? I don't have a good answer."

Trish stares. She opens her mouth, about to say something, but closes it again.

"I miss painting, Trish," I say, laughing a little because it feels good to acknowledge it out loud. "I miss it *so much.* I want to get back to my murals. And if I'm president, I won't have the time to do that."

I can tell that her thoughts are moving a mile a minute.

"It's okay," I say. "You can scream at me. Slap me, if you want. I deserve it."

"Tough call, but I'll pass." Her eyes narrow on mine. "I have an idea."

I wait for her to tell me what it is.

She doesn't.

"Okay . . . ? And?"

She stands up taller and grins. "I want to be on the ballot."

Now I'm the one squinting at her, confused. "You want to be on the ballot." I repeat her words to make sure I heard correctly.

"Yes."

"For senior class president."

"Correct."

I grin back. "Are you stoned right now?"

"I wish."

I tilt my head at her, completely lost.

"Don't you remember?" she asks. "The first day you had your 'Let's Talk' poster up in the cafeteria, you asked me to be your campaign captain, and I read through the election packet. *That* was one of the rules. Campaign captains can step in if a candidate decides to drop out. And it sounds a helluva lot like you want to drop out."

I think. "That rule's really in the election packet?"

My mind jumps back to that lunch period.

I remember being overwhelmed by what I'd just signed up for, questioning if I'd made the right decision, scared that Ashtyn was right to laugh at my candidacy earlier that morning. Then Trish and Camilla stopped by, and I handed them the packet—

Wait! *A campaign captain may take a candidate's spot, should the candidate forfeit their right to lead after they've qualified for the ballot.*

Trish is right.

Technically she could step in for me.

"Are you sure you want to do this?" I ask.

"Yes," she says quickly.

"Like, absolutely, positively sure?"

"Blaine." She leans forward so her forehead is gently touching mine. "I know I can win this thing."

We take a moment to laugh out our nervous energy before emerging from the closet, quiet and composed. Ms. Hamilton looks us up and down, still suspicious that we're up to no good, as we head back to Mr. Wells and Zach, nearly jogging.

"I'm out of the race," I announce loudly, marching into the room with Trish at my side. "She's taking my spot."

Trish waves at them. "Hello."

Mr. Wells's bifocal eyes expand in surprise. "What do you mean?"

"The rules in the election packet say that a campaign

captain can replace their candidate, should that candidate drop out of the race after qualifying for the ballot," Trish says. "That's us. That's our situation." She looks at me. "Blaine wants out, and I want in."

Mr. Wells is in complete shock.

"That *is* one of the election rules, Mr. Wells," Zach adds. "Our campaign guidelines allow for it."

"But . . ." The wheels aren't so much turning in Mr. Wells's head as they are breaking off the vehicle and spinning off the road. "You didn't give a speech to the council, Trish. You didn't debate Zach. I don't know if this could be a fair way to do it."

"Why have that stipulation in the rules, then?" Trish asks.

Mr. Wells ponders. "I'm not sure. The council added it many years ago, in case an emergency put us in a last-minute bind."

"And you wouldn't call *this*"—I gesture at the security cam footage, still paused on Joey's back walking down the hallway—"a last-minute emergency?"

Everyone sits quietly, contemplating what this curveball would mean for the race.

I understand Mr. Wells's perspective. You can't force the student council to listen to another speech at this point, and you certainly can't organize another school-wide assembly for an additional debate. It wouldn't be fair to make Zach go through all of that again either. At the same time, is it really okay to place Trish on the ticket without giving her the chance to sell her candidacy to the junior class?

"I have an idea," Zach says, rising from his chair and approaching us. "I'll give Trish access to our official class of 2023 Instagram page so she can give a virtual speech. Or do a Q and A. Whatever you want. That way you can present your argument as to why you'd make a better president than me." For the first time this afternoon, Zach's surly face shifts into a smile.

Trish and I glance at one another.

"Deal," Trish says, confidently reaching out for a shake.

Zach takes her hand in his.

The three of us turn to Mr. Wells.

"Well, then," he says, shrugging in defeat. "It looks like we have a race. And I need a vacation."

CHAPTER 30

Aunt Starr gasps from behind the wheel. "And there's a *reading nook*," she blasts into her phone, her 2003 Volvo bouncing through an intersection. "It has a freaking *reading nook*, Beth."

I grin, gazing out the passenger-side window, watching the storefronts fly by. Aunt Starr has called three friends since we left the empty apartment she's interested in renting, and each one has gotten a euphoric earful about this so-called reading nook.

Her excitement is justified, I will admit. The one-bedroom we just saw in Edgewater is a steal for the neighborhood. Plus, there's great views of Lake Michigan, updated kitchen appliances, and a teal claw-foot tub that has her name written all over it. Oh, and the reading nook. Who could say no to all that?

"Well, I haven't gotten the official offer *yet*," she explains to Beth. "But my soon-to-be boss insinuated that the job is mine, if I want it."

It's not surprising in the least that someone as personable as Aunt Starr could charm the pants off her new boss in one interview. The scheduled twenty-minute chat turned into an hour-long conversation, she told me, as they discovered they have a mutual friend, the same favorite dive bar in Ukrainian Village, and a shared disdain for Navy Pier.

So, no, it may not be official yet—but it might as well be. Aunt Starr got the job.

Which is wonderful.

But I won't lie: it's still not fun watching her get this excited about moving out of my parents' town house. I get it, because *I* wouldn't want to be living with those two when I'm in my thirties. Who can blame her?

After our talk on Monday, though, I'm feeling better about her departure. We've promised to do brinners at least once a month, check in with weekly FaceTime dates, and organize as many picnics for the Millennium Park Summer Film Series as we can in June and July. (It gets too muggy in August.) I may not see her every day, but we'll still be closer than ever. She promised.

I realize we're taking a strange route.

"You were supposed to make a left back there," I whisper at her, as to not rudely interrupt Beth, who's explaining in great detail the side effects she experiences after consuming dairy.

"Beth," she tries to interject. "Yeah, *oof* . . . yeah, I know . . . same. Ice cream is rarely a good idea for me too. But listen, I'm with Blaine and I've got to run. Can I call you back tonight?" When Beth answers back in the affirmative, Aunt Starr says, "Okay, love, bye."

She slowly veers out of our lane and into a parking space on the side of the road. "I know we're going out of the way," she confirms, coming to a complete stop in front of a row of businesses before putting the gear into park. "But I thought you should see this."

Aunt Starr points out my window.

I turn to see the storefront of Susan's Stationery—along with my half-finished mural.

I feel like I'm going to be sick.

"Oh no," I groan, looking away painfully. "I know I need to finish it."

"*Do* you, though?" Aunt Starr prods.

"Yes."

"Because it looks like you really left Ms. Ritewood hanging."

I groan louder, peeking back out the window. My guilt is staring right back.

Saturn's bubble-gum-pink surface. Its teal rings. The cobalt universe in the background. It truly is one of my favorite murals. Well, *was* one of my favorites—before my brain associated it with the Worst Day Ever at Grey Kettle and the guilt I now carry for quitting the job when it was barely half-done. Thank God Susan's Stationery is closed for the day; I'd be urging Aunt Starr to floor it if there were a chance Ms. Ritewood might spot me out here ashamedly staring at my abandoned mess.

"How does it feel seeing it?" Aunt Starr asks softly.

"Not too great," I say, opening up my Gmail app. "Ms. Ritewood emailed me on Saturday and I haven't read her message yet."

I scroll down until I spot the subject line: *I have an update about my mural, Blaine!*

I cringe, tapping it open.

> Hi, Blaine! I know you're a busy guy, but I wanted to follow up about your mural. Do you know when you'll be able to finish? We have a stingy neighborhood business association, and I was told by the athletics store owner down the block that an incomplete mural may fall into an eyesore category after a certain amount of time, which could result in a fine. We don't want that! So please drop by and finish up the job when you can, Blaine. (Is money a factor? If so, I will happily pay more. I know how talented and deserving you are!) I hope you're doing well, Blaine.

I groan again. Much louder.

"What did she say?" Aunt Starr asks, bending toward my phone to read.

"My unfinished work may cost Ms. Ritewood an eyesore fine from the stupid idiots that run her neighborhood business association," I say, gulping down a spoonful of regret. I stare out my window at Saturn. "This . . . is not good."

"You've got to let her know you'll finish, Blaine."

"Yeah."

"I mean it."

"Yeah."

"Hey." She demands my attention.

So I give it to her.

"Remember," she says, sternly but softly, in a way only Aunt Starr can pull off. "You, Blaine Bowers, are no quitter. Okay?"

I nod with an exhale.

Aunt Starr grins. "All right. Let's go."

She shifts the car into forward drive and pulls back onto the street.

I may feel like drowning in shame, but I can't let it derail my night. I'll email Ms. Ritewood back first thing when I get home later, but right now my friends take priority.

We pull up outside a town house. Trish and Camilla are already waiting on the sidewalk in front of the gate.

"Hey, Aunt Starr," Trish says, bending down and waving through the passenger-side window.

"Hi, love," Aunt Starr replies, waving back. "Good luck tonight! Blaine filled me in on what's going on. You're going to be amazing. I'll tune in!"

I step out of the car, thank Aunt Starr for the ride, and head up to the front door with Trish and Camilla.

"I cannot believe this is happening," Camilla whispers, on the verge of laughing, as we climb the steps.

From the outside it seems a lot like my town house—except much bigger, far fancier, and on a significantly more expensive block. "Are we ready?" I ask, trying to push the guilt I felt in the car onto the back burner.

Trish gives me a thumbs-up.

I knock three times on the large, oak door.

"You texted Danny about tonight, right?" Trish asks me.

I nod.

"He's not coming?" Camilla says.

I shake my head, trying not to look completely devastated. "He didn't text back."

Trish frowns at me. "He'll come around."

I don't know if that's true, but I'm not here to fret over that right now.

I'm here to help Trish win this election.

I hear footsteps approaching before Zach's face appears in the translucent, stained-glass window. He swings open the door. "Hey," he says. "Come on in."

CHAPTER 31

It's weird seeing Zach in a casual outfit. All he has on is a simple, sleeveless T-shirt, sweat shorts, and thick ankle socks. It's a Saturday night and he has no one to impress, apparently. I wish I could get to know *this* Zach more than the one pretentiously parading around school in designer sweater vests.

The Chestertons' house is sleek and intimidating. A white marble fireplace is the first thing that catches my eye in the living room to my right. The second is a towering, ornate grandfather clock clicking nearby. And the third is a very round orange cat purring at my feet.

"That's Harvey," Zach explains.

"Harvey is adorable," Trish says.

The cat slides back to Zach, who lifts him off the hardwood floor with a grunt and holds him against his chest.

"Well, hello there!" Mr. Chesterton booms, appearing behind Zach in a blue cardigan and polo shirt.

A bubbly Mrs. Chesterton also emerges, wearing a yellow sundress and ruby-red lipstick. "You must be Blaine!" she says, pointing to me. "And Trish? And Camilla?"

Trish and Camilla nod, smiling.

"Welcome, welcome!" she says, ushering us to step farther into the house. "We've heard so much about you."

Zach's parents eagerly shake all of our hands. I catch Zach's gaze in all of the hoopla; he grins and subtly rolls his eyes, embarrassed.

"Are you kids hungry?" Mr. Chesterton asks, pointing behind him, presumably toward the kitchen. "We just grabbed the steaks off the grill and there's plenty."

"Thank you, that sounds delicious," Camilla says. "We're in a little bit of a time crunch, though."

"We need to go live in . . ." Trish glances at her phone. "About ten minutes. But thanks for offering."

"That's right!" Mrs. Chesterton exclaims, backing away and taking her husband with her. "Let's let them get to work, Gary. Good luck! Oh, do you mind leaving your shoes here, though?"

"Of course not," I say, slipping my sneakers off.

Zach waits until they're out of earshot to apologize to us. "Sorry."

"For what?" Trish says. "They're so nice."

He shakes his head. "They can be a bit much sometimes. C'mon, let's go."

I assumed Mr. and Mrs. Chesterton would be similar in nature to the Olivers, seeing as Joey and Zach are cut from similar cloths when it comes to their cold, hard ambition. But the Chestertons are hardly the pretentious snobs I expected; they seem pretty much delightful. I guess not every Serious Guy comes from Seriously Awful Parents.

We follow Zach up a wooden staircase on our left to a long hallway on the second floor. He leads us past an array of framed family photos on the wall to the farthest door, where his cavernous, freakishly clean bedroom awaits.

"Dang," Camilla breathes, glancing around. "You could safely perform open-heart surgery in here."

"Yeah," Zach says, grabbing the back of his neck, clearly a bit uncomfortable having his perfectionism on display. "I like to keep it tidy."

The dozen pillows on his four-poster bed are laid out symmetrically. The books on the shelf to my right are organized by spine color—*and* cover size. There are posters of the K-pop groups he likes, spaced out equally on every wall, and the rug I'm standing on appears freshly vacuumed. (I'm getting the sense it's *always* freshly vacuumed.)

"You could say I'm a little type A," he admits, noticing how shocked we are by the cleanliness surrounding us. "Anyway." He walks over to his desk and flips on a ring light that's hovering above his laptop screen. The area gets blanketed in a warm, yellow glow. "Does this setup work okay?"

"Wow," Trish says, impressed. "You must take your FaceTime sessions very seriously."

Zach's sprawling desk is absolutely covered in the responsibilities of his full life. Everything has been intentionally (if not obsessively) placed. Binders are labeled and stacked in alphabetical order. Sticky notes are sorted by color. No pen is out of place, no to-do item is left off a list. "Type A" might be an understatement.

Zach sits down in his chair and perches his phone, which is logged in to the official class of 2023 Instagram page, on the desk. "You two have gone live before, right?" he asks, looking at me and Trish.

"Yes, Zach," I say, grinning. "We know how Instagram works."

"Just checking." He gets up, glancing at his watch. "All right, the account is all yours. Any questions?"

"You won't be here, right?" Trish asks.

"Why, do you plan on talking shit?" he asks, glaring at her.

"I mean . . ." Trish leans against his desk and cringes. "I'm not *not* going to talk shit—"

"Just kidding," he says, grinning. "This is an election. Talk all the shit you want. I'll be downstairs."

He leaves, closing the door behind him.

Camilla hops onto the immaculate bed and lays her head against a pillow. "How are you feeling, babe?"

Trish breathes in and out slowly, before licking her lips. "Nervous. But a good nervous."

She's dressed like a president tonight, rocking a purple double-breasted blazer with silver buttons. Dangling, cubed earrings drop just below the bottoms of her curls, and her eye shadow—sprinkled with just the right amount of sparkle—makes the browns of her irises shine.

"You're going to kill it," I say.

"I know." She winks at me and gestures toward Zach's desk chair. "You're up first, though. Get comfortable."

I take a seat and straighten my bow tie in the reflection of Zach's phone, going over what I want to say to the junior class before introducing Trish. I contemplated writing a formal speech, but speaking authentically in the moment feels more right.

"Ten seconds until you go on," Camilla says, watching her phone from the bed, which is just out of the camera's frame in the background. "Five, four, three, two . . ."

I tap the button to go live.

"Hey, all," I say as people start tuning in. "Blaine Bowers here, the mural kid who randomly decided to run for president."

Trish giggles off-screen.

"I have some important info about the race," I say, "but I'll wait until a few more people join."

It starts at just ten viewers. But the number quickly shoots up to twenty. Then fifty. In the blink of an eye, there are a hundred people watching—and counting. It's no surprise, really. Rumors about Joey and Ashtyn's election sabotage spread like wildfire last week, and we promised juniors an update tonight.

And they're about to get a big one.

"First of all, I want to thank each and every junior who participated in our election this year," I begin, a little weirded out by seeing myself on camera. "Whether you voted for me or Zach, being a part of the electoral process is important. And speaking of Zach, I also want to thank him for graciously letting me use our official class Instagram page to do this right now. He certainly didn't have to, but he's been a great sport."

ROBBIE COUCH

I pause, going through the mental checklist of what I wanted to get out in the beginning.

"As most of you have heard by now, the race for next year's president, um . . . the race hit a snag. Let's just say the ballots were not delivered in a secure way to be counted fairly, and unfortunately, that means we have no idea whether I or Zach earned more of your votes. However, we still need to select a president. Our senior year is the most important year of high school, and we deserve a leader who will step up, take charge, and do what's right for the well-being of our class."

I pause again, suddenly a bit nervous.

Will people hate me for doing this? Will people mock me until graduation day? One of Zach's attack lines against me in the debate was that I'm a quitter, after all. As evidenced by Ms. Ritewood's unfinished mural, that criticism isn't entirely off-base.

But I guess there's a big difference between quitting for the right reasons and quitting for the wrong ones.

I take a deep breath.

"Here's the deal," I say. "I *don't* think I'm the leader you all deserve as class president. Throughout this campaign, I learned something about myself: student government just . . . it's not for me. Painting is. My murals are what I'm most passionate about. I can be a change-maker in my own unique way by doing what I love—brightening up local businesses in our awesome corner of Chicago. That's why . . ." I pause, because I feel a lump grow in my throat. "That's why I'm dropping out of the race for senior class president."

294

The reactions and comments immediately start blowing up.

He's what????? someone writes.

R U KIDDING ME? another adds.

OMG BLAINE NO, is the last one I read before looking up at the camera again.

Avoid the comments, I remind myself. *Don't look down.*

"The person I *do* think should be our senior class president? Trish Macintosh." I glance to my left. She's standing there, watching me with a proud smile. "Due to an election rule, Trish, my campaign captain, is allowed to take my place on the ballot. And, sure, I know people will assume I'm only supporting her because she's my best friend. But that's simply not true. I think Trish will make an amazing president for the class of 2023. Here's why."

I stop to steady my breath, knowing I need to nail this next part.

"When I decided to run, it was *Trish* who proposed putting up my 'Let's Talk' sign in the cafeteria to get signatures. She knew that a campaign that prioritized listening would be a winning one." Even though I'm trying to ignore the comments, I notice a wave of heart reactions light up the screen. "After we heard from so many of you while getting signatures, it was *Trish* who was able to thread the needle between your responses and the bigger topic of mental health. And it was *Trish* who proposed the creation of our Wicker West Wellness Initiative, which she'll tell you about in more detail shortly. The bottom line is: Trish truly was the brainpower behind my campaign. So if you want someone with a vision for improving student life at Wicker West, she's your girl."

I pause to breathe again and notice the number of live viewers: 320.

Holy crap.

Don't screw up the closing, Blaine. Don't screw it up!

"That's why," I say, smiling wide, "I am beyond honored to introduce all of you to Trish Macintosh—our future senior class president of the class of 2023."

I stand up swiftly and move out of the way so Trish can take my spot.

"Thanks, boo," Trish whispers, nudging me with her elbow.

She lands in the hot seat and looks up at the camera with a radiant smile.

Of course she should be our president, I think, watching her command the camera. How did I not see this before?

"Hi, class of '23," she says, loud, clear, and as confident as ever. "I'm Trish Macintosh, and I'm asking for your vote next Tuesday. I know that I have the empathy, open-mindedness, and outsider's perspective to be a great class president. Let me tell you why."

I glance over at Camilla on the bed, who's clutching a pillow nervously, watching like a competitive parent at their kid's baseball game.

"As Blaine mentioned, I believe wholeheartedly that mental health needs to become a number one priority at Wicker West. If you're living with a mental health challenge, like I have for most of my life, our school is failing you. And that's particularly true if you're Black, Brown, Asian American, or Indigenous. If you live with a disability, Wicker West can and should be doing more. The same is true if you're LGBTQIA-plus. That's why we need my Wicker West Wellness Initiative. Here's what's included in the plan and how I know we can pay for it—*without* raising the price of prom tickets or additional class fees."

Someone taps lightly on the bedroom door. I dash over and crack it open.

It's Zach, holding a plate of garlic bread. "Hey," he whispers.

"Hi," I reply, slipping out of the room and closing the door behind me, so as to not distract Trish.

"Sorry, I didn't mean to interrupt," he says, handing the plate over to me. "My mom demanded that I deliver this to you guys."

I laugh, taking the plate from him. "No problem. Thanks."

"How's it going in there?" he asks.

"So far, so good," I say. "No shit-talking you . . . yet." I smile.

"I mean, after what I did to you, stealing the debate prep notes and all, I sort of deserve it."

I think. "Fair point."

He nods, a bit awkwardly, before turning to leave. "I'll let you get back in there—"

"Thanks again for letting us do this," I say. "That was really nice of you."

He shrugs. "Trish deserves her chance, and, I mean, we wouldn't even be *in* this mess if it weren't for our ex-boyfriend and my campaign captain trying to steal the election." He bites his lower lip, contemplating telling me something. "And, yeah . . . about that . . . I dumped Joey."

Thank God, I think. *Joey deserves it*. But instead I just say, "Oh really?"

"Yeah. He's . . ."

"A douchebag?"

Zach laughs. "Yes. And—"

"An ass clown?"

He laughs harder. "True. But—"

"A douchebag ass clown who also maybe cheated on me?"

The playfulness drains from Zach's face. "No," he says, shaking his head emphatically. "Definitely not. At least not with me."

I nod. "Okay. I didn't think so, but the time line was a bit suspicious."

"Seriously." He shakes his head harder. "I didn't so much as hold his hand until he ended it with you. You believe me, right?"

I think for a second. "Yeah," I say with a small smile. "I trust you." I slip a slice of garlic bread into my mouth. "Honestly? I almost feel bad for Joey. The only things he cares about is popularity, power, and gaining Mr. and Mrs. Oliver's approval."

"Well, he's definitely not feeling too powerful now, sitting at home, suspended from school." Zach leans in closer to me, lowering his voice. "I heard Northwestern might rescind his fall semester acceptance too. And even if they don't, his parents still might not let him go."

My eyes pop wide open as I chew Mrs. Chesterton's garlicky goodness. "For real?"

He nods, holding back a smile. "Mr. and Mrs. Oliver are mortified by what he did, and they might force him to work at his dad's firm next year. You know, to *teach him a lesson*, or whatever." He cringes. "You didn't hear that from me, though."

I zip my lips closed with my fingers. "I'm glad your parents aren't like that."

He scrunches his face. "Like the Olivers? Oh heck no. Thank God."

"It'd be terrible," I add, "living under that constant pressure to be perfect?"

He sighs. "I put enough pressure on myself as it is."

"I can see that from your desk," I say with a grin. "You should go easier on yourself, Zach. Take breaks. Enjoy the journey. Senior year only comes once—you don't want to spend it completely exhausted."

"You're right." He grins. "It sounds like the Wicker West Wellness Initiative really is rubbing off on you, huh?"

I smile.

Harvey comes slinking down the hallway and starts rubbing his sides up against Zach's ankles.

"Okay, boy, let's leave them alone," Zach says, picking him up before turning to me. "I'll see you downstairs in a bit."

"Sounds good," I say. "Tell your mom thanks for the garlic bread."

"Will do."

I reach for the doorknob to go back inside.

"Oh, by the way," he whispers from down the hallway, "what's up with you and Danny?"

My heart flutters just hearing the name. "What do you mean?"

Zach drops his chin at me with a grin. "C'mon, Blaine. It's obvious you two are into each other."

I struggle to find the right words. Zach notices.

"I know, I know, it's none of my business," he says, backing away again. "But if you ask me, I say make your move while you still can. As you say, senior year only comes once, after all."

CHAPTER 32

I roll over and give Fudge a belly rub in the morning sun before opening up Instagram.

The first pic I see is Aunt Starr's cozy reading nook in her new apartment. On one of the shelves, there's a small, stone *Tyrannosaurus rex* statue with "Field Museum" carved into the base. Her caption reads, *To new beginnings!* and there's a smiley face, a dinosaur emoji, and a green heart. I give the post a like and grin, suddenly aware that I've handled the first week of her absence much better than expected. Sure, it's likely because we leave encouraging voice memos for each other all day long. (It barely feels like she's moved out, truth be told.) But still. Despite my own worst fears, I haven't cried myself to sleep once in the past week. And I consider that a big victory.

The second pic I see is a cute selfie of Zach alongside Harvey on his front porch, posted thirteen minutes ago.

Today is going to be puuur*fect*, the caption reads, with a row of suns. I give it a like and comment with a cat emoji with hearts for eyes. Two seconds later Zach likes my response.

It's only been two weeks since he and Trish faced off on the ballot, and I'm pretty sure we set a new record for how quickly two people have gone from worn enemies to good friends.

Fudge starts getting antsy to escape my room, so I climb out of bed and freshen up before heading to the kitchen. From the staircase I can hear and smell meat sizzling on the stove, which is odd, because I thought both Mom and Dad had to work early this morning. And whenever that's the case, it's granola bars for breakfast and coffees to go.

"Brinner?" I ask, still a bit groggy, stepping into the kitchen.

Astoundingly, Mom is *not* in her scrubs for once, just a shirt and jeans, while Dad is flipping ham steaks at the stove in his pajamas.

"Morning, kiddo," Mom says, sipping her coffee. "You do know that when it's breakfast food for breakfast, we just call that . . . breakfast. Right? Not 'brinner'?"

"Yes, sure, but . . . ?" I look between both of them, confused.

They're not saying anything.

"Do you two not have to work today?" I ask.

"I decided to take the day off," Dad says, grinding sea salt over a pan of scrambled eggs.

"Both of us did," Mom adds, moving stuff off the island chair next to her so I can have a seat too. "We're going to do some spring cleaning around the house."

"And in my shed," Dad says. I open my mouth to warn him not to mess with my paints or mural items, but he cuts me off. "And, no, you don't have to worry. I won't touch your art supplies."

I take a seat at the island, feeling a little weirded out by how they're both behaving.

"What?" Mom says, laughing a little and taking another sip of coffee. "You seem suspicious."

"I *am*," I say, eyes widening. "Neither of you ever takes a day off, and now you're both on staycation together?"

"Staycation, *ha*," Dad repeats, amused with the term. "That's a bit of a stretch."

"Actually, we did decide to take the whole weekend off," Mom says, putting her mug down and turning to me. "How do you feel about a trip to William's Outfitters tomorrow?"

"For real?"

"For real." Dad rotates toward us from the stove and slides a very full plate in front of me. "We know you're having brinner at Aunt Starr's, but we're thinking we could go before that and then drop you off at her place, considering William's isn't too far from her new apartment."

I squint at them. "What's the catch?"

Mom steals a strawberry off my plate. "No catch."

"We want to spend time with you, is all," Dad says, placing eggs in front of Mom, too. "For the record, I still think William's is a pretentious rip-off."

"You can pick out a tie, though," Mom whispers. "Maybe two or three."

I smile.

"Think of it as our treat to you for running for president," Dad says, moving dirty pans into the sink.

"I dropped out, though," I say. "Did you two miss that memo?"

Mom gives me a look. "Don't get snarky, Blaine. Of course

we didn't miss that memo. We're just proud you stepped out of your comfort zone and gave it a shot."

"And even prouder of you for having the courage to speak up when you realized it wasn't your thing," Dad chimes in.

"Okay," I say, grinning. "But can I, uh . . . graciously decline the offer?"

They both pause before turning to me.

"Graciously decline a trip to William's?" Dad asks, scrunching his forehead. "On what grounds?"

"I'd rather get some new paint colors instead," I say.

They both beam. It's like I just won a Son of the Year Award or something.

I feel myself turning red. "What?"

"Yes," Mom finally answers softly. "That sounds great to me." She slices the ham on her plate into bite sizes. "Also, you should know that your dad's finishing up his work at the new building site on Wacker Drive next week."

"And on Wednesday, Mom's colleague who works evening shifts comes back from paternity leave," Dad says.

They both look at me again, like those things should mean something.

"All right?" I say, taking a bite of toast. "Congrats to your coworker on becoming a new parent, I guess?"

"What we're trying to say, Blaine, is that we're both going to be home a lot more starting soon."

"Oh." I glance between them. "Really?"

"Yes," Dad says, using a napkin to wipe his mustache. "Very soon."

Mom ruffles my hair, smiling. "Now hurry up and finish your food. You've got the Winning Wizards assembly this morning, right?"

"What's that?" Dad asks.

"The school gives out student awards from the year and praises the sports teams that actually had winning seasons, and—" I glance at my phone. "Holy crap, I'm going to be so late." I shovel the rest of my breakfast into my mouth and dash back upstairs to my room. "Thank you for brinner—er, breakfast!"

"You're welcome!" Dad calls after me. "And don't run in the house when you're wearing socks. You're going to fall!"

I throw on jeans and a light gray top, brush my teeth, and sprint back down the steps a minute later, nearly falling every step of the way. (Dad was right.) "Can you walk Fudge today, since you two will be home?" I shout from the foyer, slipping on my boots and sliding out the door. "Thank you!"

I walk-jog to school in the 80-degree heat, immediately regretting my decision to wear a light gray cotton shirt that reveals every bead of sweat my torso produces. The tardy bell is ringing right as I arrive, so I run directly to the gym, where the Winning Wizards assembly is taking place.

The gym is noisy and jam-packed. The smell of old wrestling mats and too many colognes smacks me in the face upon entering. The lingering trauma from my debate with Zach puts me a little on edge at first, before I remember how everything turned out in the end. I won't be the one in the spotlight this morning.

Thank. *God.*

"Blaine!" I hear Trish's voice above the white noise of the student body. I crane my neck around, trying to spot her in the sea of faces. I finally do, waving her hands in the very first row of bleachers on the sidelines of the basketball court.

"Why am I not surprised you staked out front-row seats?" I say, dropping down into the tight spot between Trish and a girl in pigtails.

"Why am I not surprised you're running late?" she bites back.

There are dozens of chairs lined up on one side of the hardwood itself, all facing center court. The current student council class leaders are in the first few rows, along with accomplished athletic teams, our quiz bowl squad (who apparently won the state championship, or something of the sort), and a handful of other students who've snagged notable awards this school year. Joey, fresh off his suspension, is looking particularly downtrodden a few chairs from Zach, who seems cheerful in a seersucker shirt, chatting with our class VP.

"Look at my babe," Trish says with pride, nodding toward the rows of filled chairs.

"Where is she?" I ask, eyes darting around. "Oh! I see her." Camilla is a couple of rows behind Zach, looking dope in an orange skirt and flowy white top. "Where did she get that outfit?"

"I don't know," Trish says. "But I am sure as hell lucky to call her my girlfriend."

Principal Spice stands up and wanders behind the mic at center court before getting everyone to calm down.

"It's been an amazing nine months, Wicker West High School," he says, encouraging students to respond with applause. "Today's Winning Wizards assembly is all about celebrating the big moments and triumphs that have made this year worth remembering." He checks his notes. "First up, let's hear it for our varsity girls' volleyball team!"

A bunch of very tall girls stand and wave as the crowd cheers.

"They not only won the league but went on to become state quarter finalists," Principal Spice reads from his notes. "Coach Smith, would you like to say a few words?"

"Hey," the girl with pigtails next to me says into my ear, poking my shoulder.

I turn to her. "Hi."

"You're Blaine Bowers."

"Yeah."

"Good debate a few weeks ago."

I can't tell if she's mocking me or not. "Thanks?"

"It was incredibly difficult to watch at first," she says. "But you really stuck the landing."

"I appreciate that."

"The Wicker West Wellness Initiative? Amazing idea," she says. "I hope it becomes real someday."

I smile at her.

Principal Spice runs through a couple of other teams that won their sports-ball championships or whatever, before he transitions to individual student accomplishments.

"It's coming up, it's coming up," Trish says into my ear, squeezing my arm in anticipation of Camilla's award.

"Ouch!" I squeal.

"Sorry. I'm excited!"

We still have to wait for Principal Spice to acknowledge a few more students—Cassie Moorehead, who raised a buttload of money to combat climate change using her Etsy page, and Marquis Stones, who launched an über-viral hashtag helping charitable causes while working at the Obama Foundation—before we finally get to the good part.

"Next up is junior Camilla Castro," Principal Spice begins.

"Here we go!" Trish pulls out her phone to record.

"Camilla completed an internship this spring at the Field Museum, where she studied the migratory patterns of several dinosaur species," he says. "The scientists at the Field were so impressed with her, Camilla won a spot in the museum's selective research fellowship program next fall, which comes with a nice college scholarship package. Great work, Camilla!"

Trish and I bolt to our feet and go absolutely wild as Camilla accepts her medal from Principal Spice and sends us a wink and a curtsy before returning to her seat.

"I am so happy I filmed this," Trish says, immediately playing back the story on her phone.

"Hey." Pigtail girl pokes my shoulder again.

I turn to her. Again. "Hello."

"Why'd you drop out of the race?" she asks.

"Oh." That was unexpected.

"I don't mean to be nosy," she says, totally being nosy. "Just wondering."

"It's okay," I reply. "I realized student council wasn't for me, basically."

"I'm a freshman, and I think I want to run for office at some point."

"You totally should."

"But how'd you know it wasn't for you?" she asks. "Like, I want to run, but I also don't want to be onstage in a debate when I suddenly realize I've made a bad mistake." She pauses. "No offense."

I laugh. "That's a tough question. I think I realized what *was* for me, and it helped crystallize what *wasn't*. You know?"

She thinks. "What's for you, then? If it's not student council."

"I paint murals for mom-and-pop stores around town," I say, smiling. "It brightens up the town and supports local businesses, and I make a little money doing it too. I really love it."

"I can tell," she says. "Your face lit up just talking about it."

"Yeah?"

"Yeah." She turns her attention back to Principal Spice. "It seems like you found the thing you can get serious about."

Oh. The thing I can get serious about.

I grin, looking back at center court too.

Maybe I *am* a Serious Guy after all.

"The last thing we'll be doing for our Winning Wizards assembly is recognizing next year's student council leadership," Principal Spice announces. "We had some close races this year, and some, uh, some *interesting* ones too. But Mr. Wells has assured me that next year's leaders are competent, inspiring, and more than qualified to take the reins."

I make eye contact with Zach, who sends me a grin.

"As tradition calls for, each grade's leaders will announce the student taking their place next fall," Principal Spice continues. "Let's start with the seniors. Mr. Joey Oliver, come on up here and get things started for us, will you?"

Oof.

The gym gets awkwardly quiet.

I mean, there are a few claps, here and there. But overall the stillness feels like nails on a chalkboard. Can you blame the student body, though?

No one likes a cheater.

Joey, in ripped jeans and a lopsided baseball cap, wanders to the mic, accompanied by a few boos from students— that quickly get shut down by teachers standing nearby.

Honestly? It's painful to watch.

"Hello, Wizards," he says, attempting to smile, before clearing his throat.

I really do (almost) feel bad for the guy.

Joey, clearly yearning to get the spotlight off him as quickly as possible, pulls a gavel out from behind his back. "So, I guess we can cut to the chase," he says, scared to make eye contact with the student body. "Please give a round of applause for next year's senior class president . . ."

I glance at Trish, smirking.

She bites her lower lip, nudging my arm with hers.

Joey bends a bit closer to the mic. "Trish Macintosh."

The gym bursts into applause as Trish crosses the hardwood floor in a bright pink bomber jacket and platform shoes. Lots of people are on their feet, including Zach. Camilla is hopping up and down like her girlfriend just won gold at the Olympics. I pull out my phone, eager to capture the moment.

Trish takes the gavel from Joey, and the two cordially shake hands with extremely forced smiles, pretending to at least tolerate one another. Joey sits down immediately, but Trish lingers for a bit at center court, waving up at the bleachers, basking in the glow of victory.

Trish Macintosh, president of the class of 2023.

That has such a nice ring to it.

CHAPTER 33

★ ☆ ★

Trish, Camilla, and Zach invite me to Gino's East for deep-dish pies after school. My rumbling stomach is urging me to say yes, but I can't be a flaky entrepreneur.

"Pretty please?" Trish asks for a third time, giving me sad puppy-dog eyes at my locker. Camilla and Zach, noticing her strategy, mimic the eyes too.

I stuff a textbook away and slam my locker shut. "I wish I could! But I have to finish the mural."

Camilla flashes her medal at me. "Does this mean nothing to you? I am an important scientist now, dude. You could be having dinner with the next Bill Nye."

I grin.

"Let's leave him be, ladies," Zach says, patting me on the shoulder. "We'll save you a piece."

I chuckle. "No you won't."

"Yeah, you're probably right," Trish says as the three of them start backing away. "But text me after you're done, if you want to hang out later."

"Sounds good."

They disappear around the corner, leaving me alone in the silent hallway with my FOMO. I dip into a bathroom and change into old, crummy paint clothes before zigzagging my way to the other end of the building—the exit nearest Biggest Bean.

On the long walk through the empty school, I open my email to see if Ms. Ritewood got back to me after I completed my work a couple of days ago. She did!

I'm getting so many compliments, Blaine! she begins her message, which goes on to thank me for the additional mural of Mars I painted on the back of the store, free of charge. It was the least I could do for leaving her high and dry for weeks on end. Even if Susan's Stationery didn't end up being fined for my incompetency, just the possibility that they very well could have scared me into overdrive to get the job done. *We had a big bump in business yesterday too,* Ms. Ritewood concludes in her email. *I can't confirm, but something tells me your new mural out back should take the credit.*

A smile breaks into my cheeks as I type back a cheerful response. I make sure to apologize (yet again) for dropping the ball during the campaign and promise to stop in soon to get a new sketch pad for the murals I have planned this summer.

I enjoy Wicker West in the late afternoon, after most students have left for the day, when it's quiet enough to hear the humming of the lights above and empty enough that you can smell the subtle scent of bleach wafting through the air from the custodians' cleaning runs. I like entering a vacant hallway and strutting down the middle like I own the place.

But I can't do that after rounding the corner into the Mathematics wing. There's Joey, all alone, shuffling things around in his locker a mere ten feet away.

Shoot.

I stop dead in my tracks and contemplate backpedaling, out of sight, before he sees me. But just like outside the Fat Banana, I'm caught red-handed (and this time I don't have Fudge to blame).

"Hey," Joey says meekly, giving me a sad smile. "Nice shirt."

I look down and realize that it's *his*. Well, used to be anyway. An ancient, torn WIZARDS ATHLETICS T-shirt he let me keep when we first started dating. Now it's sprinkled with the paint swatches for half a dozen murals across northwest Chicago.

"Oh." Guilt grips my insides. "I didn't mean to—"

"It's cool," Joey says, grinning. "It was an old shirt anyway. I'm sure you're putting it to good use, now that you're painting again." He pauses. "Which I was happy to learn, by the way."

I'm not even sure how to engage with him—or if I should engage at all. Hopefully any good karma I garnered from righting my wrongs over the past couple of weeks will manifest in the school's fire alarms going off, giving me an excuse to sprint away and never see him again.

"How's it going?" he asks.

"Okay," I reply. "You?"

He considers the question before his mouth shifts into a painful grin. "I've been better."

The person in front of me is not the same person who was standing on my doorstep before Grey Kettle. His eyes are sunken, and his white sneakers are uncharacteristically stained with the green of mowed grass. His hair, matted from the baseball hat he had on earlier, looks like it could use a liberal palmful of shampoo, and his ripped jeans somehow seem even holier than they were at the assembly a few hours ago.

He looks absolutely miserable. You'd think I'd be delighted to see it.

But I'm not.

"I heard you might be working at your dad's firm next year?" I ask, trying to put a positive spin on an unquestionably sad development.

"Probably," he says, closing his locker. He takes a few steps toward me.

I do the same toward him. "That's cool."

He shrugs. "Eh, I wouldn't say 'cool.' I'd rather be going to Northwestern."

I pretend to be surprised. "Whoa. Why aren't you going?"

"Blaine." He gives me a look—like he knows that I know the answer. "My parents weren't too happy with . . ." He rocks his head from side to side to fill in the blanks. "You know. *Everything.*"

"Oh. Got it."

"Maybe I'll start spring semester instead," he says. "We'll see." This is unbearable. Why am I even having this conversation? Why do I feel the need to play nice? Joey has treated me like gum stuck on the bottom of his once-polished dress shoe. He doesn't deserve another second of my time.

I need to go.

"I've got to get going," I say, moving to walk by. "See ya, Jo—"

"Hold on." His hand lands on my arm as I pass. "Can I say something?"

I pause. "Sure."

"I'm just . . ." He sighs before swallowing hard, staring at the empty space above my head to collect his thoughts. "I'm so sorry, Blaine."

I shift my weight between the tips of my toes and heels, waiting for him to continue.

"You have every right in the world to hate me right now," he says. "*I'd* hate me right now. And I'm not looking to be forgiven. I guess I just let my ego get the best of me, and I ruined your election in the process."

"Why?" I interject. "Why did you care about this election so much?"

"Why did you choose to enter just to spite me?" he asks.

"I didn't run to *spite* you," I clarify. "I . . ." I suddenly get self-conscious. "I wanted to win you back."

He clears his throat, apparently shocked by my revelation. "What?"

"Yeah," I say, turning pink. "I wanted to prove to you I could be a *Serious Guy*—the type you wanted to end up with." I let out a laugh. "Yeah, I know. How dumb was I?"

He looks lost for words.

"I've got to go, for real," I say, starting to drift away. "Have a nice life, Joey."

"A nice *life*?" he calls after me. "You're really never going to talk to me again?"

I stop, turn to face him, and feel my blood begin to boil. "Why *should* I ever talk to you again? You said I looked foolish for running. You tried to rig my election so I'd lose. You dumped me *on our anniversary*—"

"I didn't want to!" he exclaims. I see a tear forming in his eye. "Truly, Blaine. I didn't want it to end the way it did."

I glance around the hallway, totally aghast. Even though there aren't witnesses nearby, I almost wish there were so a third party could confirm that I'm not hallucinating this entire conversation.

"If you didn't want to break up"—I recap his words slowly, letting them sink in—"then why did you?"

"It's not that I didn't want to break up with you," he says, blinking away the wetness. "I know it's the biggest cliché ever, but it really wasn't you. It was me."

I roll my eyes, letting out a laugh.

"I'm being serious," he carries on. "I got caught up in what type of guy I *should* be with, instead of thinking about what guy I *wanted* to be with. And, as you know, my parents didn't help. They have a very specific person they see me with."

I think through his words. "Okay, but outside the Fat Banana, you told me your parents wanted you to break up with me. Why make it about them if you wanted to dump me anyway?"

"They wanted me to do it before Cabo," he says sheepishly.

"I kept chickening out, trying to find the least unideal moment, but it never came. Then it was the Friday before we left, and I sort of panicked, and I just . . ." He sighs, defeated. "I did it. I know, it was awful to do it at Grey Kettle. I shouldn't have."

"Yeah, you're right," I retort. "That stung, Joey."

"I know."

"It was mortifying."

"Yeah."

"And pretty much inexcusable."

Kim the custodian pushes a mop and bucket out of a nearby classroom and starts rolling it our way. Joey and I fall silent as she approaches with an awkward grin on her face, sensing that the conversation she's walking through is a heavy one.

"Boys," she says, nodding at us individually.

"Hey, Kim," I say.

Joey nods back.

The sound of the bucket's wheels fades as Kim grows smaller down the hallway and out of sight. And then me and Joey are stuck in a tub of thickening concrete silence once again.

"So," he mutters, licking his lips, unsure what to say next.

I don't know what I want him to say either. I don't know what he *could* say that would change anything, make me feel better, or justify his behavior over the course of the campaign. So I start to back away from him with a half-hearted smile, putting a final nail in what I hope is our last conversation. But then I stop.

Because if this *is* our last conversation, have I left any-thing unsaid?

"Honestly, Joey," I say, "your parents suck."

He looks up from the floor.

"Really," I continue. "Screw them. I don't say that because they don't think I was good enough for you—which, I mean, *of course* I'm good enough for you."

Joey keeps staring, unblinking and expressionless.

"I say that because your parents clearly don't have your best interests at heart," I go on. "Or, if they do, they're letting their own insecurities get in the way. They only care about how you and your brother and sister reflect on *them*. All that pressure to be perfect—all for what? So the three of you can be absolutely miserable the rest of your lives?"

He considers the point. "But my brother and sister—"

"You're not your sister or your brother, Joey," I say, cutting him off. "You're *you*." I wish I'd had the clarity and confi-dence to say all of this months ago. "Let's not forget that your dad had connections at Columbia that nudged your brother off the wait list. And didn't your mom know someone at the Gates Foundation who helped your sister get the partnership off the ground?"

He nods slowly, eyes dropping toward the floor once again.

"See? Your parents may open doors for you, but they also shove you through, whether you like it or not." I stop to take a breath.

Joey, uncharacteristically subdued, runs his tongue over his teeth behind closed lips. He'd be speaking up if he thought I was wrong. But I'm not, and we both know it.

Kim appears at the end of the hallway, pushing her mop and rickety bucket back toward us. We wait to speak again until after she slowly, awkwardly, rolls by.

"Boys," she repeats.

"Hey, Kim," I say.

Joey nods.

After she disappears for a second time, Joey places his cap back on backward, covering his disheveled hair. "You're not wrong, Blaine."

"I know."

"I need to be my own person," he says, more to himself than to me. "I need to stop comparing myself to my brother and sister, and I need to get my parents out of my head."

"Yep." I shove my hands into my pockets. "Glad you see it too."

A deep sense of relief floods my body. It feels good to tell the truth, especially when it's been building up inside for even longer than I knew it had been, unable to escape through the right words or at the most opportune moment. Now it's been said.

"You're going to be okay, Joey," I say, smiling a bit. "You know that, right?"

He doesn't look so sure.

"I never liked you because you were class president or going to Northwestern or wanted to be president someday," I explain. "I liked you for *you*. You're funny. And smart. And, despite how you've acted this semester, a good person. There are lots of other people who feel the same way."

He finally lets himself smile too. "I appreciate that."

I glance at my phone—I really, *really* have to go.

"Congrats on running a great campaign," he says as I drift off down the hallway. "And tell Trish I think the senior class presidency will be in great hands next year."

"Will do." I nod at him one last time. "See ya around, Joey."

Now I've got a mural to finish.

I breeze through the school doors and pick up the pace. It's still a humid, hot mess out here, but beggars can't be choosers when it comes to Chicagoans and their weather. The skies are clear, the birds are chirping, and the smell of freshly mowed grass accompanies me on my walk to Biggest Bean. I'll take it.

"All right, Blaine," I say to myself, arriving at the side of the coffee house and looking up at the nearly finished Ms. Nguyen. "Let's do this."

I'm always nervous to start a mural, but I was especially on edge before this one. Not because of its size (it's one of the smaller ones I've done) or because it's an overly complicated design (the quality of Ms. Nguyen's photo has been super helpful). But I knew I'd be rusty, having not painted in a while, and the thought of messing up a piece of art this emotionally connected to Bao was straight-up nightmare fuel.

Thankfully, it's coming along great.

I'm confident that I didn't lose Ms. Nguyen's infectious energy, translating her form to the mural, which was my most important priority. The flowers and plants bursting in the background pull in dozens of reds, blues, yellows, pinks, and greens. I don't know much about Ms. Nguyen, but this photo makes me wish I did.

Now I just need to finish up the very last thing before the painting is complete: filling in the details of her favorite flower—a peony—behind her ear. No, it wasn't in the original photo, but I think it'll make a nice addition.

I pull over the ladder and get to work. The sun is beating down, and beads of sweat keep blurring my view with a sting. I also keep imagining the pizza that Trish, Camilla, and Zach are inhaling this very moment across town, and feel my stomach rumbling with every pepperoni fantasy that wanders through my mind. I have to power through, though.

"A peony?" I hear a voice say to my left.

I jump, nearly tumbling off the ladder, but catch my balance just in time.

"Sorry," Danny says, biting his lower lip, embarrassed. "I didn't mean to sneak up on you."

If I hadn't been sweating before, I'd certainly be now.

"It's okay," I say, stepping down to the ground and attempting to play it cool. "I'm just finishing up."

He walks forward in a white T-shirt and blue jeans, scanning the brick wall with a beaming smile that I haven't seen since I spotted him in the crowd during the debate. "It looks amazing, Blaine."

Oh, thank God.

I gesture like I'm wiping sweat from my brow with

relief—but end up actually wiping sweat from my brow. I pull my ladder away from the wall so that he can get the best view possible. "To answer your question, yes," I say. "It is a peony. You said those were her favorite, right?"

He nods, eyes still glued to my creation.

"Once I finish that flower, I'll be all set," I add. "Well, I'll need to add a varnish once it completely dries. But *then*, that'll be it."

There's a lull in traffic, no pedestrians or bikers are in sight, and the birds in a nearby tree suspend their chirping just long enough for the silence to begin feeling heavy. It's like the entire city hit pause just to hear what we say next.

"I—"

"You—"

"Sorry," I say, grinning.

"No, no," he says, gesturing to me. "You first."

I take a breath, feeling butterflies filling up my gut. "I've missed seeing you around, is all."

His lips curl up into an even bigger smile. "I've missed you too."

"I'm sorry again for how I reacted the day of the elec—"

But he shakes his head, urging me to stop. "You already apologized for that. *I'm* the one who screwed things up."

"But you—"

"Blaine, you don't need to keep apologizing." He steps closer. "*I'm* sorry."

We're just a few feet apart. His eyes, glued to mine, aren't moving anywhere. And I'm more than okay with that.

Wait.

I notice he's holding something with both hands behind his back.

"I lied to you," he says, taking another step closer. "I said that I'd been sending you the wrong message. That wasn't true."

"No?" I swallow hard.

"No. The message that I was sending was that I like you. I like you a lot."

My heart is rapping the insides of my chest like a Wizards marching band percussionist. "I like you too."

"You're the first guy I've really fallen for," he says. "And, even though I've been out, it still felt weird and confusing at first. But it doesn't anymore. I know exactly how I feel."

"I do too," I say. My mouth can't articulate much more than two- to three-word sentences at this point.

"Blaine." He smiles, dimples creasing into his cheeks. His eyes burst like the colors surrounding Ms. Nguyen. "Can I take you out on a date sometime?"

I exhale. "Can you promise me it won't be to Grey Kettle?"

He steps even closer, letting out a small laugh. "Yes."

"Then absolutely."

Finally he pulls one arm around to his front, revealing what he's been hiding.

Oh.

It's the new aloe vera plant I dropped off with Bao yesterday—an especially green and healthy one, at home in a bright blue pot.

"This is your handiwork?" Danny asks.

I let out a soft laugh. "Well, yeah. I *did* owe you one. And a promise is a pr—"

But that's all I can get in, because—the next thing I know—his lips are touching mine. It's like I'm in a shaken snow globe. Every inch of my skin is tingling. The hand not holding the plant lands on my lower back and gently pulls me in, and our bellies press up against one another. His mouth is soft, his breath is minty, and I already know that I want this feeling to happen a million more times.

We pull apart, eyes meeting once again.

"All I ever wanted from you was a new aloe vera plant, Blaine Bowers," he says, smirking. "And you had to go and do this. . . ."

He pauses, staring—as if I should have something to say for myself.

It's difficult to think about articulating *anything*, though, I'm so overcome by his lips, and his eyes, and his smell, and the hand still resting on my lower back. "Uh," I finally get out. "What did I go and do, exactly?"

He gives me a final peck. "Made me fall for you."

I'm not sure when Chicago hit play again—when the birds started chirping, and the cars returned to the streets, and businesspeople with their black coffees re-emerged onto bustling sidewalks, smartphones in hand. But suddenly I'm very aware of all the life swirling around us, pulling me back to reality.

"So . . . ," he says.

"So . . . ," I laugh.

"Want to go inside and have a mocha?" he offers. "On the house."

Danny leads me toward the entrance of Biggest Bean, his hand in mine. Before we turn the corner, he takes a final glance up at the smiling Ms. Nguyen, surrounded by color and laughing in the sunshine.

ACKNOWLEDGMENTS

Although *Blaine for the Win* began as my excuse to write a gay, young adult version of the 2001 cinematic masterpiece *Legally Blonde*, it quickly blossomed into its own beautiful tale, thanks in large part to many brilliant people who are not named Robbie Couch. (And let me tell you: if it takes a village to publish a book, it takes a whole damn country to do so in the middle of a pandemic.)

I cannot give enough thanks to my editor, Amanda Ramirez, and the incredible team at S&S BFYR. It was an absolute joy bringing Blaine's story to life alongside all of you.

My agent, Moe Ferrara, was a rock star amid an unprecedented year of lockdowns, collective and personal setbacks, and plans gone awry. I'm beyond lucky to have you by my side.

My family back in Michigan continued to be the loudest cheerleaders and fiercest allies an author could ask for. I truly am the luckiest to have each and every one of you.

And lastly, thank you to every queer teen who's unashamedly, unapologetically themselves. You were the inspiration behind Blaine Bowers and his magical friends. Keep shining bright.